DR.
VIGILANTE

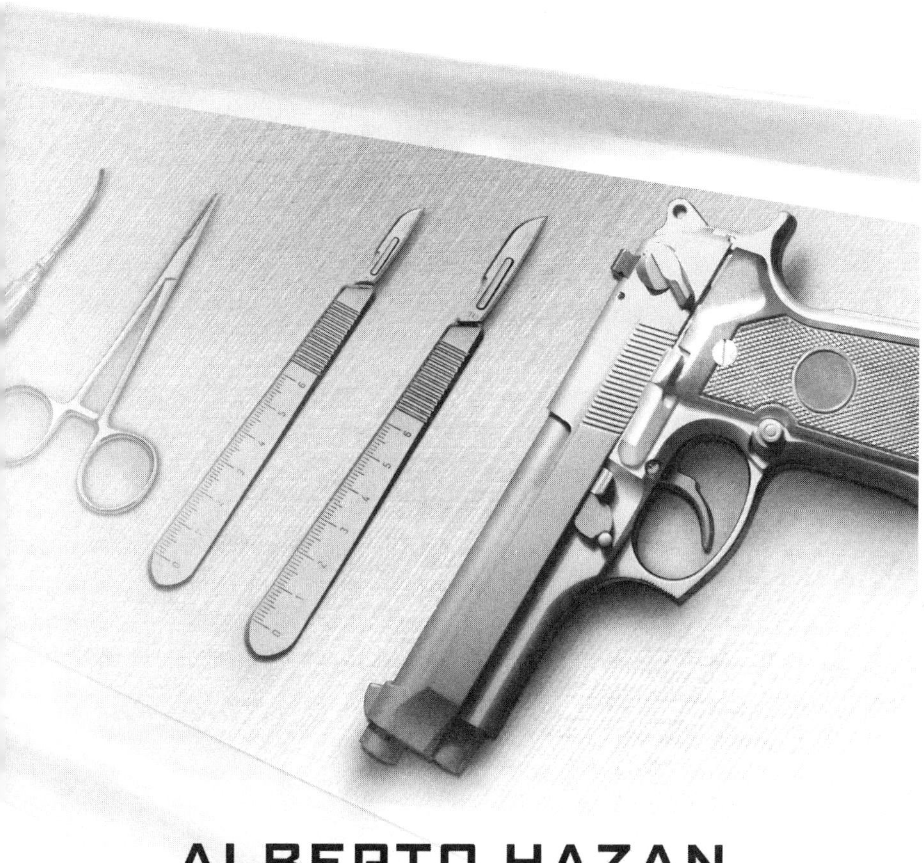

ALBERTO HAZAN

DR. VIGILANTE

A NOVEL BY
ALBERTO HAZAN, MD

A portion of the proceeds from the sale of this book will be donated to charitable foundations helping survivors of domestic violence, child abuse, and rape.

First Edition.

Cover design by Margo Murphy
Author photograph by Scott Taber

ISBN: 978-0-578-12709-5

Hearts with one purpose alone
Through summer and winter seem
Enchanted to a stone
To trouble the living stream.

—William Butler Yeats, "Easter, 1916"

a. Hugen

Prologue

Robert spotted the two men as they turned the corner.

Mid-twenties. Built like weightlifters. One tall, one squat. Voices loud, slurred. Probably heading back home from the bars.

They stopped, turned to check him out, then whispered to each other.

Robert knew he was a good target. It was three o'clock in the morning and he stood alone, in a secluded alley in Washington Heights. He carried ten thousand dollars' worth of miniaturized spy equipment, including a Bluetooth audio-enhancing earpiece and a set of night-vision goggles with high-definition magnification. Despite the unbearable heat and humidity, Robert wore his long-sleeved elastane top and his favorite pair of dark polyester pants. He didn't care that the outfit made him look unarmed and vulnerable to anyone interested in picking a fight.

It'll take them a minute to decide.

He turned his attention back to the building. By the time the two men approached, Robert would know which apartment he'd be visiting.

He switched on his earpiece and goggles and pointed a laser-thin mike toward the top floor. He knew the building's layout from a foray with a pimp two years earlier. Six apartments on every floor. Each apartment eight hundred square feet. Living room and kitchen to the right of the front door, bathroom and bedroom to the left.

Robert glanced again at the address he'd taken from Medical Records and then started sweeping the fourth floor with his equipment.

The first two apartments had kids and parents sleeping in the same room. The third looked empty. In the fourth, a television was on. TNT: Yankees vs. Angels. A lone figure sitting on the couch.

Bingo.

The two men were now ten feet away. "Hey man, how about giving us your shit?" the tall one hollered.

Not a threat yet.

Robert ignored them. He turned off the goggles' night vision, switched on the high-definition magnification, and zoomed in on the building's entrance. Double locks he could jimmy, but the doorway was too brightly lit. He panned to the side of the building.

Fire escape. Ladder eight feet off the ground.

He shifted his gaze to the target's apartment. The bedroom window was cracked open.

"My boy said he wants your shit, motherfucker. You gonna ignore us?"

Robert took off the goggles and let out a sigh. He turned slowly and studied the pair. He had underestimated their size. The squat guy was at least five feet seven, two hundred forty pounds. The tall one was six feet three, two twenty—and clearly the alpha dog. Lots of ink, including two black teardrops under his right eye, a symbol of prior kills he'd made for his gang.

Robert noticed the tall guy's clenched fist, a ridged hammerhead that would knock him out if it landed anywhere near his face. The squat guy's hand was in his front pocket, gripping a knife handle.

"Listen, boys," Robert said. "You're too drunk to make it interesting for me. Go home and sleep it off."

"What the fuck did you say?"

"Just give us your phone and those glasses, man. We're not playing."

Robert laughed and stared down at his device. "Hardly a phone, fellas. This thing can hear the swish of the janitor's mop in that building across the street. And these aren't glasses. They're the latest in night-vision surveillance. They can read the fine print on the paper in that trashcan or spot a rat crawling out of the sewer on 160th. See its whiskers twitch and all. This stuff's worth more money than you'll ever steal in your entire miserable lives."

They flushed with rage, but Robert detected a trace of surprise and worry at his confidence.

"What'd you say?" the squat one said, his chest puffing.

"Give us your shit, or we'll take it from you." The alpha dog held his friend back, then lurched a step forward, crossed his arms, and flexed his biceps.

"I have a better idea," Robert said. "Turn around, go home, and fall into that soft bed of yours. Watch the room spin a bit and get some sleep. When you wake up tomorrow, go find every sucker you ever robbed or assaulted. Visit the families of the people you killed. Apologize to them all. Then get a decent job. Do something of value. Make up for all the bad shit you've done. Trust me, you'll feel so much better than if you stay and let me kick your ass tonight. What do you say? Call it a night, or call it the end of a pain-free existence?"

Robert knew he was egging them on, but he used the time to see how each was preparing to fight. Guillermo had taught him this trick: *talk and watch.*

The knife would come out first, he decided. Then the giant would wade in with his club-like arm.

As always, Robert was right.

The squat one flicked open his switchblade and lunged. Robert turned sideways just before the blade had a chance to pierce his chest. He snatched the knife handle with the precision of a surgeon, rammed his right elbow into the man's ear, and quick-kicked his throat, paralyzing his larynx and silencing any screams that might attract unwelcome attention.

Two seconds.

Now two more.

Robert came down with his kicking leg and put all one hundred eighty pounds of his weight into the squat man's knee, splintering the patella and severing both collateral ligaments. Then he chopped into both forearms like a black belt breaking bricks. The man dropped to the ground in agony, screaming soundlessly. He wouldn't be able to make any noise for a while, not until his swollen vocal cords healed.

That is, if his larynx wasn't completely fractured.

Four seconds.

Not enough time for the slow-thinking tall guy to react, but seeing his friend writhing on the pavement in eerie silence got him moving. He swung his massive right arm at Robert's face. Robert ducked lightly into a catcher's stance as it whooshed over his head and karate-punched a one-two into the man's groin, turning his knuckles as they landed. The man's breathy howl was cut off by Robert's upward hack to his larynx, muting him like his friend.

The big man held his throat with one hand and his groin with the other, but as Robert leaned down to pick up his sweep unit, the giant heaved himself up for a last-chance knockout punch. Robert dropped to the ground, moved aside, then swept the man's leg out from under him. Rubbing the dust from his device, Robert rose up and stomped on the guy's temple, knocking him unconscious.

Eight seconds for two guys.

Not bad.

Robert brushed off his clothes and picked up the rest of his equipment. He probably had about fifteen minutes to hit his target's apartment and do what needed to be done before the ambulance, cops, and gawkers arrived.

Acting like a tired drunk coming home from a long night, Robert crossed the street. He pretended to search for his keys as he glanced back. The men were still in the mouth of the alley, one inert, the other writhing slowly. He looked around to assure himself that no one had taken notice, then dropped the drunk act, leapt up, and grabbed the rust-flaked bottom rung of the fire-escape ladder. He climbed swiftly up the moonlit stairs.

At forty-three, Robert was still quick. Then again, he wasn't a typical forty-something. He was built like an All-American linebacker with the agility of an Olympic gymnast. Most importantly, he'd been schooled in street fighting and modern warfare by Guillermo Martinez, one of the fiercest freedom fighters in Central America.

Robert reached the creaky fourth-floor landing, white with pigeon droppings. He raised the unlatched window soundlessly and entered a bedroom that smelled like the inside of a work boot. He closed the window. The ball game on TV blocked the sound of his footsteps on the floorboards.

At the doorway, he knelt and slowly peeked into the living room. The man lay snoring on the couch, feet on the coffee table, the remote and a half-empty bottle of vodka snuggled in his crotch. On the table stood a pyramid of empty orange soda cans, a tall glass with Disney characters on it, and a half-eaten plate of Chinese take-out.

No sirens yet. Still plenty of time.

Robert walked in and kicked the man's feet off the coffee table. The cans clattered to the floor. The man lurched awake in a panic and sprang to his feet, sending the bottle flying into the table edge, where it shattered.

"Jesus Christ!" he yelled, his arms waving wildly. Then he saw Robert and froze.

Robert settled down on a chair with a grin, put his own feet up on the coffee table, and started switching channels on the television set. "Sorry to wake you." He waited for the man to recognize him.

"Who the hell are you? Don't I know—haven't I—wait." Demetri's voice suddenly took on an angry tone. "You're the doctor from this morning. What the fuck are you doing in my apartment?"

"Come on, Demetri," Robert said, flipping channels. "You know why I'm here. How long did you think you could get away with what you've been doing?"

"What are you talking about?"

"I'm talking about your wife."

"My wife?" Demetri snapped. "What about my wife?"

"She's the reason I'm here."

"What's my wife got to do with anything?"

"Now, Demetri, let's not act stupid. I know you beat her until she lost consciousness, then you called the cops and told them she'd fallen down the stairs."

"I didn't touch her. She fell. That's how she got hurt. It's not my fault she's clumsy. She's always falling down stairs or tripping on shit. I told you this morning."

Robert settled on The Movie Channel, some old Clint Eastwood film, and turned up the volume.

"What does it matter anyway?" Demetri continued. "What the fuck do you care? She's doing shit like that all the time. There are clumsy bitches all over the place."

"I'm not an idiot, Demetri. You may have fooled other doctors before me with your grieving husband act. I would've applauded your tears after her first seizure, but I was too busy intubating her and connecting her to a respirator. Just to update you, she has what's known as an epidural bleed in her brain. The blood squeezed half her brain tissue against her skull bone, giving her hourly seizures. The neurosurgeons had to drill holes in her scalp to relieve the pressure."

"Damn stairs," Demetri said, shaking his head.

"If she'd fallen down the stairs, like you said, she would've broken her clavicle or a long bone. But she had no new injuries to her arms or legs, only multiple bruises on the right side of her face."

Robert held up the remote control and tossed it to Demetri, who caught it in midair with his left hand. "I noticed you were a lefty when you signed the medical forms this morning."

"Yeah, so?"

"So you prefer hitting your wife with your dominant hand."

The man shifted his bulk. He was more alert now and getting riled. "You can't prove shit," he said, looking around the room. His jittery eyes settled on a duffle bag by the TV.

"You're right. I can't prove shit," Robert said, putting his hand inside his side pocket and gripping his SIG Sauer 9mm. "But I can make you pay for what you've done."

Demetri stood up and casually inched closer to the duffle. "You're just a fucking doctor. This has nothing to do with you. You can't just break into someone's apartment. You're going to hear from the police, and you're going to hear from your hospital board. You're done, man! Get out while you still can. I'm getting my cell and calling the cops." He stooped to unzip the bag.

Robert pulled out his SIG, leaped over the coffee table, and rammed the barrel into Demetri's ear. "You're not going after your gun, are you?" He pushed Demetri back to the couch.

"I'm sorry," Demetri pleaded in panic. "Okay, okay. I won't call anyone. I promise. Just tell me why you're doing this. Why the hell do you care?"

"That's an interesting question," Robert said, taking a step back. "When bad things happen to good people, like your wife, I make sure that bad things happen back to bad people. I care that your wife was treated at six different hospitals this year, all because of violent trauma, without ever raising suspicion. At Bellevue, it was for a broken right forearm after a trip and fall. At Roosevelt, for fractures in her right orbital ridge from a car accident, except that there was never an ambulance sheet—and you don't own a car. At Beth Israel, broken ribs. You told the ER doctor she banged her chest against a banister while she was drunk, but the report sheet lists her blood alcohol level as zero. You know, Demetri, it's not so much that I *care*. It's more like I'm *pissed*. Pissed that those ER doctors were too overwhelmed with patients to pick up on the fact that you've been beating your wife for years and getting away with it."

"So you're going to shoot me?" Demetri looked anxious. "They'll find you."

Robert smiled, but remained silent. He returned his gun to his side pocket and gestured for the man to stand.

Demetri sprang to his feet and threw the remote at Robert. Without taking his eyes off his target, Robert caught the remote. He turned, raised the volume on the TV even higher, and tossed the device onto the couch. Demetri's jaw was moving sideways back and forth, his chest heaving.

Robert clapped his hands. "Class begins, Demetri. First lesson: compassion. Putting yourself in other people's shoes. I'm going to show you in three minutes how you've been making your wife feel for the past six months. And if you make it out alive, I'll make sure they put your respirator next to hers in the ICU."

Robert heard the faint sound of two sirens approaching and a small commotion outside on the street. The two muggers had been found.

This would work to his benefit. After taking care of his target, he would slip undetected from the building into the gathering crowd—and fade into the night.

PART 1

Domestic Violence Statistics[1]

» *A woman is assaulted every nine seconds in the United States.*

» *Around the world, one in every three women is beaten or raped during her lifetime.*

» *Domestic violence is the leading cause of injury to women—more than car accidents, muggings, and other forms of trauma combined.*

» *Each day in the United States, more than three women are murdered by their husbands or boyfriends.*

---

[1]National Center on Domestic and Sexual Violence

Chapter 1

Sharon Reede had no idea how long she'd been daydreaming. When she finally snapped out of her reverie, she was standing before a mirror studying the beige slacks, black chunky heels, and tan polyester blouse she was wearing.

The pants were too long, the shoes were tight, and the shirt was uncomfortable.

But the grandma outfit looked professional, and she needed to be taken seriously by the St. Jude's Hospital staff on her first day of work. Despite being twenty-eight years old—a respectable age for an emergency room social worker starting her career—her long blond hair, large brown eyes, and small frame made her look like a college freshman.

She scanned her bed, where most of her wardrobe was strewn, then looked back in the mirror and shrugged. This outfit would have to do.

Sharon found it amusing that her one-bedroom apartment in New York City was hardly bigger than her walk-in closet back home in Indiana—and yet it was four times the price! The place didn't even have a real kitchen. Instead, it had a kitchenette where you could stretch your arms and palm both walls. The living room was just big enough for a TV and sofa, the bedroom barely fit her bed, and the shower was so small that, when she stood in it, the curtain clung to the side of her body.

Nothing about New York so far had lived up to her expectations. Sharon knew she'd cry if she thought about it too much, but still she couldn't help herself. She had anticipated lights and energy. She had pictured going out, meeting people from all over the world, scoping out museums and great restaurants. Instead, she was living in a shoebox in the middle of Washington Heights, friendless and worried about money. Her first week had consisted of unpacking, sneezing from all the dust and mold, and doing a poor job of getting oriented to the city. By nightfall each evening, she was too drained to go out, and she felt unsafe walking in her neighborhood.

But she was tough. She'd fought through worse circumstances than these—taking care of dying friends and family members, cutting through the bureaucracy at her local rape crisis center, and dealing with belligerent patients. And this was New York, where she'd always wanted to live.

Sharon noticed the time on her cell phone and gasped. She was going to be late. After digging through the pile of clothes on her bed, she found her bag and hurried to the kitchen to grab a yogurt. But her fridge was empty. She had yet to go food shopping.

She left her place with a frown and a growling stomach.

The three blocks to the subway were lined with bodegas, restaurants, and four-story apartment buildings. Though unsettlingly quiet at night, the streets bustled with activity in the morning: kids heading to school, shopkeepers raising storefront gates and hosing down their patches of sidewalk. Sharon, used to greeting people passing by, had learned quickly that a Midwest "good morning" was suspicious behavior in these parts.

A train pulled in just as she slid her MetroCard into the turnstile slot. *Whump!* Her thighs met solid metal resistance. *Swipe card again at this turnstile,* the machine's LED read. Commuters were pouring on and off the train. She carefully slid the card again.

Same message.

"Do it faster, honey," a kindly old woman said, zipping her own card through successfully. Sharon could hear the subway dinging, indicating that its doors were about to shut. She swiped her card faster this time and cranked through the turnstile with her bruised thighs. The train doors shut just as she approached. She glared at the door and commanded it to open.

Surprisingly, it did.

Relieved, she took a half-step forward, but there was no room inside. Expressionless faces from a pack of suited bodies stared back at her. No one moved.

Then she saw the old lady beckoning her. Sharon hurried toward her and was pulled in as the door clattered and stuttered shut, sideswiping her butt several times. Her nose was a half-inch from an older man's slicked-back hair, which smelled like cheap olive oil. The huge backpack of a tourist thumped against her side for the eight minutes it took to get to her stop on 116th Street, Columbia University.

So far, the campus was the only part of Manhattan where she felt at ease. Unlike the noisy, crowded streets littered with used cups and chewed gum, the campus was beautiful, peaceful, and green. With its giant oaks and soft, inviting lawn, it reminded her of Indiana. Sharon heard birds chirping as she walked beside the redbrick and limestone buildings, admiring the Ionic columns of one as she hurried past.

St. Jude's Hospital, though, was nothing like the university campus. It was an enormous gray structure occupying two full city blocks. The glow of fluorescent lights came through its narrow windows, yet the building looked oddly dark.

Sharon hurried to Starko's Deli across the street from the emergency room, hoping for coffee and a bagel—but the place was mobbed with doctors and nurses, suits and construction workers. She expelled a sharp sigh and went back out.

As she headed for the ER entrance, Sharon felt a pit in her stomach. She ignored the feeling and marched inside, trying to look brisk, professional, and ten years older. She showed her new ID card to the two massive security guards and said, "Good morning." Saying nothing, they peered at her ID to compare the picture to her face, and then grimly opened the doors.

The narrow hallway echoed with loud noises and smelled like a sickly blend of mouthwash and urine. Her rotation at the small community ER in Bloomington had done little to prepare her for this chamber of chaos.

About thirty rooms surrounded the inner area, an open space sectioned unevenly by three long tables with computers where doctors and nurses filled out charts, pounded on keyboards, and looked fiercely at screens. Every room had at least one or two patients. Occupied gurneys lined the hallways. Sharon couldn't see space for anyone else, yet ambulances were lined up outside. Half a dozen people were running: technicians, nurses, residents. A man wheeling a portable x-ray machine did a miraculous job of speeding it through the traffic without any collisions.

The world spun around her as she looked for someone with authority, someone to welcome her. She approached the frowning triage nurse, an obese African American woman in her mid-forties. Her nametag read *Michelle Rivera, RN* under a photo that showed her looking fifteen years younger and fifty pounds lighter. She bounced among three moaning, bleeding patients.

Sharon wondered if that picture had captured Nurse Rivera's last moment of happiness. "Good morning, ma'am. My name is—"

"Don't call me *ma'am*, child!" Nurse Rivera snapped. "And there is certainly nothing good about this morning. Go back to the lobby. No family members back here today. Too busy."

"I'm the new social worker. It's my first day. I just want to know where I'm supposed to go," Sharon said, following Rivera from the ambulance bay to the main ER.

"*You're* the new social worker?" Looking Sharon up and down, Rivera shook her head and then grabbed an equally obese white nurse passing by. "Peggy, take a look at who the agency sent us this time."

"They graduating social workers outta kindergarten now? Sheee-it! She won't last 'til naptime."

Nurse Rivera finished registering a patient and then turned back to Sharon. "Haven't run away yet? Well, that's something. Look, we've had six social workers this year so far, and, believe me, they were about ten times sturdier than you look. I know I'm supposed to give you the tour, but it's gonna be a-bree-viated. We're up to our neck in shit this morning. I bet you'll last two, maybe two-and-a-half days, so you're gonna get the two-and-a-half-day tour."

Before Sharon could think of a response, Rivera barreled past the long tables of the main ER, pointing things out. It was impressive how fast the massive woman could move, and Sharon struggled to keep up and take in all she said, scrawling down notes whenever she could.

"The emergency department has thirty-two rooms in the main area, but way more patients than that," Rivera explained. "Hence the hallway hospitality and what we like to call the open-door policy on the rooms." She made a sharp turn down a small decline, passing by her triage desk. "The ambulances enter through those doors, and I do my thing. If they're sick enough they go to resus and—"

"Where?" Sharon interrupted.

"The resuscitation room. What'd you think I said?"

"I thought you said *recess*."

Rivera sighed as if her job were too painful for her pay scale and tramped down a dingy hallway toward a small door with a sign that read *Family Room*.

"You'll be spending a lot of time behind that door, mostly to give bad news to our patients' relatives," Rivera said. "And down there's the fast-track area. Patients with the flu, sprains, insect bites, eye crud. That's where you'll never be." She whirled to chug back to the triage desk and, without missing a beat or changing expression, redirected a paramedic wheeling a patient who was thrashing against his restraints. "Each morning, you'll report to me. I'll give you the doctors' consult charts from the night before. Finish those, then I'll give you the ones from today."

Rivera inspected her triage desk. "Where are last night's? Ah, here they are." She grabbed a thick stack of charts from under a box of rubber gloves on her desk. "Okay." She poked the top one with a fat, stubby finger. "Here's a guy in resus who got assaulted in his apartment last night. He's in a coma, on a respirator. And what's this?" She flipped through the pages irritably. "I see. His wife died in the ICU this morning. She was in for an epidural bleed from a fall and coded at 4:54 a.m. So you'll need to find any living relative he might have and give them the 411."

She pulled the next two charts from the stack and placed them on top. "But before that, do these two clowns. Scum with legs. Room 8. Ambulance scraped them off the sidewalk across the street from the guy in resus. Supposedly, some gang did payback on them, but they won't admit it. They made a ruckus about getting a social worker, and we're obliged, so lucky you. Just get rid of them quick. We need the beds."

Rivera shoved the charts at Sharon and whipped her head around as another ambulance crew arrived and called for her. She darted off and called back over her shoulder. "Just don't get in our way, Barbie, or we'll run you over. State requires you're here, but we don't. Keep your little bunny nose out of our business."

Bunny nose?

Grimacing, Sharon looked at the top two charts. They were thick with what looked like angrily scrawled notes. She juggled the heavy, crimson plastic folders as she searched for a place to sit. She'd just collapsed into a chair near Rivera's station when someone tapped her on the shoulder. "Out of my seat, sweetheart. That's for doctors. Come on, out!"

He wore a light-blue scrub top, brown jeans, and white sneakers—unlike the other doctors in full scrubs and white coats. He had a scruffy beard and didn't look friendly at all.

"Sorry about that. I'm the new social worker—"

"I don't care if you're Madame Curie. Just don't sit in my seat."

He pushed her charts aside to make room for his coffee. As she collected them, she saw him surfing the Web for news. At once, Sharon realized that she needed to stand up for herself if she was going to earn any respect.

"Wow," she said, pointing at his screen. "'Local Bartender Pickles Own Onions!' I can see why you were in such a hurry to sit down."

"Go on, Barbie. You heard Rivera."

"Could you direct me to the area where insignificant mold forms can sit?"

"Not my problem." He rolled and clicked his mouse rapidly, his eyes never leaving the screen.

Sharon reached past his mouse hand and tilted his ID up to read. "What are you doing?"

"*Dr. McKenzie,*" she read out loud. "*Emergency Physician.* A name to remember." She turned and stalked off, exaggerating the swing of her hips. She would've knocked over his cup of coffee if it weren't for his quick reflexes.

Sharon found a chair at the next table and pulled it out. "No, no, no, no, no, Miss Social Worker." It was the two-ton white nurse Rivera had stopped before. "This is for nurses only. No room for others. No room."

"But where am I supposed to do my consults?" Sharon asked.

"Not my problem."

She was already getting used to hearing that response.

Sharon grabbed her belongings and walked to the last table, by the radiology station. Four residents crowded around a large screen, studying an x-ray.

No room there, either.

She sighed, and the resident doctor pointing things out on the x-ray looked over at her. "Can I help you?"

He was a great-looking guy. Tall and dark, with broad shoulders and a friendly smile. He was a little old for her usual taste, but still attractive.

"I need a place to go over these charts. I'm Sharon, the new social worker." She looked at his nametag, but it was covered by his stethoscope. "And you're Dr...."

"Donahoe. I'm one of the chief surgical residents."

"Nice to meet you. Sorry for interrupting. I'm just trying to find a place to work."

"It's okay. Try that chair by the bathroom." He pointed to the nearby corner.

"Thanks."

"Don't mention it, Sharon. Welcome to St. Jude's." She felt him watching her as she walked away.

At least not everyone here's an a-hole.

She dragged an empty stool next to the chair by the ER bathroom and balanced her ungainly stack of charts on top. She started to look through the first chart, but the noxious smell made it impossible to concentrate. She got up to close the bathroom door and saw big gobs of feces smeared across the floor and toilet bowl.

She called to one of the ER technicians across from the bathroom. "Can you believe that smell?"

"What smell?" he answered, not bothering to look up from dipping urine samples.

"Somebody took a crap all over the bathroom!"

He scoffed. "Lucky bastard! I haven't had a good shit in weeks." He grabbed the urine specimen, wrote a note on a sheet of paper, and walked away without looking at her.

Sharon shook her head, trying not to breathe. After searching the ER for a minute, she found a janitor mopping the resuscitation room—a rail-thin, elderly Asian woman. "Hi, ma'am. I'm sorry to bother you, but somebody had an accident in the bathroom and I was hoping you could clean it up."

The woman stared at her with a blank face. Sharon wondered if she understood English, but then the woman put down the mop and walked to the bathroom. She opened the door and saw the mess, then closed the door, reached into her pocket, and pulled out a little plastic sign that read *Out of Order*. She stuck it on the door and left without saying a word.

Sharon walked back to her chair and tried her best to suppress her desire to cry. She had done so well in graduate school. She'd had her pick of jobs, including an offer to work at a pretty nursing home in San Francisco—near the water, nine to five, with weekends off for biking or hiking—and the position in Denver, with easy access to mountains for skiing or snowboarding.

Instead, she'd chosen St. Jude's.

She tried to pull herself together, taking out a tissue and holding it over her nose. She opened up the top chart and reminded herself that this was really just the start of her career. Through two years in the Peace Corps and four years in graduate school, this was what she'd been working toward. She told herself to stay strong. Nothing was going to bring her down—not hostile patients, not an unfriendly staff, and certainly not an "out-of-order" bathroom.

After ten minutes, she felt ready for her first consult. She gathered her things and headed over to room 8.

"Good morning, my name's Sharon Reede. I'm the emergency room social worker. You must be Neil Parker and Anthony Menendez, right?"

The two men were on gurneys. One had both arms casted and one knee in a black immobilizer. The other had a bloodied bandage on his head. They both glared at her.

"I understand you guys were assaulted last night. It says here that it was a gang-related act of violence?"

"Not a gang," Parker croaked. He was the smaller one with the casts and knee immobilizer. "I told the cops. It was one guy. Some crazy fucker. We were just minding our own business. He jumped us and went ape shit."

"One guy did this to you?" Sharon asked, flipping back through the chart and browsing through the list of injuries. "What did he look like?"

"How the fuck are we supposed to know? We were getting the shit kicked out of us. Damn! It was dark. He was wearing black. He had a pair of weird glasses covering his face."

Menendez turned from facing the wall and looked at Parker. "Not glasses. They were some high-tech shit, you dumb motherfucker."

"Yo, Ant. I told you not to call me that!"

"Oh sorry. I meant *dumbass*." Menendez's bulging muscles made his hospital gown look two sizes too small.

"Man, this guy must've been something else to take on big guys like you," Sharon said.

"He got lucky," Menendez said. "He knew that kung fu shit."

"But I'm gonna get me a ghetto toy and go after that mother-fucker," Parker said, squirming in pain as he tried to sit up. "He's gonna get it."

"Ghetto toy?" Sharon repeated.

"A gun," Parker barked. "Anyway, you gonna help us out or what?"

Sharon turned to the assessment page at the end of the chart. "I see that you gentlemen, and I use that term loosely, are getting discharged today. Parker, you have a follow-up with the orthope-dist next week. Menendez, you have one with the neurologist in two days. And you're both requesting a visiting nurse, right?"

"Yeah, 'cause I can't use my hands," Parker said, raising his arms, both in casts. "Unless you want to come over my house and wipe my ass for me. And no male nurse. Get me a hot female bitch, you feel me?"

"Hot ... female ... bitch," Sharon said, pretending to write this request down. She snapped the charts closed. "Okay, boys, let me speak to the charge nurse and see what I can do."

As she walked away, she heard Parker yell out, "And how about some food? McNuggets or something! All we got is Jell-O."

Sharon found Rivera at the triage station. "I was hoping you could help me arrange a visiting nurse for the two men in 8."

Rivera snorted. "For those two punks? No way. Just call the hotline and put their names on a waiting list. No service will give those guys a nurse."

"Why wouldn't they? The guys may be jerks, but Parker has a point. How's he going to wipe himself after using the bathroom?"

"He can stick his ass in the shower," Rivera said. "Listen, honey, just make the phone call, document it, and move on. You've got way too many patients to waste your time on those two scumbags."

Sharon was taken aback by the nurse's apathy. "Despite our opinions of them, they were still victims of some madman's act of violence, and they're in a lot of pain."

"Let me guess," came a voice from behind her. She immediately recognized it as coming from that ogre with the jeans and scrub top, the one who preferred surfing the Internet to being a doctor. "They probably told you they were minding their own business when some random insane guy assaulted them." He started laughing, and Rivera joined in.

"They did say that," Sharon said. "Why would they lie?"

McKenzie rolled his eyes. "Michelle, where did the agency find this girl? Kansas?"

"Actually, I'm from Indiana."

"Of course you are." He looked at Rivera. "So what's the over-under?"

"We're giving her a month," Rivera said, "but no one really thinks she'll make it to the end of the week."

"Sounds about right." McKenzie strolled back to his desk.

How can he keep doing nothing while the ER is so busy?

Sharon looked around and realized that all the work was being done by the resident physicians.

"McKenzie's in charge?" she asked out loud.

But she was speaking to herself. Rivera had gone to the ambulance bay and McKenzie had plopped back down in front of his computer screen. She went over to him, leaned forward, and spoke into his ear. "I'm sticking out the year, so get used to it."

She turned around and walked away, feeling the long look he gave her. She found a phone, called the hotline as Rivera suggested, and finished her consult with the two assault victims. Then she returned to her makeshift desk. The *Out of Order* sign was still on the bathroom, and the smell was getting worse. She put one hand to her nose and opened the chart for her next consult, the comatose guy in resus.

I'm supposed to find family for him?

She sighed, thinking of what life would have been like in San Francisco.

Chapter 2

"I'm telling you, bro. There's a ninja in Manhattan."

"You talking stupid. That's just movie shit."

Sharon stood in line for coffee at Starko's, eavesdropping on the teenagers talking in front of her.

"No, I'm telling you. My cousin and I saw him last night. We were smoking weed outside our building. This Chinese tourist dude looking all lost and shit was about to get jumped by a bunch of guys when this fucking ninja in black comes out of nowhere like Batman or something. Man, I'm telling you, he kicked the living shit out of those fuckers. The guy's like a black belt or something. Took all four of them down in like a minute!"

"Maybe you and your cousin should stay off the dope."

The kids were about twelve, drinking Red Bulls and eating chips. Sharon figured they were probably in line for cookies or donuts. She wanted to jump in on the conversation and reinforce the dangers of substance abuse, and maybe put in a few words about proper nutrition, but she thought better of it.

Two coffees in hand, she set off across the street to start her third week of work. Rivera was barking something about supplies into her cell phone while pointing peevishly to where a paramedic should wheel his patient. Sharon put one of the coffees down on Rivera's desk and grabbed a stack of charts from the side slot. She could've sworn she caught a fleeting smile on the nurse's face. It was all Sharon needed to make her morning.

She headed over to the last of the three desks in the main ER, slapped her charts down, swung her bag beneath her chair, and sat. The long hours she'd spent working behind that desk, as well as Dr. Donahoe's friendly attitude toward her, had impressed the residents enough to grant her a claim on this precious real estate. They kept to the table-end by the PACS radiology computer and let her have her space.

She'd learned a lot in her first two weeks. Lesson one was that there was no such thing as nine to five in a New York City emergency room, and overtime was unpaid. Lesson two was that even the toughest and meanest of the staff had their soft side. Once you proved strong enough to last, everyone treated you as part of the team.

Everyone excluding McKenzie.

Dr. McKenzie didn't seem like part of any team. He was sarcastic, crude, and dismissive. Except for Nurse Rivera, nobody could stand him. One of the senior ER residents, Dr. Sanchez, particularly hated him. Sanchez had been an attending physician in Guatemala, but he had to do his residency over again when he moved to the United States. Built like a boxer, Sanchez had once told her that he often dreamed of punching McKenzie out for all the times he embarrassed him in front of the other residents. Sharon tried to be supportive and reminded him that violence was not the solution. But the more she worked with McKenzie, the more she enjoyed picturing Sanchez knocking him out.

During their last interaction, Sharon had to keep *herself* from swinging at him. The case involved a battered woman she'd counseled at the end of her shift that past Friday. McKenzie had examined the victim and then notified the police. Sharon, though tired and wanting to go home, nonetheless volunteered to help. When she went back to McKenzie with her findings, he scoffed at her and blamed the woman for getting beat up. He pointed out that it wasn't the first time the woman's fiancé had abused her. It was her fault, he claimed, for sticking around and allowing the violence to continue.

Sharon waved reports in his face that showed how the woman tried to get her fiancé into anger management sessions and into a treatment program for alcohol abuse, the main cause of his outbursts.

"Those are just words," McKenzie had said. "The woman should've left him months ago. She needed this last beating to pound some sense into her."

Sharon couldn't believe her ears. She stormed away and burned the wires to secure a shelter for the woman. It took four tries and a lot of bureaucratic maneuvering, but she finally found one. Then Sharon hung around the ER for another hour to write a letter to the director of the emergency department, describing the incident and stating how Dr. McKenzie had been "unprofessional and inappropriate."

According to Rivera, though, the ER director had received dozens of complaints about McKenzie from patients, nurses, and other physicians, but he never did anything about it. There were rumors that McKenzie had saved the director's wife from a life-threatening illness no specialist could diagnose, thereby granting him lifetime immunity.

It seemed like an unfair number of her consults involved McKenzie's patients. Or maybe she felt that way because those were the ones that were memorable—largely because he was such a creep.

The one saving grace was that she also got to work quite a lot with Dr. Donahoe, the chief surgical resident. He supervised all

ER trauma cases, and many of those required a social work consult. Besides being the most attractive doctor in the department, Donahoe was also the nicest. Sharon had noticed that his left hand was ring-free, and she'd started to wonder if one day she might break her rule about not dating co-workers.

Just as she was reaching for the first chart of the morning, Sharon saw Dr. Donahoe standing by her desk. "Glad to see you've made it into your third week," he said. "For the record, I knew you would." Then he walked away.

Sharon smiled and tried really hard to keep herself from blushing. *Yes, I'm going to have to break my rule,* she thought as she took a sip of her coffee and opened the top chart, groaning inwardly when she saw Mr. Garrett's name again.

The neighborhood drunk was a frequent flyer in the ER. He always arrived intoxicated, belligerent, and requiring sedation. She'd seen him three times already in those two weeks. Each time, Sharon had managed to get him into Alcoholics Anonymous, a detox facility, and a nearby homeless shelter, but each time he broke the rules and got kicked out. This time someone found him passed out in a nearby parking lot and called 911.

"Mr. Garrett? Mr. Garrett!" She tried not to sound irritated.

Garrett didn't move. She knocked lightly on his head. "Hello! Anyone home?" Nothing. She flipped through his chart and saw he'd been violent to the paramedics, so Dr. Sanchez had given him a B52 cocktail: Benadryl, 50 milligrams; Haldol, 5 milligrams; and Ativan, 2 milligrams.

She tried ruffling his hair. "Mr. Garrett, it's Sharon, remember? You promised me you were going to stop drinking?"

Still no movement. She closed his chart and heard laughter behind her.

"Something funny?" Sharon asked, her irritation with Garrett transferring quickly to McKenzie.

"Triage your time better, Reede. Trying to fix everyone steals time from the few patients we can help. Garrett's a loser. He's scum on our little pond. Move on."

Sharon had become increasingly bold with McKenzie. From her experience in graduate school, she learned that it was the only way to gain respect from people like him. "Unlike you, Dr. McKenzie, I believe that Mr. Garrett's a human being. He has alcoholism. It's a disease. You're a physician. You should know better. If you tore yourself from your computer long enough to talk to him, you'd find he once had a wife and kids, a home, a job. Now he has nothing. He's a creep because he drinks. What's your excuse?"

"The truth is my excuse, Miss Indiana. That guy never held a job, and he sure as hell never had a family. You should hear the sob stories he gave the half-dozen social workers who came before you." He went on, doing his best Garrett impression. "*My house burned down. My child died of cancer. My whole family died in a car crash.* Last year, Garrett punched one of our pregnant nurses in the stomach. You didn't know that, did you? You think that if he punched you in the stomach while you were pregnant, and brought on a miscarriage, you'd still want to waste time on him?"

Sharon stood there gaping, wondering if McKenzie had made up that story.

Dr. Sanchez ambled over. "Everything all right?"

"Go back to your suturing," McKenzie said. "This conversation doesn't concern you."

"I was just making sure everything was okay," Sanchez said, nodding to Sharon and walking away.

"Your boyfriend smells like bottom-shelf cologne from Walgreens," McKenzie said.

"He's not my boyfriend—and I'm not giving up on Garrett. I'm not as callous as you."

"Callous?" McKenzie repeated. "Check this out." He walked over to Garrett's gurney. He made a fist and rubbed the man's chest hard with his knuckles until the patient woke up. "Hey, Charlie. You know you have a drinking problem, right?" The drunk made his eyes wider. "I do?" he said sarcastically. Then he got angry. "The only goddamn problem I have is I got no money to buy booze. You gonna give me some?" He suddenly realized whom he was talking to and shook his head. "Oh fuck. You? You ain't gonna give me shit." He turned to Sharon. "Hey honey, got a fiver?"

"You promised me you'd stay in detox, Mr. Garrett."

"My mother was raped yesterday! I just found out. I was upset."

Sharon turned to McKenzie, but he was shaking his head and walking toward resus. She took a deep breath, returned to her desk, and put Garrett's chart away. She was seething, and she wasn't sure which man she disliked more.

Chapter 3

Something felt wrong.

For the first time in four weeks, Donahoe hadn't stopped by her desk to chat. He seemed distant, exhausted, preoccupied. Sharon had hoped he'd remember that today was the day she beat the over-under. *A month at St. Jude's.* She'd made it without any major issues, other than the occasional verbal matches with Dr. Jerk-Off McKenzie.

Sharon was going to propose going out to celebrate. She had decided to break her no-dating-colleagues rule and was ready to take the lead. This was New York City, not Indiana. She could ask him out herself.

The celebration, though, would have to wait.

She'd seen Donahoe rushing out of a patient's room to call the OR. His patient, a woman in her mid-thirties, had a splenic rupture and liver lacerations from an assault and needed emergency surgery.

Not once did he look at her when he wheeled the patient out of room 14. It was tough not to take it personally. But then again, Sharon still found it difficult to understand how physicians dealt with the constant psychological trauma they experienced. It seemed like diagnosing cancer or telling people their loved ones were dead was a daily occurrence.

She wondered how Donahoe dealt with it.

"Hey, Sharon, any chance you could help out one of my patients?" Dr. Sanchez asked. He was leaning against the PACS radiology computer with a chart in his hand. "I know you're really busy with consults, but this is an easy one."

"Sure," Sharon said, pushing her stack of charts to the side. "What's up?"

"Just a medication request. This guy has a skin infection and can't afford antibiotics."

"Absolutely," she said, taking the chart and browsing through the notes. For some reason, Sanchez stood there staring at her. It was the same kind of look that guys gave her at bars whenever she'd go out for happy hour.

And that's why she'd stopped going to happy hour.

"Is there anything else you want?" Sharon asked.

"Oh, um, no," Sanchez said, and headed back to his workstation.

Sharon looked at her pile of charts and did a mental checklist of her morning consults. None was urgent. There was an elderly patient with a recent stroke requiring an occupational therapist, a diabetic woman with a chronic foot ulcer needing a visiting nurse, and another homeless man requesting placement at a shelter.

Though she was starting to find Sanchez annoying, Sharon would consult on his patient first and then tackle the rest.

Besides, this was someone she could actually help. Despite all the public health problems New York had, Sharon loved some of its assistance programs, such as the one that provided free generic medications to patients in financial need. All she had to do was stamp the prescription with the official logo and have the attending physician co-sign.

She recalled McKenzie's words from a couple weeks back about using her time for patients she could help. Well, she would show him that she was following his advice.

Sharon found the patient, a man in his late forties with left-arm cellulitis, sitting quietly in bed. He apologized for taking up her time and expressed embarrassment for requesting free prescriptions. She reassured him and reminded him that the resources were there for a reason, then finished her note and took the chart to McKenzie.

"Okay, I took your advice. I found a patient who deserves help. Mr. Elliot Jacobs. Skin infection. Just write him a prescription and sign the form. I'll stamp it, and he'll get his antibiotics for free."

"Absolutely not," McKenzie said, handing back the chart.

"Excuse me?"

"He can afford the antibiotics."

"You haven't even seen the patient."

"Oh?" He pointed across the ER. "That guy, right?"

Sharon turned and looked. "Mr. Jacobs, yes."

"You may not know this, but cephalexin is on the four-dollar prescription list at Walgreens."

"To you, four dollars may be nothing, but to this guy, it's a lot. You just want to give me a hard time."

"I won't deny that giving you a hard time provides me with an enormous amount of entertainment, but you're conceited if you think that's the only reason I'm turning down your request. Where's this guy's skin infection?"

"Left arm."

"No shit. But you need to be more specific. His skin infection is on the left antecubital fossa over the left brachial vein in his elbow pit. That's where right-handed heroin users get cellulitis. Don't let him fool you. That guy can afford antibiotics. Take a closer look at him."

Sharon turned and stared at Mr. Jacobs.

"Check out how he's sitting and fidgeting at the edge of his gurney," McKenzie continued. "He's dying to get out for a smoke. Didn't you notice his nicotine-stained teeth? Cigarettes are ten dollars a pack. Cephalexin is four dollars. If that doper really wanted antibiotics, he'd smoke eight less cigarettes today. But no. He'd rather you and I pay for them with our tax dollars. He's working the system. There's a lot of free stuff he can scam off this city. He gets clothes from the Salvation Army because he tells them he's a vet. He gets room and board from the shelters. And he gets the money for his drug and tobacco addiction by all-out mooching."

"I think you're wrong," Sharon said.

"Oh really? Check this out." He found Jacobs' phone number on the registration papers and dialed. After a few seconds, Sharon saw Jacobs dig into his pocket and pull out the latest iPhone.

"Hi, Mr. Jacobs," McKenzie said, waving to him. It took Jacobs several seconds to figure out that the call came from inside the ER. When his puzzled gaze landed on McKenzie, the patient waved back nervously.

"The social worker tells me you can't afford a four-dollar prescription. Well, it's your lucky day. I'm not only a physician but also a financial advisor with some tips. First, stop smoking. Second, stop shooting up dope. Third, get a job. Fourth, get a life. And fifth, don't show your scumbag face in this ER again or I'll quarantine your ass until you jones your puking guts out. Oh, by the way, nice phone. Who'd you steal that from?"

Mr. Jacobs grabbed his jacket, gave McKenzie the finger, and stormed out of the ER.

"I can't believe you just did that," Sharon said.

"Why? He deserved to be called out on it."

"Even if you're right about him," she said, "you have to be respectful."

"Do I? Was Jacobs being respectful?"

"No, but you shouldn't be sinking to his level."

McKenzie shrugged and picked up his stack of charts. "Look, Reede, let me tell you about some people who can really use your help. Room 3: A fifty-year-old woman who tried overdosing on Ambien because she got laid off from work and can't pay her rent. Room 16: An eighty-year-old guy with end-stage Alzheimer's who got dropped off by his family because they don't want to take care of him anymore. And last but definitely not least, room 25." He shook his head and handed Sharon the chart. "This should be your next patient, courtesy of your BFF."

"Dr. Donahoe?"

"Yeah," McKenzie answered. "He took this girl's mom to the operating room a little while ago."

Sharon flipped through the pages while he continued. "Annie Brihadara. Four years old. Brought by ambulance this morning with her mom, who caught the father raping Annie in the middle of the night. Vaginal and anal tears. Fractured orbital wall and nasal bone. Bruises all over her chest and back. Not the first time the father raped her. The girl won't talk to anyone. We'll have to transfer her to Columbia Presbyterian, the only hospital in the city that performs pediatric rape kits. It'll take another three or four hours for the paperwork before the transfer. Her mother was beaten nearly unconscious. It's a miracle she got the kid here. If the mom survives the surgery, she'll be admitted to the surgical intensive care unit. Donahoe would've requested the consult himself but, as you can imagine, he's kind of busy."

Sickened, Sharon continued to skim the five pages of documentation. There were copies of the police pictures showing the injuries. She closed the chart and looked up. "Maybe I can get her to talk."

"Maybe. You're about the same age, emotionally."

Sharon ignored the comment. "What about the father?"

"The police went to the apartment to arrest him, but he wasn't there. Apparently, the guy has a few mistresses around town. The cops are looking for him but can't go full force until the rape kit's done and all the evidence is collected."

The overhead pager called for McKenzie to assist with a cardiac arrest in resus. He grabbed his stethoscope from the desk. "The father's not your concern. Just take care of the girl. You're potentially the only good thing in her life right now."

Then he was gone.

Sharon summoned her courage and tapped on the door to room 25. She opened it to find a little girl sitting on a chair, looking lost and scared. The technician sitting with her was on his cell phone, texting, oblivious.

You're potentially the only good thing in her life.

McKenzie's words echoed in her head with a strange loneliness. She took a deep breath. "Hi, Annie. My name is Sharon."

Chapter 4

"I told you a thousand times I wanted Kurtz Lite and whiskey. Whiskey, not rum! I hate rum. Go back to the store and get me the right shit."

On the rooftop of the building across the street, Robert turned down the volume on his Bluetooth audio enhancer. The man's voice was hard to take, constantly toggling between drill sergeant and pimp. He turned on the goggles' heat-sensing function and watched one orange glowing body leave the apartment while the other took something from a drawer, sat on the couch, and leaned his head on the coffee table.

Robert flipped off the heat sensor and saw the target jolt back as if shocked, then bend down again. He turned up the volume once more. Sure enough, he heard snorting.

Cocaine.

Robert looked at his watch. Midnight. He'd been there an hour. It was time. The woman who had left the apartment now exited the building and headed south on Broadway. Using the telescope function, he swept the street and found the nearest liquor store five blocks away. Four minutes to get there, two to buy the whiskey, four to get back, plus a minute or so to take the elevator back to the third floor. He had less than twelve minutes.

Fall had arrived early this year. The nights were getting chilly. Robert wished he'd worn thermals. Normally, he planned better—but this mission was urgent. The police had already found two of the man's mistresses; it wouldn't be long before they'd find this one.

Robert had the advantage, though. He could locate anyone with an iPhone by hacking into Apple's GPS terminal. All he needed was a target's cell number. He found Mr. Brihadara's in his wife's medical records.

In case of emergency, call…

Robert considered Brihadara to be the emergency.

Fixing one end of the black zip-line to a compressed-air gun, Robert shot it straight across the forty yards to the opposite building. The grappling hook landed deep in the brick above the target's living room window. As he tightened his end of the line firmly around a nearby cement-enclosed vent, Robert heard a riot of bangs and crashes from an old *Die Hard* movie playing on Brihadara's TV.

A fan of action flicks? Robert wondered as he gathered momentum on the zip-line. Instead of braking his acceleration, he twisted backward and hunched into a ball, which increased his speed and allowed him to crash through the pane.

The sound seemed to come from the TV, where Bruce Willis was crawling through shattering office glass. Brihadara looked over his shoulder with a puzzled look and then jumped off the couch when he saw Robert rising from the shards.

"Holy shit—what the fuck?"

Robert brushed himself off and took out his SIG. "Sit down, Brihadara. Back on the couch."

"Please don't shoot—"

"I'm not going to shoot you. Just get back on the couch."

"I'll do whatever you want, man," Brihadara said, lowering his arms.

"That's exactly what I was hoping for." Robert lowered his gun and quickly glanced around, studying the apartment.

"Who are you?"

"I just want some information," Robert said. "That's all."

"Okay. Okay. Whatever you want. Just don't shoot. Please. I'll give you whatever I got." Brihadara opened the drawer and took out more cocaine. "Want some?"

Robert took a quick step and kicked the bag out of Brihadara's hands, scattering powder across the large plasma screen. Bruce Willis's eyes seemed to grow wider at the sudden snowstorm.

"Aw, man, what'd you do that for?" Brihadara sprang up, wiped a swath of cocaine off the screen, and rubbed it into his gums. "You want money? I have a shitload. Just give me a few hours. I'll get my people on it."

Brihadara was in his mid-thirties, well built, with a full head of wavy brown hair and a scruffy beard.

A New York City babe magnet.

The bad-boy type.

"I don't want your money, you dirt bag, and I certainly don't want your drugs."

"What do you want then?"

"I want to know why you raped your kid."

"That's why you're here?" Brihadara, emboldened by the coke, shook his head in disbelief. "You want to know why I raped Annie? Okay, I'll tell you. Because I'm sick, man. I'm just following the cycle started by my own daddy. I can't help it."

The cycle of sexual abuse. Robert never bought into it. Being sexually molested as a child didn't necessarily doom people to become abusers.

"Why does anybody do anything?" Brihadara continued.

"Look at you. All shocked and shit. Like things matter. You haven't learned the secret."

"What secret?"

Brihadara swiped some more powder from the screen to his gums and smacked his lips. "Nothing matters, man. That's the secret. We're all a bunch of bugs. It's a rotten life, and we're just rotting along with it."

Robert picked up an empty can of Kurtz Lite and stared at it. *Why is this piss juice the beer of choice for so many wife beaters and child molesters?*

"I believe some things matter," Robert said, looking out the shattered window to see if the woman was coming back.

"God bless you and your fairy tales, man, because they don't."

"You've scarred that little girl forever," Robert said. "You've stuffed a life of psychological torture down her throat and taped her mouth shut. I'm going to stop you from making anyone else's life a living hell."

"It won't make a difference," Brihadara said. "Anyway, what the hell are you doing here? This has nothing to do with you."

"It has *everything* to do with me," Robert said. "Your daughter couldn't defend herself when you raped her last night. She couldn't fight back when you stuffed your fingers into her mouth to keep her from crying out for help. I've taken the liberty of making myself her health care proxy."

"So what? Are you going to shoot me? I'm dead anyway. We're all dead. It won't make a difference."

Robert put the SIG back in his bag, and Brihadara's eyes bugged.

"I'm here to bring you back to life," Robert said, taking out a hypodermic needle.

Brihadara lunged off the couch, swinging a heavy fist. Robert took a precise step back. The momentum of the missed punch exposed Brihadara's jugular. Robert plunged the syringe, containing a concentrated mix of the sedatives propofol and ketamine, directly into it. A moment later, Brihadara slumped to the floor, unconscious but breathing.

Robert pulled out a set of surgical scalpels. "Here's the thing," he whispered, leaning closer. "Instead of killing you, I'm going to provide you with a whole new perspective on life."

Chapter 5

"The police are with him now," Nurse Rivera said. "He'll be moved to the surgical care unit, but I don't see what more they can do for him medically. He's technically under arrest, but he's hardly a flight risk, as you can imagine."

Sharon looked up from the chart and met the wry gaze of the triage nurse. "Yeah, I doubt he's going anywhere."

"Do me a favor," Rivera said. "Speak to the police for me. I want to feel bad for the guy, but I can't. I'm sure he's going to jail, but he's going to need a full-time nurse and physical therapist."

Sharon took her charts, dropped them on her desk, slung her bag beneath her chair, and headed to room 13. Even after five weeks on the job, she'd never seen a body as messed up as this.

Zonked on the narcotics dripping through his IV, the patient lay on a gurney. His head was wrapped in thick white gauze spotted with pink-red ooze where his eyes should be. His hands were in splints and his legs were attached to metal rods at the knees. A brownish rag, lolling from his mouth, was taped to the side of his face. Two detectives sat beside the bed taking notes.

She tried to contain her nausea and keep her composure. "Good morning, officers. I'm Sharon Reede, the social worker."

The detectives looked up. The man did a double take. Sharon was annoyed by the once-over he then gave her body. She felt like telling him to grow up, but his female partner beat her to it.

"Give the girl a break, Larry." She stuck her hand out to Sharon. "I'm Detective Macy. This is Detective Landers." She elbowed him hard in the ribs, but this only made him smile.

Sharon shook their hands, making a disgusted face at Landers. She addressed Macy. "I understand there's some paperwork I can help with?"

"Yeah, we think we can connect this case to a number of others."

"None this bad, though," Landers said, getting business-like. "This scumbag got truly helly-kellied."

"He means 'Helen-Kellered,'" Macy said with a grimace.

"Helen-Kellered?" Sharon repeated.

"It's a reference to the deaf, blind, and mute from that *Miracle Worker* movie, sweetheart," Landers answered.

"It was a book first," Macy corrected, shaking her head at him. "Whoever did this punctured the guy's eardrums and eyes, then sliced his tongue in half. It's not the first time someone's done this."

"No speaky, no looky, no heary. No evil from this monkey for a long time," Landers said. "As an extra bonus, he got shattered wrists and pulverized kneecaps."

"The puncturing could've been done by some sort of long surgical needle. Do you know of any instruments like that?" Macy asked.

Sharon was still feeling disoriented by the patient's condition and Landers's crassness. "Not that I can think of. I'm sure one of the doctors would know better."

As she said this, Sharon caught a glimpse of Dr. Donahoe striding across the main ER toward resus.

Macy nodded and looked at her notes. "You took care of this guy's daughter last week." She looked up at Sharon with honest concern. "How's she doing?"

"Oh. Annie. Yeah. Her mother brought her in. This guy raped her. Allegedly, I should say, right?"

"Not allegedly, sweetheart," Landers said. "This guy did it. DNA from the rape kit confirms it. Too bad he didn't get his dick cut off, too."

Sharon's nausea was turning into anger.

Landers raised both his hands. "Sorry, but you can't honestly be upset. The guy got what he deserved."

"Who would do something like this?" Sharon asked, looking down at the horror on the gurney.

"Somebody ruthless, righteous, and acrobatic," Landers said.

"Acrobatic?"

"There was a zip-line from the roof of the building across—" Landers began, but Macy jumped in.

"That's enough, Landers! That's holdback information."

"Reporters saw it," Landers said. "It was hanging right up there."

"Still," Macy said. "What do you think you're doing giving out information like that? Flirting?"

"What do you expect? She's pretty hot. I can't help it."

Sharon looked away and blushed.

"The problem is," Macy said, "whoever did this is turning into some kind of hush-hush hero around the station. I'm afraid some of us haven't been pursuing him with what you might call *due diligence.*"

"It'd be nice to shake his hand, though, right?" Landers said. "Maybe buy him a beer."

"You should be reported," Sharon said. "Whoever did this should pay for it. Even if this guy is a criminal, he's a victim, too."

"Sorry, Ms. Reede," Landers said, putting his notebook away. "I don't feel an ounce of sympathy for this scumbag."

"The police are on it, Sharon," Macy said. "Believe me. It's not right. I know it, and I promise you we'll get him. Vigilantes look good at first, sound righteous and all, but sooner or later they turn into the same kind of shit storm they're trying to stop. Always happens. Here's the form, if you wouldn't mind filling it out. And my card. Call me anytime about this, especially if you happen to discover any new information."

Sharon held the card, studied it, and then placed it in her pocket.

"Thanks for your help, Ms. Reede," Landers said as they were leaving. "Feel free to call me, too." He took another long glance at her body before walking out.

Sharon felt confused and conflicted. She'd spent nearly three hours with the terrified four-year-old girl. She could almost see Annie's little brain quivering in her skull like a mouse caught in a glue trap. Sharon had tried to calm her, get her to talk, but the child barely responded. When the ambulance crew came to take her to Columbia Presbyterian, the little girl started screaming and latched onto her, refusing to go with the paramedics. Sharon couldn't hold back her own tears. She promised to see her at the hospital. Then a surprise visit from out-of-town friends took up her Saturday. Sunday afternoon, she rushed into the pediatric ward and found that the girl was gone. Sharon's heart ached every time she pictured Annie waiting anxiously for her visit. She tried to get information from the nurses, but because she wasn't family they wouldn't tell her anything.

And now, so close she could smell his stink, here was the person responsible for Annie's living nightmare.

Still, Sharon couldn't help feeling sorry for him. The scope of his injuries was staggering. It was painful watching him lying there, on the bloodstained gurney, in an opioid coma, occasionally twitching and writhing. His face was disfigured beyond hope of reconstructive surgery. His arms and legs were wrapped in plaster.

She tried to imagine what it'd be like to live in constant pain and without the ability to see, hear, or talk.

Sharon shuddered at the thought and found herself wanting to confer with Donahoe. He was the one who had operated on the abused wife. She wondered if he knew that Annie's father was in the ER wracked up like this. Being on the trauma service, Donahoe would be responsible for taking care of Brihadara, a man who had beaten his wife and raped his own daughter repeatedly, and Sharon wondered how he would handle it.

She picked up the phone to page him but remembered seeing him head to resus a few minutes earlier. She wrote up her consult, partially filled in the police form, and joined the flurry of people rushing in that direction.

Chapter 6

Sharon didn't find Donahoe when she entered the room.

Instead, she was met with frantic activity verging on chaos.

Two paramedics stood on either side of an unresponsive patient on the gurney. A junior resident looked around desperately. Two interns Sharon didn't recognize botched IV insertions—one held pressure on the area she'd punctured and tried not to curse as her colleague missed a vein in the other arm. It looked like Dr. Sanchez had just entered the room to run the code, a responsibility relegated to the senior resident whenever a critical patient presented to the ER.

The only person not actively participating in the resuscitation was McKenzie, who sat on a high stool in front of the patient, staring at the cardiac monitor and shaking his head, looking bored and annoyed.

"What do you have, guys?" Sanchez asked.

The head paramedic spoke while helping to transfer the patient to the ER gurney. "Fifty-four-year-old Hispanic male found unresponsive at home. Family said he's been ill all week. Couldn't get out of bed this morning."

"Does he have a fever?" Sanchez demanded.

"Low-grade when we got there. Family says he's been coughing and complaining of shortness of breath."

"He's in ventricular tachycardia," Sanchez said, looking at the monitor.

"I got a 20-gauge IV in the right hand," one intern called, wiping her forehead.

"Good," Sanchez said. "We have to shock this guy. What's going on with the airway?"

The junior resident held a steel laryngoscope inside the patient's mouth and a plastic tube with his free hand. "I can't see his vocal cords. His epiglottis is huge. I don't want to go in blind."

Sharon looked over at McKenzie. He was still shaking his head but hadn't said a word. Across from him, Peggy, the two-ton white nurse who'd insulted Sharon on her first day of work, approached the bedside with the red crash cart. She shot a pleading look at McKenzie, as if urging him into action. McKenzie nodded solemnly.

"We have to shock him now," Sanchez repeated. "Just keep bagging him. I'll charge up the defibrillator."

"No you won't," McKenzie said.

Peggy stopped clenching her jaw and let out a sigh of relief.

"What do you mean?" Sanchez asked. "He's in unstable VT. I *have* to shock him."

"You'd be committing manslaughter if you did," McKenzie responded. "If you didn't have your head up your ass, you would've diagnosed this guy five minutes ago."

"Look at the monitor," Sanchez said. "He's in ventricular tachycardia. According to ACLS protocol, unstable VT needs to be shocked—"

"Don't bring up that advanced cardiac life support bullshit. Deal with the patient in front of you."

Sanchez pointed to the man. "The guy's been sick for a week

and has a fever. He's likely septic and needs antibiotics, but he's in VT, so we need to shock him first before we do anything else."

"You haven't even examined the patient!" McKenzie shouted.

The room grew quiet as McKenzie grabbed a pair of shears and elbowed the paramedic out of the way. He cut the patient's shirt, exposing a snake-like swelling under the left bicep. "See that? That's called a fistula. He's a renal patient."

Sanchez looked thoughtful. "But—"

"But nothing. The man gets hemodialysis three times a week, but because he's been bed-bound, he missed his sessions. Without hemodialysis, potassium has been accumulating in his blood all week and messing up the electrical function of his heart." McKenzie rifled through the crash cart, looking for something as he continued. "Did you miss that class in pathophysiology? You probably ditched another day at the Mickey Mouse Medical School you attended in Central America and went surfing instead, right? So I'll break it down for you. When potassium piles up in the blood, cells depolarize, the heart gets no excitement and dies of boredom. And that, boys and girls, is why our government uses potassium to kill all the bad people on death row."

McKenzie finally found the box he was looking for. He took out a vial, threw the box on the floor, and began pushing the medication. "Unless we stabilize this guy's heart with calcium, he'll eventually die. If you had shocked him, he would have gone straight into asystole. Flatline. Dead."

Everyone watched in suspense as the monitor slowly changed from a wide, sporadic tracing to the typical cardiac waves Sharon was used to seeing.

Sanchez looked at McKenzie and sighed. "I'm sorry."

"Sorry doesn't cut it, Dr. Kevorkian. I have to run now and check on the other kids. Will you be all right by yourself? Can you contact the nephrologist to get this guy the hemodialysis he needs? That calcium is only going to last for twenty minutes. Let's get that done stat, okay?" He ruffled Sanchez's hair and left the room.

Sharon's gaze lingered on Sanchez. An uneasy shiver ran down her spine. She could tell he was brewing with rage. She marched out of resus and followed McKenzie back to the main ER. "Dr. McKenzie," she called, catching up with him. "Do you really think mocking your residents in public is the best way to teach them?"

McKenzie charged down the hallway toward his desk. "I'm sorry, Ms. Reede, but I don't remember asking your opinion."

"You put a black cloud over the ER when you treat people like that. It makes it hard to stay sharp."

"Again, I don't recall requesting your advice. Sanchez should've stayed a family doctor in Honduras or Costa Rica or wherever the hell he's from."

"He's from Guatemala."

"I couldn't care less. He's like every other resident in this hospital: spoiled. When I trained, it was a lot tougher. It has to be in this business. We have to work hard because there's a lot to learn. There was no joint commission back then, and certainly no union to make sure residents got their so-called rights. If there's nothing more you want from me, why don't you take your social work lecture back to your little corner and save the world from there."

Sharon held his glare for a few seconds. "I realize that the stress of this job can make some of you ER doctors burn out quickly. You may be jaded, Dr. McKenzie, but you need to take it down a notch. You're allowed to be tough with your residents, just don't be a jerk."

"Whatever," McKenzie snapped.

"I was actually looking for Donahoe," Sharon said, "but I guess I'll tell you instead. The little girl you asked me to see last week? Her father, the guy who raped her, is here in the ER. He was assaulted in his home last night. He's in pretty bad shape."

"So what?"

"I just figured you'd want to know, since you're the one who consulted me on his daughter."

They reached his desk, and he immediately got on the computer.

"Listen, the guy's not my patient, and neither is his daughter anymore." He paused, gave Sharon a wry smile, and added, "I'm just glad he got helly-kellied."

"You know, people turn into what they idolize," she said. "You have about as much empathy as that screen you keep gaping at. Not good for a physician. You're *Helen-Kellering* yourself."

McKenzie emitted a series of mock deaf-mute grunts without taking his eyes off the screen or his hand from the mouse.

"Ugh," Sharon said, and huffed away.

Chapter 7

Back at her desk, Sharon steamed with anger and couldn't get herself to open her charts. McKenzie was destroying this place, and he was making her hate St. Jude's. Every time she started feeling good about her job, he kicked the legs out from under her. Part of her wanted to pack her belongings, fly home to Indiana, and never look back.

She took a deep breath, shut her eyes, and exhaled slowly.

It's temporary. I made a year commitment. The course of true work never runs smooth.

She opened the next chart.

Garrett again, the recidivist drunk. She couldn't believe he was already back. She looked up and spotted him passed out on a gurney, one grimy arm hanging down over the edge, wearing the same overalls he'd worn the week before. She could hear him snoring, and could smell him from where she sat. She slammed the chart shut. *Not today!* She had six other consults. There had to be at least one patient she could actually help.

The next chart was an inch thick but, unlike other ER regulars with complaints of chronic abdominal pain, Mrs. Castro had an identifiable cause. Gallstones diagnosed on ultrasound.

Terrible pain flare-ups every two or three months. Forty years old. Four children.

Consult requested for emergency Medicaid.

Sharon read through the chart and then went online to learn more about gallstones. After that she spent half an hour at the woman's bedside.

And now for Doctor Evil.

She headed to McKenzie's desk and gently placed the chart on top of his keyboard. "You treated Mrs. Castro earlier, right?"

McKenzie just as gently pushed the chart aside. "Yes. And?"

"You know this is her fourth visit for the same thing?" Sharon sat next to his keyboard and faced him.

"Get your butt off my table!"

Sharon folded her arms. "My butt's just fine here, thanks."

He pushed his chair back and clasped his hands behind his head. "Gallstones. I treated her the last three times. Always abdominal pain. I made sure her gallbladder wasn't infected and gave her a prescription for pain medication. Why are you even involved in this case?"

"She has four kids, Dr. McKenzie. She works two jobs to keep her family from starving, but she keeps missing work because of this pain. She needs to have her gallbladder removed so she can stop coming to the ER."

"I'm sure that would be lovely, but she doesn't have insurance. No surgeon's going to operate."

"There must be a surgeon here who isn't as callous as you."

"Nope. We're all just rusty robots looking for oil," he said, handing her chart back. "Look, it's not like she's got cholecystitis. Her gallbladder's not infected. It doesn't need to come out right now."

"Admit her for pain control. Then she can get the surgery."

"Go ahead and admit her yourself. Oh wait. You didn't go to medical school, so you can't admit anyone."

"You'd rather wait until her gallbladder gets infected and then admit her? How does that make sense?"

"I don't make up the rules."

"Rules?" Sharon repeated. "You can't use that as an excuse. You hate convention. Anything stupid makes you froth at the mouth. Since when do *you* care about rules?"

Sharon saw a transient flicker in McKenzie's eyes that made her momentarily scared. Part of her wanted to run, but the other was strangely drawn to it.

She held her ground.

A moment later, McKenzie responded with tightly controlled calm. "To get surgery, she has to have cholecystitis or cholangitis. No one operates emergently unless the gallbladder is inflamed or infected. End of story."

Sharon pulled a thick pile of computer printouts from her bag and slapped them on Mrs. Castro's chart.

"Not so. According to these articles, intractable pain *is* an indication for emergency surgery."

"Jesus, sweetheart, seriously?" McKenzie scanned the papers and pushed them aside. "Okay. Way to Google, but what Wikipedia won't tell you is that the surgeon makes the decision. And what *I'm* telling you is that no surgeon in the Western Hemisphere is going to operate on that woman. It doesn't matter if I browbeat them or not. Bottom line, she's uninsured. She should've thought about saving money for health insurance instead of popping out kids like a bunny rabbit."

Sharon glared at him. She could feel anger rising off her like heat waves from a sun-baked highway. She grabbed the papers from the desk and stood up. "I'm going to prove you wrong. I'm going to call every surgeon in this hospital until one of them agrees to operate on Mrs. Castro."

Sharon stormed off to her desk, trying to contain her

emotions. She had made an empty promise. She knew it, and McKenzie knew it. Still, she had to try to convince one of the surgeons on staff to operate. She just needed one, one who wasn't as stonehearted as McKenzie. It didn't make sense—medically or financially—to wait for someone to get really sick before treating them. Once infection hit, the chances of complications and death increased drastically.

Sharon found the St. Jude's hospital directory online and started making calls. Some doctors were already in the operating room; their secretaries said they'd relay the message. The surgeons she reached flat-out refused to take on her case once she told them that Mrs. Castro was uninsured. After nearly two frustrating hours, she lambasted her last hope—a female surgeon—for denying care to someone who so obviously needed it. The surgeon patiently replied that she did enough charity work and couldn't risk the legal liability.

During this time, McKenzie never left his desk. He listened to his residents' presentations from where he sat, chatted on the phone, and then went back to playing on the Internet.

What is it with him and that stupid computer? He could've done the darn surgery himself by now.

She was about to place another phone call when she thought about Donahoe. As one of the chief surgical residents, he had to have pull. Maybe she could talk him into asking one of his attendings to operate on Mrs. Castro.

As Sharon was about to page him, she saw him enter Mrs. Castro's room. She jumped up to follow.

"What are you doing with Mrs. Castro?"

"Hi, Sharon. I'm working with Dr. Simone today. We were in the middle of a case when he got a phone call. Apparently, you've managed to ruffle some feathers in the surgery department. He asked me to prep Mrs. Castro for a cholecystectomy."

She couldn't believe her ears. Dr. Simone had not been at his office when she'd called, but he must have gotten the message. Just as she was about to give up, her prayers were answered. There was at least one surgical attending out there willing to work pro bono. Dr. Simone was her hero, and Donahoe would be there to assist.

"I can't thank you enough. I've been at this for the past two hours."

"I can see," he said, pointing to her pile of Wiki articles. "I'm impressed. You probably know more about gallbladder pathology than most interns."

Sharon blushed. "Yeah, I guess. Anyway, I meant to speak to you earlier. Did you know that Mr. Brihadara is here? The husband of the woman you saw the other day."

"Oh, I heard." His expression darkened. "I don't want to talk about him. As soon as I'm done with Mrs. Castro's case, I have to come back and deal with his injuries. I can't stand the sight of him."

"I can imagine," Sharon said.

This may not have been the ideal time, but Sharon felt like celebrating her small victory. She was finally going to ask him out. "Listen, I was wondering if you—"

A beep from Donahoe's pager interrupted her in mid-sentence.

"Sorry, Sharon, it's going to have to wait," he said, muting the device while reading the screen. "I have to run. Talk to you later?"

"Sure, okay." Her gaze followed Donahoe as he transported Mrs. Castro through the main ER and out to the hallway leading to the operating rooms. Then she turned back and looked over at the ER physician's desk. At that moment, McKenzie stood up and headed to the resuscitation room.

Sharon felt like rubbing his nose in her triumph. Instead, she vowed to try harder to be more professional, even if he wasn't.

As he ambled off, he tossed a blank look her way.

For an indifferent glance, it packed a punch. As he closed the resus door behind him, Sharon felt her heart pounding violently against her chest.

Chapter 8

In his Upper West Side penthouse, Robert woke to his alarm at two a.m. He got out of bed immediately, stepped into the bathroom, splashed water on his face, and stared at himself in the mirror.

The bags under his eyes were puffier than usual, his eyes more haunted.

Happy forty-fourth birthday.

The aches and pains from his fights were taking too long to go away. He didn't think he could go on like this much longer. On four hours of sleep a night, he was barely surviving.

Then he remembered Guillermo, some fifteen years earlier, pushing him up a Guatemalan mountain to escape government soldiers. Guillermo had been in his sixties then. At the top of the mountain, they found a deep crevice to hide in. Robert was afraid the soldiers would hear his panting, while Guillermo's breathing was easy and regular. "Breathe with the abdomen, Roberto. Deep and slow. You can achieve harmony with the mountain that way," he had whispered to the frightened young student.

Robert did that then, and he started doing it now.

His naked body in the tall mirror was a relief map of scars and lacerations from stab wounds and bullets. He saw pancake-sized bruises near his abs and contusions over his large pecs and arms. He had a story for every mark on his body: some from his childhood, which he tried not to think about; some from the Guatemalan Civil War, where he fought with and learned from Guillermo in their battle against genocide; and the freshest ones from his private war against New York City's psychopaths.

Even though he didn't want to admit it, his life had changed during the past month. His routine was the same—he was still doctoring by day and scum cleaning by night—but the new social worker was making it harder for him to stay focused.

A wave of hate crimes and racial attacks is washing over the city, but Sharon steals precious hours of my research to deal with a fat lady with gallstones.

Robert stared at his reflection in the mirror and shook his head in disgust. He couldn't believe he'd fought to get Dr. Simone involved just because the social worker was making such a fuss. He almost ignored her plea. In the end, though, something in how much she cared—and how much work she had put into helping that lady—moved him.

After much stewing and fuming, he finally contacted his accountant, the only other person who knew about the small fortune Robert had inherited from his grandfather. Robert gave a lot of it to help people, but he hated giving the okay to wire the money to Simone.

That moldy, green-hearted bastard.

Robert hated him more than anyone in the hospital, but he also knew that he was the right surgeon for the job.

That golf-cheating money whore.

Robert could always count on an injection of Benjamins to get Simone cutting, even on someone with no insurance. The first patient he'd done that for was Ms. D'Angelo. Hers was a typical-enough story: single working mom, barely making ends meet, the mere thought of health insurance a bad joke, and abdominal pain that would double over a prizefighter. Some sketchy free clinic told her to get a CT scan, but to pay for it she'd have to kiss her life savings good-bye. Finally, after a year of horrific agony, her son called 911 and the ambulance took her to St. Jude's.

Robert had taken care of her. He could tell as soon as he walked into the exam room that she and her son were good people. The kid was a generous comforter by her side, attentive to his mother's needs. She had refused pain medication. She wanted the least done for her because she was intent on paying her bill. Even then, she was trying to set an example for her son.

The care the two showed each other had deeply moved Robert. There was a spirit in that room that even a cynic couldn't deny. Robert felt it.

It was a classic presentation: the whites of her eyes were yellow, and so was her skin, signifying liver failure. Throw in the development of late-onset abdominal pain, and you had pancreatic cancer. The case crushed him because he'd figured out the diagnosis before the CT scan results came back.

By then, Robert had asked his accountant to transfer the funds for the surgery. Then he told him to call Dr. Simone, one of three surgeons in the hospital who could perform a Whipple procedure and remove tumors from the head of the pancreas. Robert knew that Simone had the best results with the lowest risk of post-op complications.

Damn Simone.

Simone had the bedside manner of a Neanderthal. He'd been a jerk to Ms. D'Angelo and her son, despite receiving a large sum of cash for his services. If he weren't such a qualified surgeon, Robert would burst into his penthouse one fine night and pour a bag of pennies down his throat.

Just the thought of Sharon shedding tears of joy while picturing Simone as her knight in shining armor, a hero surgeon with a heart of gold performing life-saving procedures on the uninsured, gave Robert angina.

What Sharon doesn't know is that Simone wouldn't operate on his own mother if she didn't have health insurance.

Even though the social worker was naïve, Robert was very attracted to her. And it wasn't just because she was physically beautiful. She was also kind, intelligent, feisty. He loved seeing the fire in her eyes whenever she got emotionally invested in a case. It unearthed something in him that he hadn't felt in years. It energized him to keep doing the work he did. Anonymously. Making his pursuit of justice feel all the more necessary, all the more righteous.

Asking her out was out of the question. He couldn't risk getting involved with anyone seriously, especially with his double life. And he respected her too much to date her casually. He admired her resilience. Like most of the ER staff, he didn't think she'd make it past that first week, and here she was, well past her first month. That alone made her shine above the melon heads before her. She was fierce and committed. Got people food stamps and free meds. Found employment agencies for the homeless in need of part-time jobs. She knew which shelters best suited which patients and had quickly figured out whom she needed to contact at child protective services to expedite patient care.

And now she was doing medical research and calling surgeons to help get her patients what they needed!

Who does this woman think she is?

But he couldn't let his attraction get in the way. The bottom line was that she was messing up his routine. The tightrope he walked required complete control—and she was shaking the line. If she only understood that his time at work was the only opportunity he had to look up how patient information crossed with police reports. It was the only time he had to plan his evenings, check out the routes he'd take, and make sure he knew enough about the neighborhood he was working to avoid unwelcomed surprises. Recently, he found himself secretly keeping an eye on her, just to make sure she was safe. The emergency room was a dangerous place. Every year there were thousands of assaults by patients on hospital personnel. At times, these attacks led to permanent disability and death. He had developed a sixth sense of her presence on the floor. He felt better with her blip on his radar screen.

Enough about Sharon.

Time to go.

Only three hours before heading back to work. Robert dried his face with a towel, walked out of the bathroom and into his closet. He turned on the light and pressed a button hidden behind a winter coat. With a low hum, the opposite wall slid open, revealing a hidden storage compartment. He opened a drawer and took out one of seven neatly folded black outfits. They looked like thin wetsuits, but the material was much more durable, capable of protecting him from most knife blades and small-caliber bullets.

Over that, he slipped on a pair of Diesel jeans and his favorite tan cotton sweatshirt. Another button inside the drawer opened a separate compartment containing a polished steel safe. Robert pushed a combination of eight numbers and the door clicked open. Inside was his arsenal: handguns, shotguns, knives, syringes, all sorts of explosives, and some unlabeled canisters. Plus his high-tech eyewear and Bluetooth audio enhancer—his two favorite items. They made him feel omniscient, like a personal physician to the city, using his surveillance equipment to diagnose its diseases.

He stuffed the Bluetooth and eyewear into a small black duffle bag, and then added his SIG Sauer P226 and HK 45.

He made an espresso and took it out to his balcony. Looking down on Central Park, he marveled at the combination of lights and nature. Fall was fully in the air, and he loved that even in New

York you could smell the seasons change. These hours before dawn were his favorite; with so many people asleep, he could catch evil off guard.

Tonight was just about surveillance, though. He had found a new pattern of violence growing. The last patient he treated at the end of his shift was another victim of a stab wound, inflicted two blocks from the West Side Highway on Fifty-Fourth Street. Three other guys had been assaulted in that same area during the past month. He wondered if there was a new gang forming.

He finished his espresso, grabbed his bag, and headed to his private garage. He planned to take his Ducati motorcycle out for a little spin, down to Hell's Kitchen to check out what the bad guys were doing.

He didn't anticipate a fight, but if the occasion arose, he'd be ready.

Chapter 9

Sharon was already sorry she'd agreed to take the shift. It had been a favor for the weekend social worker, who was bridesmaiding in Las Vegas, but she'd forgotten how the Friday night crazies made the Saturday morning ER a living hell.

Her only consolation was her blind date after work with a criminology student at John Jay. Rivera had set them up. She described him as having "cheekbones like Bradley Cooper and the brains of a neurosurgeon. *Mm-hmm!*"

Sharon had laughed. She didn't have high hopes, but she was happy to get out for a change.

Of course, if she had her choice, she'd be going out with Donahoe. But she was starting to think it was never going to happen. It was already late fall. They'd known each other for more than two months and there was still no sign that he was going to take their flirting to the next level. Even when she finally mentioned going for drinks sometime after work, he gave her a lame excuse. And lately, she felt they'd grown more distant. He was always around the ER doing his consults, but now he seemed too overwhelmed with work to stop by her desk and chat. He also looked tired a lot. Maybe he was seeing someone. That would explain why he never seemed to be free at night.

Or maybe he wasn't interested.

Oh well. If it's not meant to be, it's not meant to be.

She flipped open her first chart.

That drunken Garrett was back again! She wondered if the man had been put on earth just to teach her that not everyone could be helped. She recalled his last visit, just a few days earlier, loaded at eleven a.m. She'd wasted three hours getting him a place in one of the few rehab centers that hadn't already kicked him out.

And now he's back.

"It wasn't my fault, Ms. Sharon," Garrett whined. "Everybody in that place hates me 'cause I'm black. I'm gonna sue 'em for racial intoleration and discriminilization."

"Mr. Garrett, you're forgetting a crucial fact."

"What's that?"

"You're *white*!" Sharon sighed loudly. "Nobody's discriminating against you because of your race. It's because you're obnoxious when you're drunk. You were kicked out for sneaking alcohol into the facility, and before that, for assaulting a patient you said was making fun of you. He was deaf! He was using his hands to sign. You told the cops he was doing 'jujitsu' on you for being a 'homey.'"

"You weren't there, Ms. Sharon." He belched the smell of liquor and vomit into the room. "Everybody hates me. I'm gonna get me a lawster and sue 'em to hell!"

"Look, Mr. Garrett. I'm going to arrange transfer to detox, but this is the last time I help you out. You mess up again, don't come back. If you do, I'm going to sic McKenzie on you."

Sharon saw Garrett's body stiffen with real fear. Then he began a trembling litany of promises to reform. She stopped listening when her eyes lit on the headline of a *New York Post* someone had left on the counter:

VIGILANTE IN DA HOUSE
Another assault averted by the Big Apple's anonymous avatar

On the cover was a picture of a crime scene in Midtown, featuring Macy and Landers, the same detectives who had interviewed her. Yellow crime-scene tape encircled an area that covered half a city block by Riverside Park. Next to the picture was a cartoon of a man wearing all black, sporting what looked like swimming goggles. He wore a cape and held a shotgun. The picture looked ridiculous, but it definitely caught her attention.

Garrett was gushing something about how hard it was for him when his two children were "abducted by the Klan." She rolled her eyes, picked up the paper, and read the blurb under the headline.

Elderly man says Hell's Angel ninja saved him from three muggers in the wee hours of the night.

Sharon looked up, recalling what the two boys at Starko's Deli had said a few weeks back, about a man in black who had saved a Chinese tourist. Could it be the same guy?

Her concentration was broken when she caught Donahoe staring at her from across the ER. As soon as their eyes met, he shifted his gaze back to his chart.

Garrett's voice, droning on and on, brought her back to the present. "I'm gonna sign me a declaration of rights against those racist mother—"

"Enough, Mr. Garrett," she said, cutting him off mid-sentence. "Like I said, I'll get you entry to your last detox facility, but that's it. If you come whining back here again, McKenzie's going to strip you naked and throw you in the Hudson. Got it?"

She handed him an entrance letter for a shelter and left him gaping.

Before she'd made it to her desk, someone grabbed her by the wrist and pulled her into an exam room. She started to yell but then realized who it was.

"Ms. Sharon! Remember me?" The woman hugged Sharon with a python's squeeze. When she let go, she continued to laugh and rubbed Sharon's arm amicably. She was a large, dark-skinned woman with bulging brown eyes and a mouth of perfect white teeth that burst from her face in the biggest smile Sharon had seen in years. Her Chipotle uniform bore a nametag that read *Manager*.

"Adele? I hardly recognized you. Look at you!" Sharon's eyes narrowed slightly. "Is everything okay? Are you depressed?"

An ambulance had brought Adele in a month earlier after overdosing on Ambien. A friend called 911 when she didn't show up at church. EMS found her unconscious in bed with the empty pill bottle and a note:

> *Husbandless, moneyless, jobless.*
> *Hopeless.*
> *Why settle for less?*

The woman's plight had really gotten to Sharon.

"I'm the *opposite* of depressed," Adele said, speaking a mile a minute and pointing to her right leg. "I sprained my ankle, that's all. Piece of lettuce on the floor. One little slimy green blotch. More slippery than a bar of soap, did you know that? Took a fall on my back like a love sick hippo!" She leaned back her head and laughed, all those teeth gleaming like grand piano keys. "I'm okay, though, I think. Wouldn't even have come, but we have to report every accident at work. Policy. And since I'm the *new manager...*" She jutted her mammoth chest out even more and tapped at her nametag. "Check it out!"

"That's great, Adele," Sharon said. "Really great. So things are going well, then?"

"Well? That's too short a word for how things are going. Things are well-well-well-well-well! The Lord gave me a miracle, Ms. Sharon. Oh yes, he did. Baby Jesus jumped right out of his crib and hit me on the head with God's own magic wand!"

"Way to go, Baby Jesus." Sharon laughed.

"Amen, child! I left this hospital ready to get right over to that homeless shelter you were so kind to call for me. I gathered up my things, got my mail, and there's this fat old brown envelope. I opened it up, and what's in there? A stack of ten one-hundred-dollar bills, crispier than Kentucky Fried. Thank you, Jesus! The Lord works in mysterious ways, his wonders to behold. And there's a note in Baby Jesus' handwriting, telling me to pay my rent, get a job, and volunteer. Signed, *Baby Jesus*. I swear. Here it is. Here's the very note. It's going to be a relic someday."

Sharon looked at the note. It was, in fact, signed, *Baby Jesus*. The note's handwriting had been made to look like a child's scrawl.

"So when the little Lord *himself* tells me to do something, writes me a note even, I do it, Ms. Sharon. Yes, ma'am I do. I unpacked my things, paid my rent, and went right out and got me a job-getting outfit, one of those real professional ensembles from Target. Matching pants and shirt. Didn't I look the picture of high-level Chipotle personnel? Got a job that very day. Oh, I know it's not going to make me no millionaire, but it pays the rent, plus burritos and chips to take home. And here's the nicest thing, Ms. Sharon. I volunteer every Sunday after church at the local Boys & Girls Club, help kids with their reading. So many of them want to read, but no one gives them the time. Makes me want to cry, but makes me want to help them even more. You know what I'm being, Ms. Sharon?" She waited a beat. "I'm being A*dele*. I'm being me at last!"

She didn't wait for Sharon to answer, just gave her another big hug and made shooing motions. "Go on now. Doctor will take care of me in a minute. Thank you for all your love, darling."

Sharon walked back to her desk, shaking her head and wondering who Baby Jesus was. It seemed too good to believe, and yet there she was, Adele, a totally different woman from a month earlier.

A sweet sensation filled Sharon's chest. She *was* making a difference.

But that feeling disappeared as soon as she opened the next chart.

Chapter 10

Andre Meyer was twenty-two, fresh out of college. A victim of an anti-gay hate crime, he was jumped in Central Park and brutally assaulted the night before, and was now requesting a bus pass back to the Midwest.

As Sharon entered the room, she found him sitting at the edge of the gurney, his arms crisscrossed around his torso, his body gently rocking back and forth. Both eyes were black, and he was pressing a soaked wad of gauze to his bloody nose. From out of his tight yellow T-shirt jutted two skinny arms, both purple with bruises.

"Mr. Meyer," she spoke softly. "I'm Sharon, the social worker."

He looked up but didn't say anything.

"You must be in terrible pain."

"Not completely. I think my right big toe doesn't hurt. Whoops, nope. I was wrong."

Sharon forced a smile despite how bad she felt for him. "It says here you're from Carmel, Indiana. I'm from Bloomington."

"Go Hoosiers," Andre said, feigning enthusiasm. "Yeah, I landed in New York a few days ago." He had a Midwest accent. "Back home, I couldn't come out to any of my friends or family, but I knew I could here. I mean, don't all the movies and TV shows promise that everyone in the Big Apple will be just dandy with my smoking love style?" He started sobbing. "I guess not everyone."

Sharon grabbed a box of tissues from the counter and handed it to him.

"First night out," his voice quivered. "Got jumped. They kept kicking me with their lumberjack boots." He wiped his tears and pressed his elbows tight into his ribs. "Such *ugly* footwear, too." He tried to smile, but it was obvious he was hurting. "They called me the dumbest fag names—no imagination or creativity—and stole my wallet. I have no money. No way to get back to Indiana. But I *have* to get back. I never thought I'd say this, but it's safer there."

He was crying uninhibitedly now. Sharon walked over and put her arm around him. It felt awkward, and at first he was resistant to being touched, but soon he was holding her and sobbing. She patted him on the back and stroked his hair, wondering if anyone in the ER was watching.

"Listen, Andre. I'm really sorry you've had such a horrible experience, but you don't have to leave New York. There are resources we can explore."

"No, I don't want to be here anymore. I want to go home, to my family."

"I'm here to help you," Sharon said. "Whatever you decide. If you want to leave the city, I can get you a bus pass on Greyhound. I can also get you a free voucher for your antibiotics and pain medications. It took a lot of courage for you to come to New York, so try not to be so hard on yourself."

She left the room and went to McKenzie's desk. She had stamped the prescriptions in Andre's chart with the state logo and now waited for McKenzie's attention. He put out his hand for the prescriptions, not looking away from the computer screen. She slapped them in his hand. He scrawled his signature quickly, gave them back to her, and went back to surfing the web.

"What?" she said. "No jokes? No remarks about wasting taxpayer money?"

"No need to make him feel worse," McKenzie said. "He already got what he deserved."

Sharon's jaw dropped. "Excuse me? Did I just hear you right?"

"Look at him," McKenzie said, pointing at Andre's room. "Black leather pants, tight T-shirt. Goes to a sports bar on bridge-and-tunnel night, on a game night, too, when the city's jammed with meatheads with hard-ons for a fight. The fair Mr. Meyer practically asked for an ass-whooping."

"He's new in town. How could he know all that? You're such a jerk!"

"Don't criticize me. Criticize him."

"I can't," she said looking back at Andre, propped up on a pillow, his eyes closed, wincing intermittently from pain. "Jesus, Dr. McKenzie. How could anyone?"

"Why were you consulted, Ms. Reede? Because he no doubt got all his stuff stolen and now wants to go home, probably somewhere in the Midwest, where he'll slink back into his cushy closet in his parents' house. Am I right?"

She made no response.

"You know I am," he continued. "What he should do instead is grow some balls and make some noise. He should go after those guys. Or at the very least, stay in New York, work out, get ready for the next time someone tries to mess with him for being himself. Instead, he's crawling back to mommy, tail between his legs, not fighting for what he believes in."

"Screw that macho crap! That same mentality made those Neanderthals attack him in the first place. You're a doctor, for Christ's sake. Try some compassion."

"You think I don't feel sorry for him? I do. I feel sorry that he's such a pussy."

A pussy?

Did McKenzie actually just use that term to describe a patient?

Sharon's hands clenched into fists and her body shook with rage. She was overwhelmed with so much anger and filled with so many objections that she didn't know where to start.

"Reede," McKenzie plowed on, "don't judge *me*. The kid is on the verge of destroying his own life. He's heading home, where he'll marry some placid girl, raise overinhibited kids, and take on a lifeless job. He'll die fifty years before his funeral. At this very moment, he's standing on the edge of an abyss and *you* want to push him in. Instead of holding his hand, you should be encouraging him to fight back. With his fists or clubs or even a gun, if he needs to. But he won't. He's a coward. His mind is clouded with doubt and his blood is clogged with fear. Most people today are like that. They make me sick. They're responsible for this cesspool world they're always whining about. This ain't the Garden of Eden. We got kicked out, remember?"

"It's not the Wild West, either," she shot back. "And besides, I did tell him to stay. But that's not my decision—or yours. And you've seen enough gunshot wounds in here to know darn well that it's not a good idea to let untrained people have guns. Because if I had a gun right now I'd … put a cap on your butt."

McKenzie stared at her for a moment, then slapped his desk and laughed loudly. Sharon almost joined in, but she was still too annoyed. "I wasn't trying to be funny."

A resident came over with a chart. McKenzie leafed through it, signed off, and handed it back without saying a word. His green eyes, now softer, returned to Sharon. "I'll let you put a cap wherever you want, but you have to admit I'm right."

"There may be a gram of truth in your pound of crap, but you have to temper this 'blame the victim' stuff. Do you think if a woman dresses in a tight skirt and gets raped, it's her fault?"

"She's not criminally at fault, no. But if she gets trashed and leaves her friends with some random guy she meets at a bar and gets raped, then, yes, it's her fault. She should know better. Is it news that the majority of guys are animals when they drink?"

"And the Jews, I suppose, are responsible for the Holocaust."

"Don't put words in my mouth," McKenzie said, "but one lesson we've learned from the Holocaust is that the first time you see an anti-Semitic sign in a window, what should you do? Rip it down. Be anything but tolerant or apathetic about it." He shook his head. "No, I'm thinking more along the lines of something I saw in Wal-Mart when I was seven. There was an old black guy on the register, and some potbellied, red-faced customer wanted a different clerk to check out his purchase. Potato chips and a six-pack of beer. 'I don't want no nigger touching my stuff!' he yells. 'Where's the manager?' The manager scurries in, all apologetic, pulls the old black man away, checks out the stuff himself while the black guy stands there, looking ashamed with his head hanging low. I'll never forget it. The manager apologized to the slob, even gave him a coupon for his trouble. Nobody protested, none of the other customers, and for sure not my sorry-ass father."

"And you think the black man should've started a fight and lost his job and been sent to jail?"

"Somebody should've done something, don't you think?"

Sharon nodded. "Yeah, I guess."

"At last!" McKenzie said. "I think we've finally reached an agreement."

"But I still don't think Andre can stay in New York. How could he? He has no money, no friends. No Uzi."

"He should stay and fight," McKenzie said.

"If you care so much about him, give him a thousand dollars and rent him an apartment in the West Village."

McKenzie's smile disappeared. He clenched his jaw. "I don't care that much. He doesn't deserve it. I'm glad he's going back to Indiana, and I hope he takes you with him."

His sudden mood change surprised her. She figured they'd almost had a breakthrough, but that last remark caught her off guard, like she'd been sucker-punched.

She scowled at him, grabbed her chart and prescriptions, and went back to her desk. On her way, she thought she heard him say something and turned around to look, but his eyes were glued to his computer screen.

A few hours later, Andre's Greyhound pass came through. Sharon waved good-bye as he limped out of the hospital and into the cold rain.

He didn't wave back.

When she turned around, she saw that Donahoe was watching, too. As he saw her catch his eye, he stood up abruptly and walked off to resus.

Chapter 11

Robert finished his chocolate martini with a flourish and set the glass down on the bar. That first syrupy sip was so sweet he'd nearly lost his dinner—but the last gulp tasted delicious.

The Animated Closet Lounge was located on Seventy-Fourth Street and Amsterdam Avenue. With its series of dark-brown shuttered windows, he'd probably passed the place a thousand times without wanting to go inside.

Until two weeks ago.

Robert turned his stool from the bar after getting another drink and took a healthy swig. Around him was a crowd of young, athletic, well-groomed men.

"Good-looking group, eh?" the bartender said, wiping the counter in front of him.

"Yeah." Robert sipped his drink. "For sure."

Before he knew it, he was thinking of Sharon again. She was getting to be like a song he couldn't get out of his head.

The pattern was obvious. For the last few months, there had been an unusual number of gay victims of Friday night assaults, nearly every other week, on the Upper West Side—always somewhere in Central Park between Seventy-Second and Seventy-Ninth

Street. It wasn't until Sharon had gotten so emotional about the gay kid from Indiana that he'd started to investigate.

The day after Andre had been attacked, Robert walked around the neighborhood and found a new construction project on the edge of the target area. Construction companies paid biweekly, like most industries. He'd bet that the bashers, probably bridge-and-tunnel rats, were hitting the town on paycheck night, liquoring up, and going hyena-pack for gay meat.

It all fit. New condo construction on Seventy-Fourth, a late-night pub a few blocks from the only openly gay bar in the area, beatings every other Friday night.

Robert's second drink was empty. He was about to order a third when the friendly bartender placed one in front of him.

"I think you got yourself an admirer," he said.

Robert looked up.

"Hi, handsome!" The man was a young-looking Asian, and his smile was devilish and funny. Even standing, he was shorter than Robert on his stool. He wore tight jeans, a flashy yellow belt, and a tight navy-blue turtleneck. "You don't look Chinese."

"I'm not," Robert said.

"Then why did I think your name was Yum-Yum?"

Robert laughed. "Let's not use names, okay? Makes forgetting more romantic."

"Oh, I like that!" He eyed Robert up and down. "I see you're packing some muscle in that tight leather. Moo shu porkable!" He put his hands on Robert's cheeks. "But why so much makeup, honey-buns? Hiding something?"

Robert saw a glint of intelligent concern in the boy-man's playful stare. Usually, Robert hated when people touched him, but he knew there wasn't any threat here.

"Honestly, honey," the Asian continued, "you'd look better without so much makeup." He shrugged. "Regardless, I'd love to take you home and lick your fortune cookie."

Robert choked back a laugh. "Sorry, little man. You're not my type." He took his admirer's cool ivory hands from his face and held them gently inside his palms. "Too short and too masculine for my taste. Go find another love god."

The man stared at Robert with a puzzled expression and shrugged again. "You're nice. Mean, too. Great combo. Not my type either, I don't think. Way too much cosmetics. Be yourself, Mr. No-Name." He laughed and walked away, calling over his shoulder, "I hope you find what you're looking for!"

Robert watched him approach a tall Indian guy, and in two minutes they were laughing, hugging, and high-fiving. Two minutes after that, they left the bar arm-in-arm.

It's so much easier to get laid when you're gay.

He looked at his watch: two a.m., the time when most people leave New York bars, when most assaults in the city occur.

He took a sip from the new drink and left the rest. Time to roll.

Robert grabbed his jacket from the hook in front of his stool and walked out. The pockets sagged from the weight of his SIG and sling blade, which he hoped he wouldn't need. A nice fight, bare hands, swinging legs—that's what he wanted.

That's what he always wanted.

Emerging into the cold night, he could see the short Asian and his tall new boy-toy a block ahead. They walked in zigzags, stopping from time to time to laugh or kiss. Robert kept a discreet distance, taking in the fresh autumn air and enjoying the scene.

The two men went into Central Park through the path on Seventy-Sixth Street.

Promising. Fewer street lights. If the meatheads were out, this was a good jump site.

Soon, the quiet of the park engulfed him and, before he knew it, thoughts of Sharon lit up his brain circuits.

Friday night. Was she on another date?

A couple of weeks earlier, he'd overheard her talking to the triage nurse about some blind date. She hadn't seemed chipper or giddy the following Monday, hadn't been texting anyone during her shift. In fact, she'd been less upbeat than usual.

That had made him happy.

It was because of her, after all, that he was spending his Friday night walking alone through Central Park, hunting gay bashers instead of his usual prey: child molesters, rapists, and wife beaters.

He wasn't used to so many conflicting emotions. He hated feeling obliged to go after anyone other than the psychopaths on his target list, but that's exactly what he was doing. For some unfathomable reason, he felt responsible for finding and eliminating the men who'd hurt that gay kid from Indiana. He had no choice...

Robert froze as he realized he'd lost the couple.

He closed his eyes, held his breath, and listened. A light breeze blew on his ears. He heard rustling leaves. Then far-away voices.

A lot of them.

Robert opened his eyes and trotted quietly toward the voices. As he turned a corner, he slowed his pace and made sure to stay hidden. Sure enough, through the cluster of maple trees that bordered a small enclosure, he saw a group of men working over the gay couple.

On the side closer to Robert, the Indian guy had been forced on his hands and knees as four men took turns hitting him in the ass with a large branch. On the far end of the enclosure, the Asian whimpered as three guys twice his size took turns pushing him around and slapping his face.

Robert sprang out from behind the tree and walked over to the group of men harassing the taller gay. "When do I get a turn at smacking that ass?"

The guy with the tree branch stopped mid-stroke and turned. The other three looked over in surprise and shock.

Robert pranced forward. "Save some for me, guys!" He pitched his voice into falsetto. "Slap some of this, puh-*leeze!*" He turned and bent slightly, grabbing a big hunk of his own butt cheek.

"I'm gonna do a lot more than slap it, queer!" called the guy with the branch.

A few seconds later, Robert found himself surrounded by the men.

When the first guy lunged, Robert yanked the branch away and rammed it back into the man's chest and jaw, putting him down. A second guy threw a beer bottle at him and Robert swung the branch, shattering the bottle into pieces, then dropped it. He wanted some plain, close-up fighting. The Indian guy got himself upright and ran to save his friend. The bottle-thrower came at Robert with a grapefruit-sized rock. Robert dropped to a half-squat and sweep-kicked his legs. As the man went down, Robert hammered his fist into the assailant's ear, then ripped the man's throwing arm out of its socket.

Two down, two to go.

Robert picked up the rock and slammed it into the forehead of the next guy, splitting his head open. The last man was short but had the shoulders and chest of a Greco-Roman wrestler. With no more emotion than a shark, he had watched Robert put the others' lights out. Now he strode toward Robert. It was obvious that the man's intent was to pick Robert up and rip him in half. Robert knew no punch or kick would slow him; his muscle mass was too thick. When the hulk got within striking distance, Robert shot out his hand and dug out the guy's left eye. The shock stopped him in his tracks, his mouth opened in a silent scream of utter shock. Robert kneed him in the crotch and then ran to help the Asian.

When he reached the far end of the clearing, Robert saw the remaining three assailants still working the Asian over. His boyfriend had jumped on the back of the biggest one, trying to pull him away, but the attacker was so beefy it wasn't doing much good. The Indian looked like a mere stripe on the man's shirt. The other two assailants, one bearded and one balding, saw Robert coming and ran at him, but then slowed when they spied their four friends in the distance writhing on the ground.

Robert turned his trot into a dash and launched a flying scissor kick that wedged the bearded guy's neck. He heard it crack like a rifle shot. He released his vise, jumped up, and watched as the bald guy went scrambling out of the park.

The last meathead standing had thrown off the Indian guy and was again going after the Asian.

"Hey," Robert yelled, and the behemoth turned to him slowly. "That's my friend you're messing with."

"No-Name?" he heard the Asian squeal.

The behemoth didn't look cowed. "I'm going to carve my name in all three of your anuses!" he shouted drunkenly, pulling out a knife. He went right for Robert.

And he wasn't clumsy.

The man slashed the knife three times. Robert dodged each attempt by a fraction of an inch. The fourth time the knife came at him, Robert stepped to the side, grabbed the man's hand, and twisted. He could feel the elbow snap back as the radial head cracked in two and the distal part of the humerus shattered into multiple shards.

The man let out a long, loud cry as he went to his knees. Robert considered silencing him, but he could already hear sirens.

Robert looked over at the gay couple, put his index finger to his forehead, and gave them a salute. The Asian applauded with rapid little claps and a cheer.

"Keep this between us. Okay, boys?" Robert winked and disappeared.

Chapter 12

"I'm telling you, she's being abused."

"Okay, whatever you say, Ms. CSI," Dr. Sanchez said, not bothering to look up from his charting.

"Stop writing for a second and listen to me," Sharon demanded. "Just because I don't want to go out with you doesn't give you the right to act like a turkey."

He looked up, a little startled. "Would you lower your voice, please? And show some respect. There's no need to bring personal stuff up in public."

"I'll show you respect when you start taking me seriously. Every time I ask her a question, she looks to her husband for permission to speak. And her body language is classic abused woman—head hanging, hunched back, strangled voice."

"Okay, I've listened," Dr. Sanchez said, shutting his chart. "Now it's your turn to do the same. I asked you for a social work consult so my patient could get emergency Medicaid. Can you just do that for me? Then, once she's admitted to the orthopedic service and no longer an ER patient, you can do whatever you want with her." He handed her the chart and stormed off.

The woman had multiple contusions on her face, and her arms

were a fresco of black-and-blues. After the exam, she had quickly put her sweatshirt back on, and then a heavy winter coat on top of that—even though it was only mid-October and the day was unseasonably warm. Sanchez hadn't even bothered to ask the obvious question: If she broke her fall with her cracked forearm, how did her face get so messed up?

The mechanism of action didn't make any sense.

Sharon considered her options while looking around the ER. Rivera was in the middle of triaging a long row of ambulances. Donahoe was in a room with a patient.

Knowing full well she might regret her decision, she headed over to McKenzie.

"Look, no lame sarcastic remarks, okay?" Sharon began.

"My sarcasm is never lame," McKenzie said. "It's the best there is."

"I highly doubt that," she said, sitting next to him. "I know you think all abused women are worthless weaklings who should know better, but I want you to pretend for a moment that the woman in room 23 is your sister, and her husband is systematically beating her. What can we do about it?"

"You're talking about the hangdog battered woman with the facial contusions?"

Sharon let out a sigh of relief. "Yes. Thank you."

"You'd have to be as brain dead as Sanchez not to realize she's being abused. Look at their interaction."

The woman was still sitting at the edge of the gurney, eyes cast down, while the man paced up and down the small room, talking on his cell. Every time he came her way, she flinched.

"So what can we do, Dr. McKenzie?"

His eyes widened. "Has she admitted to the abuse?"

"No, but our judgment counts for something, doesn't it?"

"Not until she admits it. Then you have to ask her if she wants help. She has to say yes, or you can't do anything."

"I thought by law we had to report any suspicion of domestic violence to the police. No matter how trivial, no matter what the evidence."

"That's for children. If there's any suspicion of child abuse, I'm obligated by law to call child protective services and get the police involved. Even if the kid's parents were voted 'Parents of the Year' by *Parenting* magazine, I wouldn't get in trouble. The law leans over for kids. In fact, if I ever pass on a kid with a bruise who later turns out to have been a victim of abuse, I could lose my license. But it's different for adults, even if they've been raped or beaten."

"The law should protect battered women in the same way."

"Sorry to break it to you, sweetheart, but it doesn't."

"So there's nothing I can do?"

"I didn't say that," McKenzie said. "There's always a way to finagle around the law."

"How?"

"Ah, Ms. Reede, I like how ready you are to break the law."

"I'm willing to bend it. Just tell me how."

McKenzie grimaced and shrugged. "Trick her sorry ass into admitting something's going on at home that requires police intervention, and I'll make sure she gets help."

"But how?" Sharon turned her gaze back at the exam room. "As long as her husband is with her, she won't talk. And there's no way he's going to leave her alone."

McKenzie leaned over and knocked lightly on her forehead. "Is there anything inside that pretty little head of yours? Figure something out. I can't do everything for you."

Pretty little head? Is he flirting or poking fun at me?

Sharon didn't mind the jab. At least it was better than being called Barbie.

She stood absorbed in thought as McKenzie went back to his computer screen. Then her light bulb turned on.

"Ah!"

"What?"

"I'll be right back." Sharon sprinted to her desk. She picked up the chart and brought it back to McKenzie's desk.

"I could page him about his car, but I don't know what kind of car he drives."

"Call the parking attendant and find out. Make up an excuse. Tell him you're Fritz's wife and want to make sure your husband didn't take the car. Or tell them you're concerned that the car's been stolen."

"I like that last idea."

A moment later, Sharon had Mr. Fritz's information.

"Okay," she whispered. "How do you page someone here?"

"Star eight nine," he said, handing her the phone.

She dialed and made her voice sound bored and nasal. "Will the owner of a gray Ford Taurus with license plate number GFY108 please see the parking attendant?"

The man inside room 23 snapped his cell phone shut and rushed toward the exit.

"You're on, Ms. Reede," McKenzie said.

Sharon marched into the room and shut the door.

"Okay, Mrs. Fritz, I'm working on your emergency Medicaid, but I need to get something clear first. I think you're being beaten by your husband."

The woman looked up with an expression of fear. She shot a look past Sharon toward the small window in the middle of the door.

"Don't worry, Ginger, he's gone. At least for the next two minutes," Sharon said. "We don't have much time. You're not fooling anyone. I know your husband's been hitting you."

"Please, don't get involved," the woman pleaded.

"Mrs. Fritz, I can imagine you're scared, but let me try to help you."

The woman continued to crane her neck to see through the little window in the door. "There's nothing you can do! You're just making things worse. He hasn't touched the kids in over a month. Just leave me alone. Nobody can help me."

"The police can help," Sharon said. "We can get a restraining order, and then you and your kids will be safe."

The woman shook her head violently and started sobbing. "I tried that once. It ruined everything! They couldn't find enough evidence, and my husband convinced the court I was lying to get custody. They refused the restraining order." She cut her crying off abruptly, wiped the tears from her eyes, and fixed Sharon a steely look. "He's got a gun. He said he'd use it on the kids if the police ever showed up again. You have no idea who you're dealing with. The man doesn't make empty threats."

Sharon felt a sudden breeze from the fast-opening door. "What's going on here?" roared a voice that hurt her ears.

She turned around and faced the woman's husband. He towered over her by a foot. He was puffing out his massive chest and she smelled alcohol somewhere behind his heavy cologne.

"Back off, Mr. Fritz, or I'll call security. There's no need to get in my face. I was telling your wife that we're working on the papers for the emergency Medicaid. You want that, don't you?"

Fritz didn't step back. "We've been here long enough," he growled. "This hospital sucks! You make us wait four hours to see an airhead doctor. Then some stupid parking attendant gives me a false alarm about my car being stolen. This is bullshit." He grabbed his wife's arm. "Come on, let's go. We don't need this."

Sharon pleaded with them, but was nearly run over as the man dragged his wife from the room. She rushed to McKenzie, who was talking with Rivera.

"He's forcing her to leave. Please do something. She admitted to being beaten."

"So why is she leaving?" McKenzie asked.

"Because he has a gun and threatened to shoot the kids if she calls the police again. She thinks he will. She tried getting a restraining order once, and the police believed him and not her. Come on, do something! Michelle, call security before he gets her out of the building."

Rivera shook her head and put her big hand on Sharon's shoulder. "No, no, honey. If the woman won't put up a fight, we can't do anything about it. It's horrible, I know, but we can't."

"That doesn't make any sense," Sharon said, struggling to dam her tears. "Dr. McKenzie, you said you'd help if I got her to confess!"

McKenzie glanced up at Sharon. There was a look in his eyes that she hadn't seen before. It was powerful, electric even, yet also calming and reassuring, as if she'd been yanked into the eye of a hurricane. When he spoke, there was no trace of the complete jerk she once thought he was. "I promised you she'd get help, and she will. You can have as much faith in that as you do in that cross you keep tucked inside your shirt."

Sharon reflexively put her fingers to the cross her grandmother had given her for her First Communion. She looked at McKenzie with a dazed expression. She had always been careful to keep the cross hidden.

Questions flooded her mind, but she kept them to herself.

She wasn't exactly sure how it would happen, but Sharon knew that Mrs. Fritz would be helped.

Chapter 13

There was no time for pleasantries.

Sharon put a cup of coffee within reach of Rivera, who held a phone to one ear and directed the paramedics to various spots on the bay with her free hand. As she whisked up her charts and walked to her desk, Sharon saw the line of gurneys extending all the way to the bay.

By the heft of the stack, she knew her shift would run past midnight.

She arranged the paper and files on her desk, still thinking of the *New York Post* article she had read on the subway. Mr. Fritz had been assaulted in Central Park the night before. The former wife beater wound up with a dislocated jaw, two broken wrists, and severe injuries to his lower back.

There had been a cluster of Central Park assaults lately. The article suggested a connection with the brutal beatings of a gang of construction workers, but quoted Detective Landers as saying, "No way. Forget about it. It's not the vigilante. Neither of them." Detective Macy, however, "refused to comment," which the *Post* interpreted as confirmation of a connection.

Sharon heard a ruckus in the resuscitation room and hurried

over, hoping to speak to McKenzie about what had happened to Mr. Fritz. As she got closer, she heard an explosion of yelling and arguing.

"Don't even think about performing a thoracotomy!"

She recognized the voice of Dr. Singh, the short, pot-bellied head of cardiothoracic surgery. Usually so calm, he had definitely lost his cool.

"I'm the one who decides who gets chest surgery," Dr. Singh continued, "not impulsive, inexperienced, and uncertified hospital traffic cops like you, McKenzie. You performing a thoracotomy on this patient is *not* going to happen. There's no clinical indication for it. He's not a trauma victim."

"But there *is* a clinical indication. You of all people should know that. And as far as inexperienced, I've cracked more chests than I can count. The guy's got a ruptured triple A. He needs to go to the operating room. Stop wasting time and get him there, or I'll perform the thoracotomy right here and force you to finish the job in the OR."

"You're an emergency doctor, not a surgeon. You don't decide how to treat a ruptured abdominal aortic aneurysm—I do. The guy's aorta is seven centimeters. That thing is leaking and he's coded twice." Dr. Singh paused, growing red in the face. "He's hypotensive, in his sixties, with multiple medical issues. Surgery would kill him. His chances of surviving are less than one percent."

"The default is death," McKenzie shot back. "If he doesn't go to the operating room, he has *zero* chance at survival. Don't you like saving people, Raj? Or do you just hate the idea of tainting your surgery record? Is that the most important thing here?"

"What's important, cowboy, is being realistic. It's his time. The only thing keeping him alive are those IV fluids. It's a decision for a surgeon, McKenzie. You ER doctors are nothing more than triage nurses."

As they continued arguing, Sharon got the background story from Donahoe, who was standing in the back of the room with the rest of the residents.

"The patient came in an hour ago," Donahoe explained. "Stomach pain. He became unresponsive and coded. McKenzie intubated him and brought him back. Then he did a bedside ultrasound, which showed that the patient's aorta is leaking blood into his belly. Singh has a point. That's a death sentence for a guy like this."

"Do you think McKenzie's wrong?" Sharon whispered.

"Technically, no. The only way to stop the bleeding is to surgically open the guy's chest and clamp the artery above the bleeding site. That's what McKenzie wants to do. Then Singh can take him to the OR and fix the vessel. The problem is that the patient has lost so much blood that he pretty much has no chance of survival."

The monitor overhead started beeping, hushing everyone. The man's heart rate shot up to 150 and his blood pressure plunged to 80/40. McKenzie opened a thoracotomy tray, pulled a scalpel from the crash cart, and placed it on top of the tray. He snapped on a pair of latex gloves, spread a sterile dressing on top of the patient's body, and poured Betadine over the chest. He picked up the scalpel and sliced neatly into the man's left thorax. Meanwhile, Singh went into a fit of rage, throwing things, threatening to write McKenzie up, and demanding he stop the procedure immediately. One of the male ER technicians held him back.

McKenzie and most of the others in the room disregarded Singh completely. Everyone's gaze was fixed on what McKenzie was doing. Sharon marveled at how steady his hands were, given that he'd just been in a screaming match. McKenzie seemed to have entered another dimension, one without doubt or distraction, a state of pure flow. In less than a minute, the ribs were spread, the lungs and heart exposed, and a long metal clamp had stopped the aortic blood from filling the abdomen.

The monitor stopped beeping, and the man's heart rate and blood pressure immediately returned to normal.

McKenzie snapped off his bloody gloves and threw them on the floor. "Ball's in your court, Raj. You got a couple of hours to repair the vessel. If you don't take him to the OR, he'll die, and you'll lose your medical license and won't be able to buy that second Porsche."

Singh trembled with fury as he stormed out. Following close behind him, Donahoe and another surgery resident wheeled the patient out of the room. Before he left, Donahoe glanced back at Sharon, but her eyes were fixed on McKenzie.

Sharon felt her heart beating violently in her chest.

Was it the excitement of the case?

She started to move toward him, remembering she wanted to talk to him about Mr. Fritz, but another gurney appeared with a paramedic doing chest compressions. She stepped aside to let the gurney pass and watched McKenzie listen to the paramedics give their brief history.

No time for updates. They both had work to do.

Noticing that the main ER had become even busier, Sharon hustled to her desk and took a sip of her now-cold coffee. She dropped the cup into the trash and attacked her chart pile.

Garrett again! She looked up and saw him in room 17-C, sitting in a chair reserved for asthmatics or people awaiting x-rays. He was blustering forth to a beautiful young woman getting inhalation therapy. The woman leaned back every time Garrett leaned closer.

Sharon strode angrily toward the room. The ER was overflowing. She didn't have time for this man any more. For the first time, she was going to deny a patient social services.

"Get up, Mr. Garrett."

"Hey, Ms. Sharon. How's my girl?"

"Come on, Mr. Garrett. Other people need that chair." There were four people awaiting x-rays and three other asthmatics. A mom stood holding her three-year-old, who was getting a nebulizer treatment.

Sharon felt she would explode as Garrett slurred on. "You said not to come back if they threw me out, but some douche bag motherfucker spiked my coffee when I was helping this old lady cross the street. It wasn't my fault, I promise."

The mother covered her kid's ears at Garrett's language. Sharon yanked the drunk to his feet and tugged him down to the family room, the only vacant place left in the ER. She pointed to a chair by the long table and shut the door. The shades were closed to give family members privacy in their grief. She turned on the light.

"All right, Mr. Garrett. I have to write my consult recommending that this hospital refuse you further services. It'll just take a minute."

"Please, Ms. Sharon. Don't be a hater," he protested, lurching to his feet. "There's gotta be a place in the city that understands people like me. You're the only one I can count on. The only one who understands me, sees me for who I really am. Come on. I'll stay off the booze, I swear it."

Sharon could smell him inching closer as she hurried to finish her note. She looked up sharply, and he veered away. She resumed writing as he kept talking, pleading with her to stop and listen to him.

"No, Mr. Garrett," she said, stabbing the final period. "We're done here. I've exhausted all our resources trying to help you."

Sharon heard the door lock behind her.

When she looked up, Garrett stood with his back to the door. His eyes looked wild. Gone was the apologetic drunk. She was looking at a violent criminal.

He lunged at her like a lion targeting its prey. She swung

the edge of her chart into his head, but it only made him angrier. Before she knew it, he lifted her by the throat and slammed her against the wall. He held her off the floor with both hands around her neck, squeezing.

"You stupid bitch! You give me what I want, you hear? What I want, when I want it. I'm gonna tell you what I want, and I'm gonna get it, or you're gonna have to do without breathing. Got it?"

Sharon felt her head expanding. She was losing oxygen. She thrust up her pen, lodging it deep into Garrett's left thumb muscle. The pain made him let go of her. She pushed away and ran for the door, fumbling for the lock, but Garrett was too quick. He grabbed her from behind, pulled her toward him, and flung her onto the long table. Sharon tried to yell, but her inflamed throat could only rasp. She tried to scramble away, but he dragged her under him as he climbed on the table and fell on top of her.

She could smell piss and alcohol on Garrett as he pushed his face inches from hers. "I'm gonna get what I want, okay? And you're gonna give it to me. You're gonna learn how to give and keep giving. Right bitch? Stop fighting me!" He elbowed her jaw so hard she almost lost consciousness. The blow left her dizzy and disoriented, but still she fought to wrench free with every ounce of energy she had left. He slammed his heavy forearm across her sternum and pinned her while his other hand fumbled its way down her body. She sensed his hand groping her crotch and her panties being ripped out from under her long skirt. He threw them on the floor and reached for his zipper.

Sharon was too weak to fight the man. His body was shot from drink, but he was still far bigger and stronger than she was. She kept struggling but felt herself wanting to give up. The more she tried to scream, the weaker the rasping sound got. She moved her torso back and forth, trying her best to escape as he worked his zipper. She tried pulling her arms, lifting her head, pounding the table. Nothing helped. Her adrenaline was wearing off. Nausea and excruciating pain flooded in.

She found herself looking with a terrible ache at the window in the door, covered with a polite curtain so nobody's eyes could intrude on the room's privacy. She heard ambulance sirens and the sounds of chaos in the near distance, and she could hear people walking back and forth in the adjoining hallway, the sound filling her with unbearable sadness.

Slowly, she stopped fighting.

She stopped moving.

She felt cold, numb, empty.

And she felt anger at this awful city in which she'd so stupidly hoped she'd be able to make a difference.

Chapter 14

Every movement Garrett made seemed to make the room spin and her vision blur. Her arms were pinned over her head. Her torso was a throbbing lump. Her legs were lead. Only her feet moved.

Sharon felt the chill of being naked under her uplifted skirt, then the pressure of his fist screwing into her stomach as he tried to push himself inside her, his knees grinding into her thighs. She attempted one last yell, but nothing emerged. A sharp pain knifed through her brain. Burning tears welled from her eyes as she squeezed them shut.

She heard a crash so loud her insides jumped. Then Garrett seemed to fly backward and up, as if suctioned out of an airplane midflight, smashing into the far wall.

Sharon saw McKenzie's face leaning in close to her. She wrapped her arms reflexively around his neck, and he picked her up so tenderly she had to grind her teeth not to break into sobs. He carried her from the room and lowered her onto an empty gurney in the hallway.

McKenzie carefully turned her face to the right and left, examining her head and throat. He looked closely at her wrists and then the rest of her body, delicately lifting her skirt to inspect her thighs. She saw him glare back into the room, where her underwear lay on the floor, and look back at her, eyebrows raised.

"He didn't ... get a chance. Thanks ... to you."

McKenzie nodded and whipped his gaze back into the room. Garrett was getting to his feet. McKenzie patted Sharon's hands and charged into the family room.

Sharon watched him dodge a chair Garrett threw at him as he entered the room. Grunting like a juiced-up weightlifter, the drunk picked up the long table. As he held it wobbly over his head, McKenzie took two steps forward and chopped both of his armpits. Garrett's arms dropped, and the table came down on his head with a sickening bang. He fell with the table crashing over him, but immediately jumped up with insane energy, blood pouring from a gash in his scalp.

"I used to wrestle, motherfucker. You didn't know that, did you?" With a roar, he charged.

Sharon couldn't quite believe what she saw. Garrett threw his arms around McKenzie, but before his hands could lock in a bear hug, McKenzie slipped to the floor and, kneeling, punched both of Garrett's kneecaps. While Garrett screamed in agony, McKenzie stood and flipped him head first over his shoulder. It happened so quickly that Sharon feared she had a concussion and wasn't seeing straight. Garrett got up from the floor, gasping but smiling insanely.

"You think your jujitsu shit's gonna stop me, asshole?"

With unnatural calm, McKenzie stared at the drunk.

"You gonna call security on me, Doc?" Garrett shouted, breathless.

"Not a chance," McKenzie said, widening his stance.

"You want a piece of me? I'm gonna show you some varsity shit now. None of this JV bullshit!"

This time Garrett approached McKenzie more carefully. He kept throwing out a long arm, trying to grab McKenzie, but

McKenzie kept hacking it away. The third time Garrett grunted in pain. Still, he managed to herd McKenzie into a corner, grinning as he readied for the kill.

A few staff members clustered around the doorway, among them the charge nurse and Rebecca Gordon, one of the new ER interns. Sharon heard Rivera calling security.

Garrett rushed forward, screaming at the top of his lungs. McKenzie shot his palm straight into Garrett's nose. The drunk came to a dead stop and grabbed his face while McKenzie delivered six lightning-fast left-right punches to his crotch and walked away. Garrett melted like sludge to the floor, unconscious.

Then there was a large commotion as three security guards scrambled into the room.

McKenzie walked over to Rivera and Gordon. "Rebecca, take Sharon to the physicians' lounge and do a thorough exam. If there's anything suspicious, do a rape kit." He took Rivera's elbow. "Call the cops. Get that trash arrested for assault and attempted rape."

"You bet I will," Rivera said.

"Wow, Dr. McKenzie," Rebecca said, "I didn't know you had it in you!"

"He's a falling-down drunk. A Girl Scout could've put him down with a box of cookies." He walked away into the main ER.

Sharon found herself back on the gurney, surrounded by a group of nurses. Rebecca Gordon held her hand. The security guards picked Garrett off the floor and dumped him onto a gurney. The housekeeper, the same one who months earlier had placed the out-of-order sign on the bathroom door, started getting the family room back in order.

As Rebecca wheeled her toward the physicians' lounge, Sharon felt her voice returning. Her throat still burned, and she was light-headed and trembling. She felt like crying, but no tears came.

As they crossed the narrow stretch that connected the lounge to the ER, Sharon turned her head and saw McKenzie back on his desk. Everything around him seemed to glow with a kind of blurry, otherworldly light.

He lifted his gaze and their eyes met.

Sharon felt a kind of dreamy delirium creep over her.

Are you Michael the archangel or Lucifer before the fall? she wondered as he faded from view.

And so did the light.

Chapter 15

Three days after the attack, the staff was still buzzing about Robert's heroics.

He responded by acting like a bigger jerk than ever.

He felt like a pressure cooker about to blow. He hated the attention. He liked being a lone wolf, not a hero.

The only saving grace was that Sharon had taken a few days off, so he'd been able to get things more or less back to normal. When she finally returned to the ER, people seemed more concerned about her well-being than about how Garrett had ended up with a shattered ethmoid bone and a pair of crippled testicles. She'd arrived to a whole circus of *oohs* and *ahs*. Staff members hovered around, taking her hand, patting her, and recounting their own ER horror stories. Robert's prowess was no longer a big deal.

Robert hoped the urgent demands of the ER would quell his inner turmoil and force the staff to forget the incident. As the morning progressed, he was glad to see everyone soldiering back into the rigors of their work, and was especially relieved to see Sharon tackling the hefty pile of charts that had accumulated in her absence. Robert dodged every approach she made in his direction, but when he came out of the bathroom after lunch, there she was, smiling at him with bright eyes.

"I knew I could catch you here," she said. "Even Batman has to pee."

"Let me guess. You want to tell me how you're forever grateful, how brave I was for saving your life, and how you'll never forget what I did. Blah, blah, blah."

"I mean that sincerely," she said. "Especially the *blah, blah, blah* part."

"You're welcome. Now get back to work."

"There's something else we need to discuss."

"Are you going to tell me about what a dumbass you are for getting yourself locked in a room with someone I told you a thousand times was a psycho? Or about how you left us short-handed these last three days? Or maybe about how much of my time you're wasting right now?"

She hadn't expected that response. And before she could reply, he stomped away.

The day chugged on. Some of the people who passed by Robert at his station gave him a respectful glance, while others just ignored him. As far as patients, it was a typical shift: a tourist with a pulmonary embolus, a fifty-year-old with a ruptured appendix, a toddler with a penny in her throat. Deep lacerations, a subarachnoid hemorrhage, two cardiac arrests.

Dr. Valentine, one of the other ER attendings, appeared just before five o'clock to relieve Robert for the late shift. Robert signed out his patients, grabbed his bag, and hustled off.

Friday. Weekend off. He had successfully avoided Sharon since their encounter.

By Monday things should be back to normal.

But the moment he got outside, thoughts of her and that awful day flooded in…

Robert recalled not having Sharon on his radar after returning to his desk from resus. Something was wrong. Where was she? Where was Garrett?

He had felt a black cloud gather. He knew his instincts. He lived by them.

He had walked around the ER. No Sharon. No Garrett.

He tried the family room. The door was locked. He backed up five steps, then rammed forward, splintering the door and crashing it open. He had saved her life and disabled that frequent-flying scumbag—

"Dr. McKenzie, wait up!"

Robert flinched, but kept walking. He didn't need to turn. He recognized her voice.

Despite his desire to give her another stern lecture about the Garrett incident, he wanted to put the week behind him even more.

"Dr. McKenzie, please! Wait up," she called again.

The pedestrian signal started flashing *Do Not Walk*, but Robert knew he could make it across in time. His motorcycle was only a block away. He could make a clean getaway and avoid Sharon until Monday.

He trotted across the street and hurried on. Seconds later, he heard multiple horns, people yelling, the squeal of brakes, and a sweet-toned voice calling, "Sorr-reee. My fault. Thank you. Sorry!"

She had dodged through the traffic.

"Why do you keep trying to get yourself killed?" Robert yelled as she approached.

"I don't mean to," she said, catching her breath. "It just happens."

"Well, that's your problem."

"We need to talk."

"No, we don't. My shift's over. See you Monday." He turned and kept walking.

110

She ran to catch up. "Dr. McKenzie, stop! Please. Slow down for a second."

"I told you, we have nothing to talk about." Robert could see his motorcycle now. As soon as he put on his helmet, he was home free.

"I know you're the vigilante!"

This time, Robert stopped. He looked frantically around. No one else had heard.

"What did you just say?"

"I know you're the vigilante." Sharon approached and lowered her voice. "At least, I think I do. There's a lot that doesn't make sense, and that's why I want to talk to you."

"You know nothing."

"Dr. McKenzie, I *know*," she said. "I've spent the last three days doing nothing but research. It all fits. Times, places. The man who raped his daughter, the Harlem thugs, the gay bashers. I even figured out who paid for Mrs. Castro's surgery and a dozen others. You're the one who gave Adele a thousand dollars in cash." Sharon smiled. "You're Baby Jesus!"

Robert's mind raced along with his heartbeat.

How had she figured it out? What exactly does she know?

"I was lucky to have you," she went on, "and I'm willing to keep this information to myself, but we need to talk."

He felt torn apart by unreserved anger on one hand and astonishment on the other. How the hell had this twenty-something Hoosier unraveled his tightly plotted labyrinth?

"What do you want?" he asked coldly.

"I just want to talk, that's all. There are a few things that don't make sense. For example, why did you—"

"We're not doing this here," Robert said, putting on his helmet. "Tomorrow night." He climbed on his cycle, started the engine, revved it three times, and kicked up the stand. "There's a

Mexican restaurant called El Tercer Piso three blocks east of your apartment. Eight o'clock."

Robert didn't wait for her confirmation. He felt anxious and vulnerable as he peeled out of his parking spot into the Amsterdam Avenue traffic.

He was no longer anonymous.

He was no longer a lone wolf.

PART 2

Child Abuse Statistics[1]

» *Five children die every day as a result of child abuse in the United States.*

» *Up to sixty percent of child fatalities due to child abuse are not recorded as such on death certificates.*

» *More than ninety percent of child sexual abuse victims know the perpetrator in some way; seventy percent are abused by family members.*

» *One-third of abused and neglected children will go on to abuse their own children.*

---

[1]Childhelp, National Child Abuse Statistics

Chapter 16

On the five-minute walk to the restaurant on St. Nicholas and 164th Street, Sharon's head was a jumble of thoughts. She realized she was putting off coping with the brutal attack from three days prior to concentrate on McKenzie's secret identity. She had a long list of things she wanted to know about his life as a vigilante. But almost more pressing were the questions about their relationship.

How did McKenzie know where she lived? Why had he chosen to meet three blocks from her apartment? Was he stalking her?

When she found the place, sandwiched between a barbershop and a twenty-four-hour bodega, Sharon's questions were overshadowed by a more pressing thought: she was overdressed. Why had she chosen to wear her black silk dress for such an informal occasion?

Nobody seemed to notice. The restaurant was small and packed with families, couples, people of all ages—laughing, eating, drinking. A four-piece mariachi band played in the corner; a few people were singing along. The restaurant was festive, almost to the point of absurdity. Not exactly her vision of romantic, but charming nonetheless. And the place smelled amazing: fresh herbs and spices filled the air and transported her to a different world, one far away from Washington Heights.

It took her a while to pick McKenzie out of the crowd. At first she didn't think it was him—the guy at the bar wearing Diesel jeans, a fitted blue T-shirt, and Adidas sneakers. He was laughing so hard it looked like he might fall off his stool. The bartender was having a drink with him, and the two seemed to know each other well. How could this be McKenzie? She'd barely seen him crack a smile. There was so much she didn't know about him.

She approached and leaned on the bar next to him, waiting to be noticed. When he turned and saw her, his face stiffened. He nodded his head in recognition but didn't greet her.

The guy on the stool next to her got up, and she took his seat. She swiveled to watch the crowd. McKenzie watched with her.

"This is a cute place," she said.

"I know."

A waiter walked over to McKenzie and whispered something into his ear. McKenzie answered in perfect Spanish.

"Impressive. I didn't know you were fluent in Spanish, Dr. McKenzie."

"I spent some time in Guatemala. I guess I picked up a few words." He paused and looked at her. "Please don't call me Dr. McKenzie. We're not in the hospital."

"Okay, Roberto." She turned to the bartender. "*Por favor, una cerveza. Dos Equis.*"

"You speak Spanish, too? Let me guess. You spent a spring break in Cancún?"

"Puerto Vallarta." Sharon shrugged. "I picked up a few words."

Robert suppressed a smile. He nodded at the bartender, who called one of the waiters over. A minute later, Robert and Sharon were ushered to the last empty table by the window.

"They seem to know you here," she said.

120

"It's the only place in New York that makes food the way it tasted in Guatemala, so I come here often."

"I thought this was a Mexican restaurant."

"Mexico and Guatemala share a border. They have a lot in common."

Sharon picked up her menu. "They must have great arepas here. I've always wanted to try one."

Robert shook his head. "Arepas are Venezuelan, not so much Guatemalan. This place is known for its enchiladas and chiles rellenos."

"I see," she said, glancing at the menu. "How'd you end up in Guatemala?"

Robert picked up his beer and downed half of it. "Through some sort of Doctors Without Borders offshoot designed for medical students. I signed up thinking I'd shadow a physician, and maybe learn a little Spanish at the same time. When I got there, the only physician there to shadow was myself. Besides the local medicine man, I was the only doctor-like creature in a fifty-mile radius. The patients were sick, some even critical. And there were a lot of them. I had about a month to do the equivalent of a three-year residency."

"You started treating people just like that?"

"First couple of days, it was awful. Kind of like being thrown into hell and asking the person in charge to turn the heat down."

Sharon smiled and rearranged her napkin.

"I was in way over my head," Robert continued, "but there was no alternative. I had to do whatever I could manage or just leave and let people die."

The waiter came with her beer and a refill for him. Sharon took a drink. "You must've done a lot of good," she said.

"Why do you say that?"

"This is the most animated I've ever seen you."

"I was fortunate to have had that experience," Robert said. "I'd always known that I had a good memory, but it was there that I realized how much I could do with it. I'm not sure whether it was adrenaline or necessity, but I managed to recall things I'd read about months before in random medical journals and textbooks. I treated a lot of people using that knowledge—and a suitcase filled with medical supplies. There were only a handful of people I couldn't help."

They sat quietly for a moment. McKenzie glanced around the room while Sharon studied him. He had a great jawline. He looked more attractive to her at that moment than ever.

"What else?" she asked.

"What do you mean?"

"There's something else about Guatemala—not just the medical part."

"You know, Reede, you may look young and fresh in that little black number you're wearing tonight, but sometimes you're frighteningly perceptive."

"Was it some hot *señorita* you left behind?" she said, blushing. "A story of unrequited love?"

"It was a love story, I suppose. But not what you think. It was between a teacher and student, not between lovers."

"A teacher?"

"The medicine man I mentioned. His name's Guillermo. He was also a brilliant general, responsible for directing a number of forces scattered in the hills. Freedom fighters. There was an awful war going on the whole time I was there. It was genocide."

"He taught you how to fight?"

"He taught me how to live. But, yes, he also taught me everything I know about how to protect myself and how to attack when necessary."

"I'd like to thank him," Sharon said. "What he taught you saved my life the other day."

"It did," he said. "I'll make sure to tweet him later."

"I'm sure he doesn't tweet!"

"No," Robert laughed, "but we do e-mail."

"He's still alive, then?"

"Yeah, amazingly. It's a testament to just how smart he is. Most people wouldn't have lasted a week in his position."

They were quiet again. Sharon took another sip of her beer and allowed his story to sink in.

"How do you deal with it, Robert?" she said, breaking the silence.

"Deal with what?"

"Death," Sharon said. "I'm sure you experienced your fair share of it in Guatemala. And I know you deal with it at St. Jude's on a daily basis. It's such a part of your job, but for me it's like a wrecking ball that swings away for a long arc and then comes back at me when I'm not expecting it. I guess I'm still having a hard time handling it on an emotional level."

"There are worse things to deal with than death." Robert called the waiter over. "Anyway, we're not going to talk about that now, are we?"

Sharon opened her mouth to answer, but the waiter arrived before she could speak. Robert placed an order, and since she couldn't think of anything else, she ordered the chiles rellenos and enchiladas. The waiter took their menus and left.

"If we can't talk about death," she said with a sardonic grin, "what can we possibly talk about?"

Robert made no response.

The waiter delivered two new beers; Sharon made a mental note to pace herself.

"What about your parents?" Robert asked. "Are either of them social workers?"

"Teachers. My dad's an English professor. Mom teaches third grade. Social work's like teaching, too, I guess. Teaching people how to empower themselves. At least that's how I look at it."

"You mean how to utilize resources?"

"Their own—"

"And society's," Robert said, finishing her thought.

"Right," she said, feeling a little glow from being understood.

"You're good at what you do. You learn quickly and make the right choices."

Sharon blushed. He was being very different from the jerk of the emergency room. Was he being genuinely nice, or was it an act to keep her from exposing him? She wasn't sure. She took a slow sip.

"How long have you been a vigilante?"

Robert's face paled and a shadow passed over his eyes. The change was sudden. "How did you figure it out?"

"I became suspicious after Adele, the lady with the Ambien overdose. She told me about getting a thousand dollars cash in the mail. She didn't have friends with that kind of money. I started checking medical records, matched them with human-interest stories about random acts of kindness. Your name cross-indexed way too much."

"That can't be all."

"It was really the violent acts that caught my attention. The wife beater, the child molester—whoever assaulted these guys knew exactly where to hurt them, almost as if the attacker understood anatomy. It had to be a doctor. I pulled up your schedule and noted that you were off every night of the attacks. And so many of the victims were relatives of your patients."

Robert closed his eyes, shook his head, and sighed.

"I already told you," she continued, "your secret's safe with me. I just want to know why you do it. I understand the nice things: getting surgery for the uninsured, money to help the poor get out of a hole. What you did for that orphan a few months back—tuition to City College—was incredible. And I understand wanting to stay anonymous. You don't want the ER flooded with people asking for free stuff. Smart. But hunting down people you run across in the ER?" She lowered her voice. "Assaulting and maiming them? That's totally insane, Robert. You're a physician. Not only is it wrong, but it's immoral, indictable, and dangerous. You could get put away, or even worse, you could get yourself killed."

The waiter brought their food just as Sharon finished the sentence. Robert put out two fingers and pointed to Sharon. The waiter understood, and a moment later brought back two shot glasses and a bottle of tequila.

"Like I said earlier, there are worse things than death. But all right, you want to talk and I want to drink. So unless you drink, I'm not talking." He poured a shot and handed it to her.

Sharon smelled the alcohol and instantly recalled the first (and last) time she drank tequila. Her first college weekend. New independence, new roommate, an off-campus bar that never asked students for ID. After downing multiple shots, she'd felt the room spinning around her. She stopped drinking, but by then it was too late. She threw up her dinner (a bowl of Frosted Flakes) on the sidewalk outside the bar. Ever since, she made a point of keeping close tabs on how much she drank, and stayed clear of tequila.

She raised the glass and toasted. "Okay, but if I vomit on you, it's not my fault. Let's drink to talk and talk to drink." As the liquid went down, her throat tightened and a trail of fire burned all the way to the pit of her stomach.

She looked at the two giant plates that had appeared in the middle of the table. "Whoops," she said. "I guess I ordered a little too much." She shrugged and placed some of each dish on her own plate. Then she washed down the shot with a sip of beer, gave a little shudder, and dug in.

Robert watched her with approval, still holding his shot. He tossed it down as if it were water.

"I don't like that term," Robert said, filling his own plate.

"What ... term?" Sharon asked between bites.

"Vigilante. It's inexact for what I do. A vigilante goes out and punishes those who've broken the law."

"And you don't?"

"I don't target people just because they've broken the law. I go after a specific group of people. Those who commit atrocious acts and show no remorse—the psychopaths."

"Isn't everyone who commits a violent crime a psychopath in some way or another?"

"Not at all. People commit crimes for different reasons. Mostly because they're idiots, made stupid by greed, power, or jealousy. Take away their idiocy and they're just like you and me. Maybe given certain circumstances, our desperation might outstrip our judgment, and we'd do the same stupid shit they do."

Robert took a bite of the chiles rellenos and another swig of his beer. "It's the psychopaths who have to be stopped; the guys who do harm just for the hell of it. They don't care about repercussions. They lack remorse. They can't be helped."

"There are studies that say some violent criminals are treatable. I think everyone has the potential for change. There are new drugs, experiments with different environments—"

"No one has found any sure way of rehabilitating these guys. They need to be put out of commission."

"But it's—"

"I wish there were another way, but if I don't stop them, they'll keep hurting innocent people."

"Robert, you could make a mistake. You could get hurt, or hurt someone you shouldn't. You could end up in jail with a whole crew of psychopaths for neighbors."

"See, that's exactly the problem. There are thousands of savages in this city alone getting away with rape, murder, and violence every day, sometimes for years, because people don't take a stand against them. Everyone assumes that someone else will take care of them, that someone else will do the dirty work. They believe that the forces of law and order are structured to protect them. Psychopaths know that's a myth. They count on the hollowness of that trust. They understand that there are huge cracks in the system, and they know that they can slip right through. They don't play by the rules, so the rules don't touch them."

"But then what are we left with? How does society stay intact?"

"The only way society can continue to function is if people decide to take personal responsibility and go after these psychopaths. If there's anything I learned in Guatemala, it's that you can't play by the rules to stop monsters from taking machetes to pregnant women or from burning down orphanages full of children."

"I don't know. I don't see this ending well at all. It's too much like a comic book. You're not Batman. If you don't get killed, chances are you're going to get arrested—and then you'll certainly get fired."

He didn't say anything.

"You're too good a doctor to jeopardize your career."

He smiled. "Thank you. I appreciate that. Especially coming from you. But don't worry about me. I've been doing a pretty good job staying out of trouble so far."

Sharon felt all sorts of emotions. She was angry with him. She was worried about him.

And she was falling for him.

She pushed the plate of food away, poured herself a shot of tequila, and held it in her hand. Robert poured one for himself and tapped his glass against hers. They locked eyes and tossed the shots down, lightly slamming the glasses on the table.

"Whoops," Sharon said. "That was one too many." She grabbed her glass of water and took a large sip.

"There's a folk tale in Guatemala about why God invented drink."

"Well, that's something I'd like to know," she said, aware that she was on the edge of slurring her words.

"You would, wouldn't you?"

"As far as I know, alcohol causes only bad things to happen: broken homes, hangovers, car accidents, violence. So what do the Guatemalans say?"

"The natives say that God gave men drink to make dancing less awkward."

She laughed and let out a little burp. "Oh. Excuse me," she giggled.

He stood up, grabbed Sharon's hand, and led her to where a few couples were dancing on a small wooden section of the floor. He cupped his left hand over her right and placed it carefully on his chest while laying his right hand gently on her waist. A warm shockwave went up her back.

"I never thought in a million years I'd be slow-dancing to Spanish music with Dr. Jerk Nut McKenzie."

"I told you not to call me Dr. McKenzie in public." He smiled and they started moving together. "I don't mind Jerk Nut but, for your information, this isn't Spanish music. This is a ranchera, the traditional music of Mexico and Guatemala."

"I love this song," she said, looking around. Everyone appeared to be having a great time.

"I'm glad," he said. "It happens to be my favorite."

"This might be a rash decision for such an important thing," she said, "but I think it's my favorite song, too."

"It's by Rafael Rodrigo. The song is about a country poet who falls madly in love. Even though he's convinced that he found his soul mate, he breaks up with the girl and leaves town after

128

realizing that being so much in love was interfering with his writing. He sacrifices his happiness to live in misery and die alone. In doing so, he composes the most incredible poetry the world has ever known."

"That's beautiful," Sharon said, moving closer.

"Beautiful?" Robert laughed. "That's kind of stupid on his part. Then again, I'm no romantic."

"I can see that."

They swayed silently to the music. She put her cheek against his chest. "Do you miss Guatemala?"

"Is it obvious?"

"Ever think of going back?"

"I'd go back in a heartbeat."

"You would?" she said, looking up at him with a mock pouty face.

"There might be a couple things I'd miss," he said, smiling. "But I hate practicing medicine in New York. People feel too entitled. They complain if they have to wait thirty minutes to get an x-ray for their sprained ankle. Meanwhile, the rest of the world waits hours with potentially life-threatening problems. In Guatemalan clinics, people camp out for days just to be seen, and then they're grateful to be treated. We spend billions of dollars keeping people alive in vegetative states, people with no chance at neurological improvement. There's no way they'd ever think of doing that in Guatemala, or in most other places in the world."

"I never thought I'd ever tell you this," she said.

"Tell me what?"

"I think I'd miss you if you left."

He pulled her closer to him.

The universe could implode, but she wouldn't care. With his arms around her, Sharon felt nothing could hurt her.

Chapter 17

Robert stood close behind Sharon, his breath on her neck, watching her dig through her bag for her keys. When she finally found them, she aimed one of the keys at the lower lock on the door. After a few errant attempts, she got the tip in the keyhole, but it wouldn't go in. She tried the key in the upper lock. Didn't work there, either. Robert's breath suddenly struck her as funny. She started to giggle.

"No go!" she chirped and fumbled through her other keys. "You know what? There are way too many keys and not enough locks. Or are there too many locks and not enough keys?" She turned to Robert and threw her hands up in defeat.

He was smiling.

"There's probably one that works." He took the keys from her hand, studied them, chose one, and slid it in easily.

"How'd you do that?"

Seconds later they were inside her dark apartment. She groped her hand around on the wall until she hit the light switch.

Robert stood just inside the doorway and took in his surroundings. It was a typical Washington Heights railroad apartment; a small entryway led to a tiny kitchen, which gave way to a small living room and then a bedroom with a postage-stamp bathroom. "That sangria at the second bar went down like Kool-Aid," she said. "Do you remember Kool-Aid? I used to love that stuff. I'm glad you got me out of there before I started seeing twelve of you."

Sharon teetered into the living room, flopped onto the sofa, took off her shoes, threw them over her shoulder like spilled salt, and began massaging her feet. "I have to get new shoes. I know they make me look cute, but they really hurt my feet."

Robert ambled around the apartment. The furniture screamed "garage sale," but she definitely had taste. There was an old record player and a retro set of floor and desk lamps. The blue sofa had large velvet pillows. A vintage cedar chest took the place of a coffee table.

There were printouts and books all over the place. Robert itched to pick some up and start reading—or to scan the titles of the library that overfilled her small mahogany bookcase—but he knew it was time to go.

"I guess this is good night," he said.

"What do you mean?" Sharon asked and burped again. "Excuse me! See? I'm just too classy for you to leave … just yet."

"You're also too drunk. Go to bed and sleep it off. I wanted to make sure you got home all right."

"I like chatting with you," she said, moving a pile of papers and two thick books from the sofa to the floor. She patted the cushion next to her. "We have to finish our conversation."

"Which one? I think we started a dozen and never finished any of them."

Instead of taking a seat on the sofa, he walked to the bookshelves. He fingered a few of the bindings, then stopped abruptly and removed one volume. "You have a copy of Machiavelli's *The Prince?*" Robert asked and stared at Sharon with curiosity. "A social worker shouldn't be reading stuff like that."

"Are you still surprised that I'm smart?" Sharon said, twirling a finger through her hair. "Remember, I'm the one who figured out you're the vigilante."

"That's not what I meant. I just didn't expect you to be reading Machiavelli, that's all." He put the book back on the shelf. "Anyway, please don't bring up that vigilante stuff."

"Is it hot in here? It's hot in here. Are you hot?" Sharon asked, unfastening the two top buttons on her dress.

"Not at all," Robert said. "Seriously, I really do have to go—"

He stopped mid-sentence and stared past her, at the bold title of a printout on the floor. He walked over and picked it up. "What's this?"

Sharon grabbed at it, but his reflexes were too quick. He held the pages above her head and turned his body from her, using his other hand to straight-arm her away.

"Don't read that," she urged. "It's not ready yet!"

"'The Political Report Card: Changing the Way America Votes in the 21st Century,' by Sharon Reede, PhD candidate."

There was scribbling all over the margins, with a number of capital Es and Cs circled. "I don't get it," he said after perusing the writing. He handed back the cover sheet, plopped down beside her, and started going through the stack of papers on the table.

"Well, okay, go ahead. I suppose you should get comfortable and help yourself to the still undigested research I've spent the past three years of my life working on. But for the record, if you get me started on my dissertation, you're not going to be able to shut me up."

Robert was too absorbed in speed-reading to comment. After a minute, he looked up at her.

Sharon's eyes were shut, but she opened them immediately when she sensed his gaze. "What?"

"You're trying to figure out an objective way to profile political candidates running for office?"

"For re-election, specifically."

"A mathematical formula using objective markers for"—he flipped through some pages—*"how each candidate weighs in on the economy, environment, education, and crime?"*

"I need an algorithm for foreign policy, too, but that's much more complex. I'm sticking to local politics for now."

"Who comes up with this stuff?"

"I do," Sharon said, sitting straighter. The topic of conversation seemed to sober her up immediately. "I got tired of the same politicians running for office and winning, despite how little they've done for the people they represent. I figured there had to be objective ways of measuring the progress made by an elected official—"

"And objective ways of finding real leaders who can make a difference instead of doing the same thing year after year."

"That's right! It's frustrating to see unemployment soar, school grades fall, teen pregnancy skyrocket, the environment turn to crap, and the rate of homicides and rapes rise. Meanwhile, the same people get re-elected. It's like there's this ritzy club of professional politicians who stay in power, but they don't do anything except fundraise and campaign. We need real community people in office: teachers, economists, doctors, and—"

"Social workers," Robert said.

"You bet your butt!"

Robert laughed. "This is smart, Reede. Incumbents shouldn't have the advantage just because they're incumbents, unless they've done something during their term in office that's made a real impact on society." He scanned the title page again. "But what's up with the math in your thesis?"

"It's used to objectively gauge the progress an incumbent made during time in office. I came up with the idea, not the formula. I have a math whiz friend for that. She worked out how to integrate all the parameters. You're going to think I'm a nerd."

"I already do," he said. "But go on."

"It uses regression analysis to measure non-quantitative variables. Like, see, right here?" She pressed against him to point out a bar graph with a complex arrangement of numbers, headed with bold capital letters. "We have to lower the margin of error by calculating each parameter separately. Obviously, lowering unemployment one percent shouldn't be the same as lowering the homicide rate by the same amount. Same with teen pregnancy and education, so these letters represent different variables."

He pulled away, looking at her in half disbelief. "I had no idea you were working on anything like this. You have your own double life." He picked up another printout. "What about this stuff here about prison reform?"

"That's part two," Sharon explained. "After presenting the theory in part one, I wanted to give some praxis showing what an elected official could actually do once elected—to ensure that they make an impact on all these variables."

"You really believe in rehabilitation, don't you?"

"I know you disagree, but if it's done appropriately, anyone can be rehabilitated."

Robert shook his head. "I don't buy that."

"As it stands now, prisons are overpopulated. Most inmates get out before their sentence is up. And what do they do? They go back to society and commit more crime. Right now, prisons don't serve their function. They can't rehabilitate prisoners because of the way they're set up."

"How they're set up?"

"That's right. What I'm proposing is a way to completely revamp how we house our inmates. This will help us deal with the overcrowding and the rehabilitation issue." She paused. "You see, prisoners are mashed into one another like this." She put her arms around him and pulled herself close.

"If they could only be so lucky," he said.

Sharon laughed. "Imagine my apartment is a prison. Right now we're in the area where education happens, okay?"

"Okay."

"And say my kitchen is where constructive work gets done. For example, we can have a recycling facility there where prisoners go through garbage and separate recyclable goods from regular trash."

"That could work," he said.

"And the bedroom is—well, you know what happens in the bedroom, don't you?"

"That's where prisoners sleep," he answered, grinning.

"Right! So here's my proposal." She pulled away. "I say prisons should be divided physically into three separate units, and inmates should live their time behind bars as shift workers. The prison will always have a shift of prisoners in each of its three areas. Eight hours for education, eight for productive work, and eight for sleep. In our current system, when one of these areas is being used, the other two are not."

"If you always have a shift in each area," he said, "you can triple the prison population."

"Well, yeah, but more important, you can provide inmates with a sense of structure, ensuring that they get proper sleep, an education, and solid work experience."

"But what you're saying is that a third of the group might be sleeping in the middle of the day? How's that going to work?"

"If physicians have to be on-call at night and sleep during the day, why can't prisoners?"

Robert stared at Sharon without saying anything.

"What?" she asked. "I know what you're thinking. You think I'm crazy. You probably think—"

Robert leaned in and kissed her.

Sharon threw her arms around him and kissed him passionately, pressing her body into his.

Suddenly he lifted her off the sofa.

"I think our shift's about up in this room," he said, "don't you?"

Chapter 18

Sharon was humming as she entered the ER on Monday.
"Good morning, Michelle," she said, dropping off Rivera's
coffee and picking up her pile of charts. She was surprised by how
light they were—only two consults—and by how quiet the ER was.
"Mm-hmm! Someone got lucky this weekend."
"Excuse me?" Sharon said.
Rivera looked at her up and down. "Girl, you can't hide it from
me. You got that FFL."
"The what?" Sharon asked.
"Freshly fucked look." Rivera cackled. "So who'd you bang?
Donahoe? Nah, it can't be him. He's a workaholic. How about that
new internal medicine resident with the braids? Or the cardiology
fellow with the salt-and-pepper goatee?"
"Stop it, Rivera!"
"It couldn't have been Sanchez," she barreled on. "Hmm. Oh!
The respiratory tech—what's his name? Alex? The one with the
bad-boy smile who's always coming down here for no reason but
to check out your butt?"
"I'm sorry to disappoint you," Sharon said, "but I'm not about
to confirm your theory."

"No, no, baby. I've been a nurse for fifteen years. I can read body language like the blind read Braille."

From the corner of her eye, Sharon saw Robert a few feet away, sitting like a statue in front of his computer.

"Even if I did get lucky—incredibly, amazingly, mind-bogglingly lucky—I wouldn't talk about it at work."

"I knew it! My cute little social worker finally got a little something-something in her. It's about time! Make sure you hit it as much as you can before you quit it. Honeymoons don't last long." Still laughing, Rivera walked over to the ambulance bay to speak to the EMS crew who'd just brought in a patient.

Biting down a smile, Sharon looked over at Robert.

Still a statue.

She walked to her desk and browsed through her consults, every once in a while sneaking a peek at Robert, who continued to stare at his computer as if it were insulting him.

A minute later, one of the nurses came up to Robert and murmured something in his ear. He got up abruptly and walked over to room 8.

Sharon scanned her charts quickly and grabbed the consult for room 9: *Request for alcohol detox, male, 25.*

She found the patient asleep and didn't bother waking him. She moved to the doorway and pretended to write a note while tuning in to what was happening in the room next door.

Robert was at the bedside of an Asian man in his mid-fifties. His white busboy outfit was splashed with blood. The man's face was horribly bruised but, to Sharon's surprise and admiration, his demeanor was calm.

Next to Robert stood a student from Columbia medical school. Sharon had helped her with orientation a week earlier. Most medical students were hard to take. They thought they knew more than they did and behaved toward the staff as if they were already physicians. This one wasn't like that.

"A lateral canthotomy? For this guy?" Robert asked in his usual obnoxious tone. "What the hell for?"

"Because of his facial trauma, Dr. McKenzie," the student continued, barely taking a breath. "He was beat up by three men on his way home from work last night. He can't see out of his left eye. It's bulging—proptotic, right? His loss of vision could be secondary to a retrobulbar hematoma. There could be a clot behind that eye compressing his optic nerve. If so, we can relieve the pressure and save his vision by cutting the lateral canthal ligament, but we'd have to do it real soon. We can always confirm the diagnosis by doing a CT scan of his orbits."

"No, there's no time for that. And how'd you know he got jumped last night? The guy doesn't speak a lick of English."

"I speak Mandarin. I spent two years in China before med school doing—"

"Yeah, yeah. Peace Corps. Spare me the details." Robert held the man's face with one of his hands and compared the two sides. "Ask him where it happened."

She did. The man answered so quietly that the student had to ask him twice to speak up.

"He says two blocks from the restaurant where he works in Hell's Kitchen, Fifty-Fourth and Broadway. The guys dragged him to an alley."

"Ask him what they looked like."

"Um, okay, but what's this have to do with—?"

"Just ask him," Robert barked. "I have family in that neighborhood, and I want to make sure I tell them what streets to avoid at night."

Sharon knew exactly what Robert was up to. She couldn't believe he was doing his investigative work so openly. Seeing him in action and knowing his intentions gave her a rush.

"He says they were big guys, maybe in their late twenties, white, didn't steal anything, and had, you know, shaved heads and lots of tattoos."

Robert opened a drawer and took out a laceration kit, setting it on top of a table by the patient's bed. He lifted its lid and withdrew a pair of scissors and a clamp.

"All right, Miss Mandarin, ever done a lateral orbital canthotomy?" He took a syringe from his pocket and some pre-sealed lidocaine, withdrew some from the bottle, and put the syringe on the table by the scissors.

"I've read about it."

"That's obvious from your blathering mini-lecture a minute ago. Info spew won't make you a good doctor. It's what you do with the knowledge that counts." He grabbed a swab of Betadine from the drawer and dabbed some next to the man's bulging eye. "What are you waiting for? Put on sterile gloves and switch spots with me. You're going to do the canthotomy."

"Dr. McKenzie, I'm just a fourth-year medical student, not an ophthalmologist. What if I mess up?"

"I'm not going to ask you twice. Either you want it or not. I can do this procedure in my sleep, and there are three residents out there who would kill their mothers to be in your position. So what will it be?"

"Well, um, sure. Yeah. Yes!" She fumbled into a pair of sterile gloves and started the procedure.

Sharon heard her patient waking up. As she went to his bedside, she could hear Robert snapping off instructions. She began the interview with her patient, a bright young research assistant at NYU with a drinking problem. He told her that he'd tried quitting multiple times but couldn't because of the shakes. As they talked, she kept a sharp ear out for the goings-on next door and almost cheered when she heard the man happily exclaiming, with the student translating, that he could see again.

When her interview was over, Sharon managed to accidentally-on-purpose bump into Robert as he came out of room 8.

"Good morning," she said.

"What's so good about it?" he snapped and went back to his desk.

Sharon stared at him. Her brows lowered, and lava began swirling in her gut as she walked back to her desk. She spent ten minutes writing up her note for the young researcher and then carried the chart over to McKenzie.

"Robert, can you do me a favor?" she asked. "I'm arranging detox for this guy, and I was hoping you could write him a work excuse for a few days."

He stared blankly at the chart and turned back to his computer. "First, show some professionalism and address me as Dr. McKenzie. Second, writing work notes is not in my job description. For the tenth night in a row that disgrace of a human being stayed up until who-knows-what time getting wasted with his friends, and now he's here because he missed another day of work and wants an excuse. I'd be happy to call his boss and explain everything to him. But give that kid a work excuse? Not in a million years, sweetheart. Unlike you, I believe in personal responsibility. You obviously don't since you're wasting my time. Am I making myself clear?"

Sharon stood dumbfounded, frozen and burning at the same time. She tried to regain her composure. The medical student, Rivera, and a resident who'd approached Robert with a question heard it all. The student's jaw dropped. Rivera clucked and shook her head. The resident didn't move.

Sharon took a deep breath and found her voice. "I apologize, Dr. McKenzie. You're right. I should address you with respect. But since we're on the subject of professionalism, I have to insist you do the same. No more calling me sweetheart or Miss Indiana, and no more insulting me or making ungrounded accusations about my intelligence or sense of responsibility. Your tone of voice when you talk to me from now on had better be civil. I'll start showing you some respect when you start doing the same. Am I making *myself* clear?"

It seemed as if the entire ER grew still. The only sounds came from a gurney rolling down a distant hall and a bedpan clattering to the floor in a faraway room.

"Nurse Rivera," Sharon said, turning away from McKenzie and handing her the chart, "this patient is officially discharged."

Back at her desk, Sharon opened the chart for her next consult, shocked that McKenzie could have so quickly returned to his old self. She was furious with herself for allowing him to sweet-talk her, and for allowing herself to think of him as anything but the total jerk he truly was.

Chapter 19

Robert stood in his living room staring at a grid of Manhattan on the large plasma television. He touched the screen and zoomed in on several areas, dotted with three-dimensional icons of various colors: red for homicides, orange for rapes, yellow for assaults.

He was on the verge of putting together a life-or-death puzzle, but couldn't quite get the last pieces to fit.

One thing he was certain of: there was something horrible brewing in New York City.

He could feel static electricity sparking from his bones, making his brain twitch. It was the same buzz he got when a sick patient showed up in the ER and he knew the diagnosis before running any laboratory or imaging studies.

It was already after ten p.m. Robert sipped his second espresso as he tried to clear his mind of everything but the grid and what it prompted.

A Chinese guy, kicked and beaten brutally.

A busboy going home from work, carrying his under-the-table shift money ... and the dirt bags let him keep it?

Shaved heads. White. Multiple tats.

Swastika tats?

Neo-Nazis in Manhattan?

Robert touched the screen and expanded the Midtown West area—Hell's Kitchen, from Thirty-Fourth to Fifty-Ninth Street. He tapped the date menu for felonies in that section. There had been a big upsurge in hate crimes during the last three months, mostly targeting minorities—blacks, Hispanics, Chinese.

And that poor Hassidic Jew.

The case had made headlines and caused a huge uproar in the Hassidic Community. The student had visited a friend at Fordham Law School on Sixtieth Street and Columbus Avenue, then headed for Times Square and was assaulted on Fifty-Fourth Street. He claimed he was beaten up by guys with swastikas, but the fact that his Fordham friend was also his lover became the main story. The aftermath was a story about homosexuality and Judaism—not about hate crime.

Robert winced in disgust and looked out his wide living room window. Beyond his balcony, the city glittered quietly.

He shifted his focus and stared at his weary reflection. Though he'd fought them, there they were again: thoughts of Sharon.

What was his problem? Why had he been such a jerk to her? He had fallen into his badass ER act that morning without thinking. But as soon as he started it, he couldn't stop.

Grow up, Robert.

The game had changed, and he didn't know how to play with new rules. He was pissed, too. He felt betrayed, but he couldn't figure out why. Was she going to turn him in? He assumed his secret was safe with her, but how could he be sure? Maybe she was out now having drinks with the nurses and yapping about his true identity.

Did she have any idea what was at stake?

The truth was, he had looked forward to seeing her at work that morning, had felt his spirits lift when she sauntered in. When he overheard Rivera ribbing her, he had to force himself not to smile. But then the anger came. He couldn't control it.

Where does that rage come from?

Robert picked up his espresso and downed it. He walked to the bathroom, splashed cold water on his face, and stared at himself in the mirror.

He had to get her off his mind. There was work to do.

But she was different than anyone he'd ever met. He half-wished she had never entered his life and half-wished he could see her tonight after his mission.

Now is not the time. Stay focused. You have a job to do.

He'd had affairs with a lot of the female staff members and had been able to keep them a secret. They all seemed to understand his day-after jerk act instinctively. The last dimwitted social worker had stayed quiet about their affair even after she'd been fired and walked out of the ER in tears.

Sharon, however, was no dimwit—and she was as passionate about helping society in her way as he was in his.

It also didn't help that she was so damn cute.

Would she be okay with what you are about to do?

He stared at the mirror again.

Definitely not.

He dried his face with a towel and left the bathroom. Tonight was all about recon. He wasn't going to seek a fight, at least not intentionally.

He chose an all-black outfit and secured a SIG Sauer P226 on his calf and a Glock 17 around his shoulder. He went to the code box hidden in the closet and pressed the numbers, plus the pound sign twice. A cylindrical part of the ceiling came down to reveal a large metal box, which opened slowly. Robert surveyed his urban warfare arsenal of light arms, an INA .45 caliber submachine gun, stun and flash grenades, knives, a host of bugging and surveillance devices, and his pet shotgun.

He reached in and grabbed the shotgun, almost purring at the friendly feel of the varnished stock. He cocked it back, saw two shells in the chamber, and then flip-snapped it back, loving that sound. He hoisted it up and slid it through a slit in his black leather jacket. He shrugged it into a comfortable position and patted it.

Just in case I end up running into any neo-Nazis.

He grabbed his surveillance bag, walked out of the apartment, and took the elevator down to his private garage, the entire time humming the love song about the stupid country poet.

Chapter 20

Fifteen minutes later, Robert was zooming toward Hell's Kitchen on the West Side Highway. His bike had just hit one hundred twenty miles per hour and wasn't stopping there.

His radar detector was state of the art; it could spot a cop a mile away.

As he passed car after car, Robert felt better and better. Within a minute, he was speeding off the Fiftieth Street exit and hanging a tight left. His bike's aluminum frame was light and powerful, allowing him to turn on a dime.

Robert raced north on Tenth Avenue. He swerved through traffic and sped down side streets when his radar lit up fuzz alerts on his night-vision lenses. He knew exactly which corners, main drags, and alleys were not policed at any moment.

Robert revved the engine as he made the turn on Fifty-Fourth Street and then lowered his speed. Suddenly, all was quiet. Riding along slowly, he checked his surroundings. A light fall breeze swept over the streets, which were oddly empty. It was almost midnight. In the distance, he heard three garbage bags being tossed out the back of some restaurant. Then calm and quiet again.

Robert aimed his night goggles at the surrounding apartments and activated the audio. Instantly he heard more sound, more activity in front of him: intermittent television chatter, murmurs of conversation, and random spikes of noise—generators, electric toothbrushes, pets, clanking silverware, alley rats.

He went to the corner where the Chinese man had been assaulted and looped around the block. He stopped at a four-way intersection. When the traffic light turned green, he didn't move; there were no other vehicles behind him. Methodically, he scanned each building, using the heat-sensing function to detect unusual activity.

After a minute he found four large lumps of glowing orange, hunching close together. The sight sent a zing into his heart.

Bingo!

Robert headed for the run-down building that housed his suspects. Decade-old posters stamped its boarded windows and metal scaffolding. It looked abandoned, but inside it bustled like a mini-city.

He shut off his engine, put the kickstand down, and got off. His legs still vibrated from the ride, but they felt strong.

Four people on the top floor stood in something like a make-shift office.

He squinted up. The metal scaffolding looked unsteady. He did a pull up to test it out. It held him firmly, without making a sound. He dangled a few seconds, stretched his neck from side to side, and pulled up and twisted in a half circle, landing deftly on the higher pipe.

He was on the roof in less than a minute. Once there, he stretched his back and rubbed his arms.

Still got it.

He walked around and scoped the place out. Peering through the skylight, he found his targets: four white hulks shouting and laughing. Robert ducked away from their sightlines and readied his Eye-Spy, a crack-thin stick on a wire thread that was strong enough to pull a tractor. He plunged it through the slit around the skylight hinge, connected the video link to his goggles, thumbed the direction/zoom wheel for the lens, and sat back to enjoy the show.

Four men. Lots of beer.

Kurtz fucking Lite!

Signs and placards hung on the walls:

"White is Right"

"One Rule: We Rule"

"If you're not smart enough to speak English, you're too dumb to be American."

"Immigration? Invasion!"

Robert had to resist the urge to burst in and beat the ignorance out of them.

A bushy-red-bearded guy jabbed his index finger at a map on the wall. He had a tattoo of a large swastika on his freckle-splotched forearm. Robert shook his head in wonder at how stupid these guys were for being so easily found. If they read, maybe they'd know it's easier to track a gang who operates in one area than a gang who hits targets at random. This was one of Miyamoto Musashi's basic principles in *The Book of Five Rings*.

He carefully pulled his Eye-Spy back into the chilly night air. He had all the information he needed for now. Should he tell the police or take care of the Nazis himself?

The problem was that if he let the police know, he'd have to do it anonymously. An anonymous tip, however, would have to seem legit. Who would believe a neo-Nazi gang was rising to power in the middle of Manhattan?

Robert heard a shout from below and peered over the edge. Redbeard was leaving the building and calling up to a comrade leaning out a window ten feet below where Robert stood.

As Redbeard began his bull-like swagger down the street, Robert made out a gun bulge in the small of his back under his sleeveless sweatshirt.

Escalating from beatings to deadly weapons already?

It took Robert a matter of seconds to climb down and get back onto his bike. He began following Redbeard's path. He didn't want anyone shot on his watch.

He passed a cop car, empty, in front of a twenty-four-hour Starbucks. He saw the officers inside waiting for coffees. He stopped and scribbled a note: "Man with red beard, hooded sweatshirt, walking north on Tenth Avenue. Gun in small of back."

He tossed the note onto the front seat and sped off.

For now, Robert would let the cops handle it.

He had other pressing business to take care of.

Chapter 21

Sharon stood in front of her door, searching through her purse for the keys. She remembered the last time she had key issues and thought of Robert. Still angry with him, she took it out on her bag, dumping its entire contents onto her doorstep. The keys landed between a gum wrapper and a pamphlet entitled "Alcoholism: A Disease with a Cure."

She picked up the keys, crammed the rest of her belongings into her purse, and began trying to find the right key for the lock. Again, she remembered Robert and his Jedi key trick. *Ugh*. She needed to get that creep out of her mind. Her feet ached, her lids felt as heavy as half-dollars, and all she wanted to do was get inside, drop everything on the floor, climb into bed, and push her mind's *Off* button.

She plopped down in front of her doorway, the keys dangling clumsily in her hands, feeling as if she was about to cry. She'd gone out with the ER staff to get her mind off Robert, but instead he was all she could think about. Every time his name came up in conversation, she wanted to blurt out everything she knew about him. Just to spite him.

Sharon shook her head and sighed.

What is it about men?

She wanted to believe Robert was different. She felt so good when the day began. Then he ignored her. She thought that was bad enough, until he embarrassed her in front of everyone.

She was *not* going to cry, especially not outside her doorway like some crazy person. She forced herself up again and peered very closely at her keys, determined to find the right one.

"You really should consider labeling those things."

Startled, she gasped and dropped the keys.

Robert appeared from the shadows.

"You scared me. Now is not the time. I'm in no mood for you."

Robert picked up the keys and unlocked the door. Sharon shoved it open and stormed past him without saying a word.

"You should also consider getting better locks," Robert said, studying the bolts with his hands. "Seriously, any amateur thief could jimmy these. Two thin metal rods for the top lock and maybe a number six Allen key for the bottom."

He followed her inside and shut the door.

"You're not invited in." Sharon paced to the kitchen and back, stopping in the middle of the room with her arms folded. "Seriously, what do you want, Robert? I mean, what do you want, Dr. McKenzie?"

"Okay. I guess I deserve that."

Sharon glared and turned away.

"I came to apologize," he said.

"Apology *not* accepted."

"Listen, Sharon. I'm sorry. I totally overdid it," he said. "I didn't need to act like a total jackass, especially with you. I'm sorry."

"You ruined my day. I was excited to see you."

"I'm sorry. I was childish and inconsiderate."

"I don't understand why being a jerk is your default."

"I don't want people knowing that I care about you."

"Now you care about me?" she said. "I find that hard to believe. We went out and had a great time together, or at least I thought we did, but then you disappeared before I woke up the next day. And when I finally see you, you embarrass me in front of our co-workers. You were really mean. I can't help feeling that I should stay away from you. I'm usually a good judge of character, but I'm all over the map with you. I don't know what to think."

"You should give me another chance. I really like you, Sharon." She was trying not to look at him.

"Sharon?" He gently turned her toward him. "Why don't you think about it while you eat?" He handed her a warm brown paper bag. "It's from a little Venezuelan restaurant in the West Village—Rosa's Kitchen."

She hesitated for a moment before reaching inside the bag and unwrapping a fragrant cornmeal patty with melted cheese. "An arepa?" She smiled despite herself. Then she took a big bite and closed her eyes. "Mm-hmm!" She took another bite, feeling her anger slowly dissipating. "Delicious!"

"The restaurant was closed, but I bribed one of the cooks."

She nodded several times and swallowed. "Thank you, Robert. I didn't eat all night." She kept talking as she inhaled the rest of the patty. "The ER nurses went to some swanky sushi place where each tiny piece of fish was a zillion dollars."

"Well, then, I'm glad I brought you more than one," Robert said as he pulled out another arepa.

She took it, tore off the wrapper, and took a healthy bite. "Yum. Okay. This doesn't mean I completely forgive you, but you're temporarily off the hook."

"If every guy knew that an arepa is the way into a woman's heart, that restaurant would be booming."

"I can't speak for anyone else," she said. "But for me, this is what life is about."

"An arepa?" Robert asked.

"Tasting each moment," she said, mumbling through the food. "I think I like making you happy more than I like pissing you off."

"I'm afraid you still like being a pain in the butt a little too much."

"If it cuts through bullshit, yeah. I hate phoniness more than I like happiness. But you're not a phony, and that's why I'm sorry about today. It won't happen again."

"I don't mind if you stay tough," Sharon said between bites. "It saves a lot of time. I get it. Just don't cross that line. And don't do it with me."

"Being a jerk helps, you know."

"I know. It's a perfect cover for your secret identity. Anyone that mean can't be New York's finest superhero."

"That's right," Robert grinned, "but it also helps me know which residents will be shitty doctors. If they hate me but hear what I say and soldier on, I know they care about medicine. If they kiss my ass, then I know they care more about their careers than helping the sick."

"Maybe that's true," Sharon said, grabbing the wrappers and placing them inside the paper bag. "But the Buddha says, 'You don't have to be an asshole to know what shit is.'" She carried the garbage into the kitchen.

"The Buddha actually said that, huh?" he said, standing up and ambling over to the bookshelves. "I suppose I could do it the old-fashioned way and use my judgment."

Washing her hands in the sink, she called out, "Why not? Then you wouldn't have to be a phony yourself. I don't have to pretend to be callous to know which residents are good or bad—and I certainly don't spend one-tenth of the doctor time with them that you do."

"Ah, here's that Buddha book. I thought I saw it last time I was here." He pulled *The Eightfold Path* from Sharon's collection just as she came out of the kitchen, smiling and drying her hands. He walked back to the couch and plopped himself down. "Damn, you highlighted the hell out of this! Where's the quote about being an asshole?"

"I was kidding, silly," she said, taking a seat next to him. "I made it up, but he did say, 'Rub my big belly and you'll get good luck.' See, right ... there." She pointed to a highlighted part of the introduction.

He laughed loudly and kissed her forehead. "I'm really sorry, Sharon."

"It's okay, I guess." She let him hug her. "I'm glad to know I didn't make up everything between us."

"You didn't," he said, then kissed her on the mouth.

"It's nice to see you happy," she said, pulling back to look into his eyes. "Is there anything else that puts a smile on your face?"

"You mean besides going after child molesters, wife beaters, and rapists? Nah, not really."

"I'm being serious, Robert," she said, running her fingers once through his hair. "What about family or friends?"

"Don't have much of either. I'm a Buddhist that way. Human life is suffering, so I tend to avoid human contact. It keeps suffering to a minimum."

"I'm sorry to break it to you, but Buddha was a big flop about that issue."

"Says who? You?" Robert laughed again. "Are you going to tell me his billion followers are all wrong?"

"Buddha was the son of some rich guy, who physically sheltered him from the real world. One day, Buddha decided to venture outside his palace. He saw how much others suffered. He realized then that it's best to lead a simple and honest life, free of worldly attachments. I agree with that part, except that he also included freeing yourself from relationships, which I certainly don't agree with."

"And I happen to agree *only* with that part," he countered playfully.

"Connecting makes us human, Robert. It's the only thing that makes the suffering worthwhile. Confucius said so."

"He did, did he?"

"Get right with your family first. Then continue to build strong bonds with your neighbors, colleagues, and friends. That way you create a beautiful and solid ever-expanding network of relationships whose foundation centers you here on Earth."

"Damn, Professor Reede! That was a great lecture," he said. "But there's a huge flaw in your logic."

"And what might that be?"

"The main fact of life."

"I'm afraid to ask."

"People are no good."

"Oh *that.*"

Robert shrugged. "It explains a lot, you have to admit."

"So does Greek mythology, but it doesn't mean the stories are true."

"I love how smart you are, Sharon. Really. But I'm afraid people are going to disappoint you."

"I'll take my chances," she said without hesitation. "You know, Robert, you pretend you're a realist when you're really just socially awkward. And you label me naïve when in fact I'm an idealist."

"What's the difference? Naïve or idealist, they're both the same."

"Being naïve is thinking that the world is perfect when it is not. Being idealistic means knowing that the world is far from perfect, but trying to do something to make it a little better. How can you make this world a better place without having a firm grasp of what the ideal world looks like?"

She started to put her arms around him, but Robert stood up. "I should go. You need your sleep."

She stood up right with him. "At least give me a hug before you go."

She put her arms around him and he tentatively put his around her. She sighed and made humming sounds, then moved her hands up his back and stopped. "What's this?"

"It's a shotgun."

"I know what it is," she said. "What are you doing with it?"

"I did recon tonight on some recent neo-Nazi muggings."

"Really? Let me see that thing," she said.

He reached behind him and pulled the shotgun through his jacket slit in one smooth motion. He cracked it open to make sure there was no accidental firing.

She reached out and ran her hand along the stock.

"This is beautiful wood. You take great care of it."

"I do."

"My father used to take me on hunting trips to Salamonie. My parents had a cabin by the lake. I remember eating a rabbit I killed. Took us two hours to clean it. There was hardly any meat left after we picked out all the buckshot."

"You know, Reede," he said, running a finger down the side of her face, "I'm not sure how you did it, but I'm glad you've come into my life."

"It must be a kind of hell living the double life you do, Robert. I don't know how you do it, but I do know you want to help people as much as I do."

Robert moved his other hand along her spine and stopped just at the edge of her hip. He unzipped the back of her skirt and slid his fingers beneath the back edge of her panties. "It can be tough," he said. "But once you look, you can't just look away."

He kissed her hard on the mouth and pulled her body into his.

"Okay. My legs are shaking. If we don't make love right now, I think I'm going to explode."

She turned around, letting her skirt fall to the floor, revealing a lacy white thong. She walked slowly toward the bedroom, swaying her hips seductively. "But stay the night this time, okay?" She looked back at him over her shoulder. "You never know what I might want to do to you in the morning."

Chapter 22

Sharon slipped quietly out of bed, opened the window, and inhaled the crisp November air. Her naked body glowed golden in the morning light as she marveled at the array of activity below. She could see the entire city skyline. Robert's penthouse was a whole lot nicer than her little flat. She still found it hard to believe she'd spent almost every night with him for nearly a month.

Robert looked at her from his bed. "My view's better than yours."

She turned, beaming. "So glad you like it."

"What time is it?"

"Guess."

"Eight thirty?"

"Nope."

"Eight thirty-two?"

"Ten."

"What? You're kidding me!"

"Nope."

Robert sat up, stretched, and spoke while yawning, "Thah sa longst I shlet sih ah wa ayee!"

"Sorry, I don't speak yawn."

He smiled, looking so relaxed that she walked right over to him, knelt on the bed, and hugged his head to her breasts.

"Mm … I said, that's the longest I slept since I was a baby."

"Did you know when you sleep, you don't move?"

"I'll have to take your word for it." He grabbed a bottle of water from the nightstand. "I think I could sleep another twelve hours."

"I can't believe you still refuse to sleep at my place," Sharon said, shaking her head.

"Your apartment is a dump."

"It is not!" Sharon frowned. "I happen to think it's quite charming."

"I'll give you that," he said, "but mine is much nicer."

"Whatever," she said, rolling her eyes. "Anyway, what do you want to do today?"

"I was hoping we could have sex all day."

"No way," she said. "Let's do some sightseeing. I want to check out New York. Come on, Bobby. Show me around your city."

"Oh no. You're not calling me Bobby."

"You're Bobby until you're out of bed." She scooted away and put on one of his T-shirts. Robert threw the covers off, stood up, walked over to Sharon, and pulled the T-shirt off.

"Hey there, Bobby," she said.

Soon they were back in bed making love again.

Around noon, after he made them breakfast, Sharon stood side by side with Robert in his private garage.

"Ducati, this is Sharon. Sharon, Ducati."

"Nice to meet you," she said, taking a seat on the bike and wrapping her arms around Robert.

"Where to?" he asked.

160

"I'm embarrassed to admit it, but I haven't been over the Brooklyn Bridge. To live life to the fullest, we need to go to that famous pizza place that's supposed to be the best."

"Grimaldi's? Not sure it's the best, but it's pretty damn good. Okay. Brooklyn, here we come," he said, and the motor roared to life. "What does it mean to 'live life to the fullest'?"

"This!" she yelled back and hooted loud and long as Robert grinned and gunned the beast out of the garage and into traffic. She hugged him tightly as they sped down the FDR weaving through the cars. When they reached the other side of the bridge, Robert found a parking spot and the two walked up the cement steps that led to the street above.

"Why is it called Dumbo?" she asked. "Were there elephants around here?"

"Down Under the Manhattan Bridge Overpass," he explained.

"Lord," she said, laughing. Her face was fixed in a permanent smile. The bridge was incredible. The weather was perfect. She slipped her hand into Robert's.

"We're holding hands now?" he asked.

"Seems like it." She pointed to a bird on the railing fifteen yards away. "Look!"

"The pigeon?"

"No, it's a piping plover. Do you know how rare it is to see one in the city, especially this late in autumn? Look at how beautiful it is." They slowed, approaching the bird as they would a sleeping baby. It flapped a few yards up to a higher mast.

"Cute little ball of chub," Robert said, gazing up with her. "Like a mini-penguin." The plover took off and sailed out of sight.

"I don't think he liked being called that," Sharon said.

"I'm pretty sure he did. He just left to tell the other plovers." Robert lifted her hand to his lips and kissed it. "You're going to tell me you're a bird watcher, too? Is there anything you don't do?"

"Nah, I don't know much about birds. I read about the plight of the plovers in last week's *Times*. I never thought I'd see one."

"The plight of the plovers," he mused. "Sounds like a bad action film."

For a while, they walked in peaceful silence.

"You know," Robert said, "it's good for me to be with someone as upbeat about life as you are. How can you have such a great attitude, especially with all the stuff we see in the ER?"

"It's not that difficult," Sharon said. "The key is to be honest with your feelings. It's impossible to work a day in the ER without being traumatized by what we see. I don't ignore the experience. I try to feel as bad about a situation as it warrants. Suffering deserves respect. It keeps me serious about doing what I can to help, and it makes the things I love all the better."

"Things like what?"

"Days like this, yoga, a good cappuccino, crying over some cheesy romantic-comedy, laying out a nice paragraph or two for my dissertation. You must have your own list of things that make you happy. Don't you?"

Robert shook his head. "Not really. The only thing on my happy list is going after dirt bags and kicking their butts."

"Come on. You also give to charity and make sure good people get their surgeries."

"That stuff is okay, I guess, but it doesn't compare to kicking the crap out of the bad guys."

They walked in silence.

"What about me?"

"You're okay, too."

She elbowed him in the stomach, but he didn't flinch. "Ouch," she said. "I think I just broke my elbow on your six-pack."

Robert laughed and ruffled her hair. Then he sighed so deeply she felt a chill run up her spine.

"What was that about?"

"The thing is," he said quietly, "I think we're doomed."

"The Earth?"

"That, too, especially if terrorists get their hands on nuclear weapons," he said. "But I was thinking more about us."

"Oh, that."

They reached the end of the Brooklyn Bridge Promenade and turned on Front Street without saying anything.

"I want to say there's hope," Robert finally said. "But vigilantism isn't exactly your lifestyle of choice. And singing 'Kumbaya' isn't my idea of contributing to society."

"Come on, 'Kumbaya'?"

"I'm a soldier, Sharon, and you don't believe in violence."

"I do," she said. "At least I do now. How could I not? You couldn't have pulled that rapist off me without violence."

"True. But you don't agree with my lifestyle."

"Not necessarily. The question we should be asking is, when is violence appropriate? I think you and I still have time to see if we can live with each other's answer. But with a gorgeous day like this, let's not talk about violence or about us being doomed or about work."

"Yes, Ms. Reede. Sorry." Robert gave her butt a little pat.

Suddenly, Sharon heard a man's voice yelling a short distance behind them. She turned and saw a teenage kid on a mountain bike zooming down the street, a smug look on his face.

"That's my bike!" the man's voice called.

Sharon marveled at how Robert's eyes instantly clicked into tracking mode, zeroing in on the kid's approach. A car screeched to a stop, nearly hitting the kid and making him swerve dangerously.

Robert nudged Sharon aside as the boy regained his balance a few feet from them, then he took one precisely calculated step and shot his palm against the boy's torso. The bike swerved out of control across the street and hit a parked car. The boy flew five feet in the air and hit the pavement.

The bike owner arrived at the scene as a crowd gathered. The man grabbed his bike—which was smashed and dented in the front, but still functioning—thanked Robert warmly, and rode off.

"The kid's in pain," she said.

"Let him respect that. He needs to learn a lesson."

"Come on, you're a doctor."

"The paramedics will take care of him when they get here. Don't worry. He didn't break anything."

She resisted and stared at the boy on the ground, wondering if she should stay and help. But Robert tugged lightly at her elbow. "Like you said, no work today."

Chapter 23

Robert had barely settled down in front of the computer to check the crime blotter when Sanchez, fast becoming his least-favorite resident, approached him with a chart in hand.

"Dr. McKenzie, this guy's full of it," Sanchez began. "His stomach's supposedly killing him, and he's been vomiting for three days, but he looks great. He's hydrated. He's got moist mucus membranes. His abdomen is totally soft, not tender, and not distended. The guy just wants narcotics. He's another illegal immigrant wanting to get high on our tax dollars. Am I right or what?"

"Where's the patient?" Robert asked quietly.

"Room 22."

"Follow me."

On the way, Robert saw two medical students at the PACS station, looking at an abdominal CT scan. "Enough with the imaging," he called as he passed by. "Neither of you is smart enough to go into radiology. Come learn something useful."

Robert had seen the patient and his brother walk into the ER an hour earlier. He had studied their interaction as Rivera triaged them. He knew exactly what was going on.

The patient on the gurney was in his early twenties, wearing jeans, a tan shirt with the logo of a local restaurant, and a new pair of black high-tops. Out of everything Sanchez had said in his presentation, this much was right: the guy on the gurney was not sick.

"What brings you in today, *amigo?*" Robert asked. He took a couple of steps back and leaned against the wall, where he could see everyone in the room: Sanchez, the two medical students, the nurse setting up an IV, the patient, and his brother, who sat by himself in the corner.

"I start vomiting for two days. Then my stomach hurt right here." The patient pointed to the middle of his abdomen. Robert could tell from his accent that he was from southern Mexico. "But now the pain is here," he said, pointing to the right lower side. "It kills me to eat or to walk. I need antibiotics."

This is too easy.

Robert put his hand on the young man's shoulder and gave a gentle squeeze. "I know how bad you're feeling. It's going to be fine."

Robert saw him blink back tears and nod gratefully.

Sanchez sidled up and whispered. "By antibiotics, he means Dilaudid, right?"

"Stand with the students," Robert barked at him. Sanchez shrugged and tried a cool walk back.

"Dilaudid junkies," Robert explained to the medical students, "are getting more and more common in the ER. Word seems to have gotten around that Dilaudid, or hydromorphone, is seven times stronger than morphine, but this guy here is no junkie. Melanie, stop what you're doing."

The nurse had the tourniquet on the patient and was about to insert an intravenous line. Puzzled, she stopped and looked at Robert.

"The person who needs the IV is sitting in that chair," Robert said, pointing to the brother.

They all looked at the boy, slouched in a chair in the corner, and then back at Robert as if he were crazy.

"Dr. Sanchez, your biggest problem, the thing that's preventing you from being a competent physician, is that you think you know more than you actually do. That makes you a dangerous person in the ER. You make one simple observation and warp it with a deranged and prejudiced conclusion. The guy on the gurney is not sick, but that's the only thing you got right. If you were paying attention, though, you would've recognized that his brother's the real patient."

The puzzled looks in the room now turned nervous.

"You see, kids, the man on the gurney has a job. He works at Gordito's, a fine eating establishment that would never hire people without giving them full benefits, including health insurance. This guy doesn't want narcotics. He wants to get medicine with his insurance and give it to his brother, the *real* patient."

The boy in the chair was pale. His skin was covered in sweat. Hunched over, he clasped his hands on top of his stomach.

"He doesn't speak English," the guy on the gurney said, sliding off the bed and standing humbly. "I am sorry doctor, but he is in pain."

"It's all right. I'd do the same thing for my brother."

The young man nodded.

"The problem, Miguel," Robert said, looking at the chart, "is that your brother—what's his name?"

"Eduardo. Eddie."

"Eddie has appendicitis and drugs aren't going to help that. He needs surgery, a very common surgery. He'll be better by tomorrow morning."

They all watched Miguel translate this to his brother, who looked to be about eighteen. The tears in Eddie's eyes burst forth when he understood. Looking at Robert apologetically, he murmured, "*Gracias.*"

"Melanie," Robert said, addressing the nurse, "get Eddie on the gurney, place an IV, give him two liters of fluids, and start him on cefotaxime. Draw a CBC, a CMP, and get him to CT when he's done with his contrast." He paused. "Oh, and give him as much Dilaudid as he wants."

He started to walk out, but then stopped and addressed the brothers in Spanish. "I know you're worried about the cost. I'll see that it's taken care of."

Robert felt like humming the classic Mexican song "Canción Mixteca" as he walked from the room, but he restrained himself. He spied Sharon hunched over a bunch of reports by her desk, her hair pulled into a tight ponytail. She pushed her reading glasses closer to her face and started writing a note, oblivious to the world around her. He smiled and headed to his desk, picked up a clump of charts, and started tending to patients.

Two hours later, feeling energized by all the bedside interaction, Robert made his way to Sharon's desk.

"Pardon me, Ms. Reede, I was hoping you could see one of my patients."

Sharon looked surprised to see him by her desk.

"I'd be glad to, Dr. McKenzie. Who's the patient?"

"He's a forty-four-year-old crime-fighting male who needs an emergency social work consult."

"Sure, absolutely." She seemed to be holding back laughter. "Let me finish up here, and I'll go see him right away."

Robert looked around, made sure nobody was watching, and then leaned forward and pointed to something in the note, whispering in her ear. "How about grabbing dinner after our shift, Ms. Reede?"

Sharon's lips formed a smile.

"The usual place?" he asked.

She nodded.

A sudden commotion made them both turn. Four paramedics wheeled a bloodied body to the trauma bay.

Sharon and Robert looked at each other. "Go," she said. "I'll see you tonight."

Holding onto his stethoscope, he strode toward resus.

Inside, Robert could tell that the guy on the gurney had no shot at surviving. A trail of blood marked the man's route from the ambulance bay to the resuscitation room. Robert guessed that the patient had lost three pints already. He recognized the paramedics as the ones who were always in Midtown. St. Jude's was their closest trauma center, and it was over fifty blocks away.

"This is a twenty-three-year-old Hispanic male. Stabbed in the chest multiple times on the way to work. Bystanders report he was jumped by five white guys with shaved heads and tattoos. Sounds like they were a bunch of neo-Nazi bastards."

The room started to spin. Robert squeezed his eyes tight to stabilize. The note about Redbeard, left inside the cop car, had led to nothing.

What was I thinking?

He opened his eyes and watched as the paramedics continued CPR. Time slowed down. His chest felt hollow. The poor kid was a lost cause.

Anger flooded into him, diverting his concentration from the patient. He should've lit that whole building on fire. Their gang was getting more violent by the week. He could have prevented this.

Robert could sense residents scurrying around, an IV being placed, the patient being intubated, CPR in progress.

More chaos in the room—and in his head.

Focus, Robert.

A split second later, his mind became still and the room grew silent. He looked up at the boy and knew exactly what to do.

"Rivera, have a tech run to the blood bank and get six units of uncrossed blood, six units of platelets, and six units of fresh frozen plasma. Now!"

Rivera ran out.

Robert pulled his sleeves up, put on a pair of gloves, and slid a scalpel from his pocket. "Sanchez, grab a thoracotomy tray. We're going to crack this guy's chest."

"I don't think that's a good idea, Dr. McKenzie. Policy is that all thoracotomies go to trauma surgery."

"I'm not waiting for them," Robert said, walking to the head of the bed. "Stop compressions, keep bagging the patient. Feel for a pulse and tell me what's on the monitor."

Robert knew he had less than a minute to get inside the man's chest. He gripped the scalpel and made a firm incision from the man's breastbone to just underneath his left nipple, between the fourth and fifth ribs. By the time he finished cutting, the tray was open right next to the bedside. He grabbed the rib spreaders, placed them inside the chest, and cranked the lever. In five seconds, the ribs were spread, the lungs exposed. He snatched a large clip and closed off the aorta. Then he turned his attention to the heart, which was abnormally large.

Robert realized right away that the stab wound had pierced the outer part of the heart and left a massive clot within the surrounding pericardial sac, squeezing the heart and preventing it from pumping blood appropriately.

With this in mind, he made a small nick across the pericardium. Blood gushed out. He stripped the thin membrane, found the clot, removed it, and then placed a tight figure-eight suture over the laceration.

The heart gave a little flutter.

"Transfuse the first unit," Robert said as Rivera walked in with the supply of blood products. He began compressing

170

the heart, which was still deep in the chest cavity, between his two hands.

"Get me the internal paddles. The patient's in ventricular fibrillation."

The paddles arrived just as Dr. Cheng, the chief of trauma surgery, stormed into resus with Dr. Donahoe and the rest of the trauma team.

"Damn you, McKenzie," Dr. Cheng said. "You were supposed to wait for us."

Robert ignored him, placed the paddles along each side of the heart, and gave a shock, followed by more compressions.

In the background, Cheng continued his litany of expletives. Robert thought about a quick back kick to Cheng's nuts, but then felt the patient's heart starting a regular beat. He stepped aside and looked at the monitor. Normal sinus rhythm. Robert's own heart lifted. The patient's hands moved slowly. He was waking up.

"Rivera, start the guy on propofol for sedation," Robert said. He slotted his gloves into the garbage. "Now that we've saved the patient, you surgeons can take him to the OR and put him back together."

Robert left the room, disregarding the yells of rage coming from the trauma team.

His heart lifted even higher at the thought of paying a visit to the neo-Nazi warehouse before dinner.

Chapter 24

Sharon arrived early at the Mexican restaurant. They'd been there many times since their first date, and she was always greeted with the same colorful scene, the same Mariachi band playing, the same air filled with the smell of chiles and cumin as the waiter and bartender she recognized served another sizable crowd.

But Robert wasn't there.

After almost thirty minutes of nursing a beer and eating chips and salsa by herself, she started to fear something was wrong.

He'd said "the usual place." Did I mishear?

She took another sip of her Dos Equis and phoned him on her cell.

"Hi, Robert. It's your favorite social worker. Just wondering where you are. I'm at the restaurant. Get your butt over here. Kisses."

After an hour and three more unanswered phone calls, she was really worried. She paid for her beer, left the waiter a generous tip, and headed home.

She placed another call, but at midnight there was still no word from him. Sharon decided to try to sleep. She tossed and turned, wondering where he might be. She had known that this was the risk in caring about him. Something bad was bound to happen at some point.

An hour later, she heard a noise from the living room and bolted up in bed.

Adrenalin coursing, she took stock of her surroundings. Robert had warned her about getting new locks. Her stomach dropped.

Then there was a loud crash.

"Robert?"

She jumped out of bed. There were more noises now. Clinks. A whoosh. A bang.

She stood still as her heart raced. She knew she should lock herself in the bathroom and call 911, but decided against it. Slowly, she crept toward the living room. Her ears were tuned to the tiniest sounds, but now she heard nothing.

"Hello?" she called.

She peered from behind the doorway, saw a large shadow on the couch.

"Robert, is that you?"

Silence. Then more heavy breathing.

Sharon looked around for something to use as a weapon. She grabbed an umbrella and walked cautiously toward the couch, gripping the handle tightly as she approached.

"Oh Jesus. It *is* you." She threw the umbrella on the floor. "Why didn't you say something? You scared me to death. Where were you?"

"I had to take care of something." His voice trailed to a whisper.

Robert's words blew a flame of anger up from her smoldering embers. "The gang that cut that boy you saved today? You saved his life. Wasn't that enough?"

He didn't say anything. He was breathing hard. It was dark and she couldn't see him very well. She went to turn on a light.

Then came another thump. She stopped and turned. Something had slipped from his hand onto the floor. It rolled a short distance, turned on its side, and stopped moving.

His motorcycle helmet.

Through the dark, she could see Robert's hand dangling off the side of the couch. She heard a soft dripping sound. A dim ray from the kitchen window shimmered on a small puddle under his fingers.

She rushed to turn on the lamp by the couch and gasped at what she saw: deep red blood under his hands and feet, jacket badly torn, bruises on his cheeks and neck. His face was the color of old teeth. He was staring into space, panting like an exhausted dog.

"Robert!" Sharon screamed, grabbing a pillow. She eased him into a supine position. She took his shirt off slowly and saw more bruises on his chest. His body was smeared with blood. There were cuts all over. The deepest one, by his right shoulder, had a soaked T-shirt wrapped around it, seeping blood down onto her floor.

"I was careless," he managed. "Outnumbered. No plan." He was breathing hard. "I just reacted." He gave her a blank stare. Then he shut his eyes and took several deep breaths.

Sharon ran to retrieve a towel. She cleaned up the smaller wounds before she got to the one by his shoulder. When she gently peeled off the wrapping, it started squirting blood.

"Oh my God," she said, stanching the blood with the towel. "Hold this. I have to call 911."

"No!" Robert said loudly, his old voice rising up strongly. He panted a few times and then continued weakly but urgently. "Don't call. Stab wounds ... paramedics ... they'll have to notify the police."

"What should I do? Tell me what to do! I'm not going to watch you die. I have to call an ambulance."

He grabbed her hand and tried to pull her close. "Listen to me. I promise. I'll be fine by morning. Please. I will. I'm in here. See?"

She looked long into his eyes. They were jumping a little, but there was a steadiness in there she recognized.

She gave a weak nod.

"Pass me the towel." He squeezed the wound on his right deltoid and shuddered. Grinding his teeth, he pointed across the living room. "My bag ... by the door."

She fetched the heavy bag and placed it on the coffee table, shoving aside her papers.

"First-aid kit ... side pocket," Robert said between breaths.

She opened the bag and saw the shotgun, two handguns, and a collection of gadgets that looked like alien insects. She was nervous about touching the guns as she searched the bag for the pocket.

"They're all on safety." Robert grimaced.

She opened a dark-blue box. The sides were lined with scalpels, tweezers, scissors, and needle clamps. In the cavity were bandages, medications, and suture material.

"Needle driver. Scissors. 3-0 Ethilon suture," Robert instructed.

Sharon fumbled through the kit until she found the items. She handed each to him, one at a time. Robert used his left forearm to compress his wound as he extended his arm to receive the instruments. With his left hand, he clamped the needle of the 3-0 suture onto the driver while the scissors dangled from his little finger. Despite the awkward position, Robert's hands still managed to be graceful.

He gave the needle driver to Sharon, eased his hold on the wound, and isolated the bleeding source. He tucked the corner of the towel in place and said, "Figure-eight stitch. Simple thing. Needle into ... here ... then out ... here. Then again—I'll show you where—then a knot."

Her hands shook as the needle pierced through the skin by the stab wound. "Like this?"

"Nicely done. You're a natural," he said, managing a weak smile. "Now take the needle off the driver and turn it one hundred eighty degrees."

The needle was cold to the touch. Sharon twisted the sharp end and snapped the driver back around the metal hub.

"Go back in through here and out through there," Robert instructed.

She did what he said, her hand no longer shaking.

"Perfect. Now put the needle under the stitch and pull up."

The skin came together beautifully, compressing the artery below it. There was no more blood.

"All right, Sharon, you've got a couple more steps." He was breathing more comfortably now. "Cross the two ends of suture ... twice ... bring the bottom end around. First knot. Three more and we're done."

A minute later the wound was tightly stitched. He twirled the scissors into position and snipped off the suture ends.

A minute after that, he was snoring.

Sharon slowly pulled off his shoes, cut his pants off, and then stuffed his bloody clothes into a garbage bag. She soaked paper towels with soap and water and finished cleaning him up as best she could while he slept. There were so many fresh cuts and bruises—and dozens of old scars.

She recognized the circular ones along his forearms as old cigarette burns. The old linear wounds across his back came from a pipe or broom handle. She'd seen similar marks on abused children. When she'd asked about his scars after their first night together, he had refused to explain and quickly changed the subject.

She continued to wash each part of him. By the time she had scrubbed the floor clean of blood, his breathing had settled into a normal rhythm.

She sat on the floor for a while and looked around the living room. She'd have to replace the couch.

The phone rang, jolting her.

At this hour?

Caller unknown.

She let it ring again, getting nervous.

Maybe it's the police, wondering if Robert's here. Could they be on to him?

Another ring.

Not the police—too unlikely. Had the neo-Nazis followed him here?

The phone stopped ringing.

Robert slept on.

Chapter 25

Even though Robert looked better on Saturday, Sharon wouldn't let him get up from the couch. He didn't want to eat, but she cajoled him into sipping puréed vegetables and chicken broth. By nightfall, he was taking normal food and shuffling around the apartment.

When she woke on Sunday, she found him doing sit-ups in her living room. His scarred, sculpted body glistened with sweat. She got herself some coffee and watched him.

He grunted between ups and downs. "I'm getting stir-crazy … I'll take a shower … and take you out … for breakfast. Show my gratitude … to my live-in … nurse."

Sharon laughed. "Okay, Rocky. No hurry. I'm enjoying the show."

He smiled, winced, and walked to the bathroom, breathing fast.

After brunch, they took the subway to Battery Park. It was chilly despite the sun, and the trees had lost most of their leaves. Sharon made a mental note to go shopping for a wool hat and scarf.

"Did you know I've never been ice-skating before?"

"I didn't," he said. "I guess it's something we'll have to remedy."

"I've never been to the Alps either."

"Now you're pushing it," Robert said. He leaned over to kiss her but stopped midway. He clenched his jaw and narrowed his eyes slightly. It seemed like every nerve in his body buzzed with a life of its own.

"Don't look to your left," he said. "Detective Macy is about thirty yards away. She hasn't noticed us yet. I'm splitting from you. Keep your back to her. Head out of the park. We'll keep in touch by cell."

She veered to her right, thinking of the unanswered phone call the night Robert was bleeding on her couch. Was it Macy? Did she know anything? Could Sharon get arrested for not reporting a stab wound?

On the outer rim of the park, she took a seat on a bench and carefully glanced over her shoulder. Macy was sitting by the fountain, biting the corner of a sandwich. She quickly texted Robert: *She's just having lunch.*

After a few moments, her cell blipped and she read the text from Robert: *Don't be so sure.*

Where R U? she texted back.

"Well, well. If it isn't New York City's hottest social worker, St. Jude's pride and joy."

Sharon looked up, startled. Standing in front of her was Landers, smiling as he bit into a large meatball hoagie.

"Good morning, Detective," she said, feeling a chill run down her spine.

He sat down next to her and took another dripping bite. The sound of his chewing repulsed her.

"What brings you to this neck of the woods?" Landers asked.

"Just going for a walk," Sharon said. "I'm heading home now."

"To Washington Heights or to your boyfriend's penthouse on the Upper West Side?"

"My boyfriend?"

"Didn't handsome, rugged Dr. McKenzie save you from getting raped a few weeks ago, using some amazing martial arts moves?"

"Listen, Detective," she said, "I don't think there's anything for us to talk about. I'm not doing anything wrong, am I?"

"I'm not so sure," he said, then took another big bite. "Please send my regards to the good doctor."

Sharon stood up and strode out of the park without saying good-bye. As soon as she was a block away, she called Robert.

"What'd he want?" he answered in lieu of hello.

"I'm not sure," Sharon said. "The guy's a creep. I think he was flirting with me, but he does know we're together."

"Damn it," he said, "I think he and Macy suspect me. They're sniffing at my heels."

"He's not smart enough."

"Don't let his pig act fool you. He graduated top of his class at the police academy."

"You're kidding!"

"He's all politically incorrect to distract you, Sharon. Macy may be nicer, but she's certainly not the better cop."

"Where *are* you?"

"I'm right here," he said, stepping out of a convenience store just as she walked past its entrance. He held a shiny violet spyglass about three inches long.

"Darn it, you scared me," she gasped. "Do you always carry spying equipment with you?"

"Only when I think it's necessary," he said. He grabbed her hand and led her across the street, toward the subway station on Chambers Street.

"Landers thinks you're my boyfriend because you saved me using martial arts."

"Shit."

"I know."

There was an uncomfortable silence as they continued walking. Sharon stuck her cold hands into her pockets.

"Shit," he said again.

Her answer was a long, audible sigh.

"They don't have anything on me," he said. "They couldn't."

"But they're watching you now. You can't go after that gang anymore."

"I can't sit back and allow them to fill the ER with victims."

"You can't stop all the crime in the city, Robert! The problem's too big, and you can't pull out its roots with weapons and spy equipment"

"What roots?"

"Poverty, access to guns, crappy education, violence in the media, drugs—"

"Those aren't the roots, Sharon. That's the worst kind of sloppy liberal thinking I've ever heard."

They stopped on the sidewalk in front of the subway station. Lots of people passed, most of them too involved with their smart phones to care that the couple was arguing.

"All I'm saying is that you shouldn't hold yourself personally accountable for getting rid of every wife beater and child molester in Manhattan. You got to stop this vigilante stuff, especially now that the police are onto you."

"I can't stop, Sharon," he said, his voice faint in the background city noise.

"Can't you at least lay low for a bit? Let the police do their job—let them take care of the bad guys, just for a little while."

"The police? They don't take care of anything. I tipped them off to that gang weeks ago. Look what good it did."

"Well, you can't do it all. And you're hurt."

"That's pretty obvious."

"Just take a break. Until things blow over. For me?"

He looked away and rubbed his shoulder. "I guess I can rest up until my wounds heal. I'll lay low, but only until I get better."

They went down the subway stairs. "Are we going separate ways?" she asked.

"I was hoping you'd stay at my place tonight."

"Won't that clue in Landers and Macy?"

"I don't think it matters. They seem to already know."

"Okay," she said. "I guess I can spend the night."

Sharon couldn't tell if it was joy or fear that was making her heart race.

Chapter 26

Robert stared at his watch. The man lying on the gurney had been medically dead for nearly five minutes. Meanwhile, the ambulance bay was piling up with EMS gurneys. The ER was getting hit with the early-afternoon rush. Robert started to pace up and down the room. He was wasting time. Part of him started to regret his plan.

Where was Sharon? Where was the man's wife?

"Dr. McKenzie, the guy is still in asystole. Do we need to continue CPR? He's got no chance of surviving."

"More compressions and less talking, Sanchez."

A minute later, Sharon arrived with the patient's family.

"Dr. McKenzie, this is Mr. Howard's wife, Estelle, and their daughters, Monica and Julia."

"Nice to meet you." Robert shook hands with each woman. "As you know," he began in a quiet, but clear voice, "Mr. Howard's cancer metastasized to his brain. This morning he was transferred here from his skilled nursing facility in an abnormal cardiac rhythm known as PEA—pulseless electrical activity. We tried a whole cocktail of medications but nothing's worked. I've asked the resident to continue chest compressions so that you all can have an opportunity to say good-bye. The only thing keeping him alive at this point is the CPR Dr. Sanchez is providing."

The resident looked over, beads of sweat pooling on his forehead. He gave the family a neutral nod and continued doing compressions.

The two daughters were crying. They thanked Robert and walked to either side of their father, each taking a hand. The patient's wife made her way to the foot of the bed and stood there, silent and motionless.

"Dad, we love you," one daughter managed.

"And that's not going to stop," the other said, tears flowing. "Thank you for all you gave us."

"Bye, Dad. You're a beautiful person. We're going to miss you so much."

"Bye, Daddy. We were so lucky to have you as our father."

Robert stood in respectful silence as the sisters wept for a moment, then he walked over to their mother. "Mrs. Howard, would you like to say good-bye?"

"I already have," she said calmly. "My husband and I said our good-byes months ago, while he was still lucid. But I want to thank you, Dr. McKenzie, for giving my daughters an opportunity to say good-bye in their own way."

As if mirroring each other, the sisters got on their knees. Each placed a cheek against the hand she held. Then each ran out of tears, stood, and placed the hand over her heart.

Sanchez continued doing chest compressions.

Finally, the daughters looked forlornly at their mother. Mrs. Howard, her gaze intense and unwavering, turned to Robert and nodded.

"Okay, Dr. Sanchez. Thank you."

The resident stopped compressions and backed away from the bed, rubbing his forearms. Everyone watched the red line on the monitor stop spiking and go flat.

A deep quiet took over the room.

The nurse turned off the monitor and gently put a palm on the shoulder of one of the daughters.

Sanchez snatched his white coat and left the room.

Robert and Sharon left soon after and headed toward the ER's main desks.

"Are you okay, Robert?"

"Yeah, I'm fine. Why do you ask?"

"The way you were looking at the patient. It's as if you'd seen a ghost or something."

Robert gave her a dismissive smile. "It's nothing. Besides, now is not the time to talk about my ghosts. We can talk about them tonight—that is, if you're still planning on sleeping over."

"You're a good man, Dr. McKenzie," Sharon replied. "I think I will."

"You realize that's ten nights in a row," he said.

"If you keep doing nice things, then I'll keep coming back."

"That's good," he said, "because I'm making steak frites, and we're going to watch *Le Diner de Cons*, one of the funniest movies of all times."

"*Ooh là là*," Sharon sang. "Sounds exciting. I think I'm getting addicted to dinner and movie nights at Chez Bobby's. You should get hurt more often."

"Don't get used to it, *ma cherie*. As soon as I'm feeling better, I'm going after the bad guys again."

"Not if I can help it." She walked to her workstation.

Robert headed back to his desk but stopped midstride. At the ambulance bay stood Detective Landers, next to a guy in handcuffs getting triaged. The prisoner had bruises on his face and a small laceration over his eyebrow. Rivera was taking down the information from the paramedics who had accompanied the patient and the police officer.

Detective Landers caught Robert's eye and waved.

Robert waved back and sat down at his desk, grabbing a patient's chart and pretending to check test results on the computer system.

Something about Landers's look made Robert uneasy.

Chapter 27

It was midnight before the dark-blue Ford Fusion Hybrid pulled out of the parking spot in front of Robert's apartment building. He put down his binoculars and breathed a sigh of relief. He wondered whether Landers was on the clock or doing extracurricular spying of his own.

Either way, Landers had left.

"Come to bed," Sharon urged.

He walked back inside and closed the door behind him.

"Is he gone?" she asked.

"Yeah, I think so," Robert answered. He got under the covers and wrapped his arms around her.

"Should I be concerned that the NYPD is stalking you?"

"Not really. I'll let you know when you should start worrying."

"Can I ask you something, totally off the topic?"

"That depends on what you want to know."

"The elderly man you saw this morning," Sharon started, "Mr. Howard. It's like you were a whole different person when we were in the room with the family. You were pale, and didn't look like yourself."

"It was nothing."

"I don't believe that," she said. "Remember, you told me we would talk about it tonight."

"I did?"

Sharon nodded.

"Right," Robert sighed. "He reminded me of a patient I had when I was an intern, that's all."

"Who was it?" Sharon said.

"Nobody."

"Come on, Robert. You promised you'd start opening up."

"When did I do that?"

"Maybe you didn't promise, but I want to know. You never talk about personal stuff, and every time I bring up your past, you brush it aside. We can't grow closer if you don't let me in."

For a minute they lay together in silence, side by side but not touching.

"Okay," he finally said. "It's a long story."

Sharon rolled onto her side and placed her hand on top of his chest. Robert put his arms behind his head and stared at the ceiling.

"It was my first cardiac resuscitation," Robert said, closing his eyes. "I was a brand-new intern working an overnight shift. An old man had come in by ambulance in cardiac arrest. We worked on him for an hour. It was like he didn't want to leave this world. Every time we were about to call it, his heart would lurch back into normal sinus rhythm and he would regain his pulse. Finally, whatever made him go into cardiac arrest in the first place, probably a massive heart attack or pulmonary embolism, was too much for his body to bear. We pronounced him dead, and I was in charge of going outside and telling his wife.

"The ER was full of patients waiting to be seen, but she kept talking. She went on and on about how they never had kids, about how they were just about to celebrate their fiftieth wedding anniversary, about how he took care of everything from paying the bills to helping her dress when her arthritis flared up. I knew I should've tried to be more sympathetic and comforting, and maybe get her to talk to a social worker or a psychiatrist, but I didn't. I finally blurted out that her husband was dead and left. To me, he was just an old man who croaked, and I had a lot of patients to see."

He inhaled deeply and looked up at the ceiling. "Almost a year later, just before I started my second-year rotations, I went for a long run in Central Park. It was May, I had the day off, and it was gorgeous outside. My intern year had been brutal. It was before the Bell Commission changed resident work hours from the insane thirty-six hours on, twelve hours off schedule. We were always understaffed, and the ER was always packed, always filled with mayhem. I hardly had time or energy left for exercise, but I knew I needed it. Central Park has always been my haven. That is, before you came along."

He reached over and laid his hand on her stomach. Sharon smiled and held onto his hand. "On the path into the park on Sixty-Sixth Street, I noticed an old couple walking in front of me. They must've been in their eighties. Moving slowly but arm in arm, doing fine, not falling. Something about their pace seemed like bliss after the ER, so I slowed down and watched them. At one point, they had to climb a step to the sidewalk. The man took the first step and then turned to give his wife a hand. And ... then ... I just lost it. I don't know why. It seems odd, looking back. I started crying, right there on the path."

"You didn't know why?"

"Not right away, but then I realized that the couple reminded me of the old woman and her dead husband. I had a flashback of them today."

"Is that why you were acting strange?"

"Yeah. The family this morning reminded me of both couples." Robert's eyes were moist, but no tears escaped them. He clasped his pillow. "I always think about that case. I should've stayed and talked with her," he continued, thinking of the first grieving widow, "or at least held her hand. Instead, I went to see the next patient, who happened to be a goddamn alcoholic with an ankle sprain. That's who I saw instead of comforting the old lady. I should've let that drunk fucker wait and sat with the woman a little longer."

"It's okay," Sharon said, drawing closer to kiss him.

"No, it's not okay." Robert pushed her away and stood up. "I spent an hour trying to revive the dead and thirty seconds comforting the living."

"You were an intern," Sharon said. "You didn't know any better."

"I *did* know better," he said, heading to the bathroom.

Sharon trailed after him. "Robert, you're only human. Stop beating yourself up. That happened years ago."

"Just because things happened years ago doesn't mean you should forget about them."

"I wasn't implying that," she said. "I just think you shouldn't be so hard on yourself. What you did today shows that you've learned from that experience."

"Maybe. I don't know."

"You're a good man. Give yourself a break."

Robert remained silent.

"Come on, let's go back to bed."

"I can't. I have to go." He pulled on his black jeans and started stuffing his duffel bag with equipment.

"What are you doing? Are you going out now?"

"I have no choice," he said.

"Of course you do. Think rationally. What about the cops?"

"If they have a tail on me, I'll know it and abort."

"And if they don't, you'll go after some psychopath? Is that how you deal with your feelings?"

190

"I can't lie around with you all the time whining. Stop trying to heal me. You're not going to change who I am."

He zipped up the bag and pulled on a black nylon shirt.

"I know what you're doing," she said. "You're just trying to drive me away, but I'm not going anywhere."

"Suit yourself."

"Please, Robert. You're overreacting."

As he walked out the door, he raised his hand absentmindedly. "Feel free to let yourself out."

A minute later, Robert emerged from his private garage on his Ducati, dressed in clothes as black as the starless sky.

Chapter 28

Robert had all his senses on alert for any cops who might be shadowing him.

Wearing a black hoodie and a pair of sunglasses, he hunched over to look less imposing and limped like a wino to a nearby bench. A homeless man snored on one end.

Robert turned on his audio enhancer and aimed a pinky-sized laser mike at the neo-Nazi hideout across the street. Their voices floated to him on a low wash of static.

While Robert listened to the bastards talking, he shook his head in disgust and massaged his bad shoulder, thinking about the incident that almost took his life. He had broken into the warehouse when he thought no one was around and taken pictures of their maps and files in the office. The group had documented all their atrocities in loathsome, gloating language that still made his blood boil. He was in the midst of destroying some counterfeit money when a large rock hit him on the temple. Redbeard had thrown it from the landing outside the open window, through which three of the other men then swarmed and started kicking him with their steel-toed boots. By the time Robert had oriented himself, Redbeard had taken out his knife and stabbed him.

He still had no idea how he'd been so careless. He thought he was keeping an ear out for any return. He'd dodged another blow just in time, then fought his way out of the warehouse and lurched into the street like a gored beast. He was back on his bike before the pain from the stab wound announced itself. He had been lucky to get out alive. He was certain the men would've tortured him for a long time before killing him.

Now, as he sat on the bench listening to their moronic drivel, he felt the wound with his fingers. It was healing. Not quite ready for full combat, but it would have to do.

He felt dizzy.

How could I have been so careless?

Maybe he let himself get too emotional about all the shit the neo-Nazis had done. Or maybe he'd been thinking about getting to the restaurant to meet Sharon.

He shook his head and the dizziness faded, just in time to catch Redbeard sauntering out of the warehouse, mindlessly rubbing his chest.

Robert slowly stood and swayed, taking up his act as a deadbeat wino. Redbeard glanced his way, hawked a gob on the sidewalk, and stomped toward the next avenue to look for a cab. As the man slammed the taxi's door shut, Robert eased onto his cycle. He'd follow far enough behind to avoid detection.

Fifteen minutes later, Redbeard got out on Canal Street, lit a cigarette, walked east and then south on Mulberry Street. When Robert saw him trot up some steps into a four-story redbrick apartment building on the corner, he parked and activated his heat-sensing equipment.

From across the street, he traced Redbeard up three flights of stairs into an apartment already occupied by a smaller adult and a child.

Robert turned on his laser mike.

"Hi, honey," Redbeard said. "How are my two favorite girls doing?"

Robert followed the large orange glow as Redbeard approached. "How's my little Lacey?" he leaned forward to the smaller blob of heat. "Have you been a good girl for mommy?"

"She just woke up a minute ago. I think she can tell when you're coming home."

Redbeard moved closer and picked up his daughter. There was some undecipherable noise from the baby. Then laughter.

Robert took off his mike and gripped it tightly.

The bastard scumbag is a family man.

How could that be?

Robert sat back in silence watching the three blobs interact with each other. What was he going to do? He had intended to incapacitate Redbeard, but now he had to rethink everything.

He felt a flurry of mixed emotions. Neo-Nazis were racist, soulless, ignorant. They preached hatred and made the world a living hell. They weren't supposed to be doting husbands and loving fathers.

To quiet the noise inside his head, he put the Bluetooth back on and listened to the three blobs eat dinner and talk.

An hour later, Redbeard left the apartment and headed back outside. He stood in front of his building, looking for a cab, but the streets were empty.

From across the street, Robert drew his gun and aimed it at his target. He hit Redbeard in the left groin, exactly over the highly vascular femoral canal.

But this was no ordinary bullet. It was a blank Robert had adapted to release etomidate, a powerful but short-acting anesthetic. In a matter of seconds, Redbeard dropped to the ground with a thud. Robert shook the wino act and crossed the street. He looked around, confirmed that nobody was watching, and kneeled down to get face to face with the man who almost took his life a week and a half earlier.

"If I didn't know better, I'd think you were a good man," Robert said, getting within inches of the man's face, "but I know who you are. I know what you've done, and I know what you stand for."

Redbeard's body was motionless, but his eyes were wild.

Robert stooped closer toward Redbeard's ear and whispered. "I'm going to give you one last chance. Go back to your warehouse and end this racist bullshit. Stop hurting innocent people. Tell your pals to do the same. If you guys don't, I will find and kill every one of you."

Robert stood and walked to his bike. The half-life of the sedative was approximately three minutes. He climbed onto his motorcycle and sped off.

He wasn't sure if his warning would work, and he wondered whether Sharon's optimism was infecting him at all.

Chapter 29

Back at St. Jude's, Robert sat at his desk staring mindlessly at his computer.

Outside, winter had finally descended. The temperature had dropped below freezing and the sky was perpetually covered by a blanket of gray, preventing any of the sun's rays from reaching the city.

It had been a week since he'd torn himself away from Sharon. He hadn't spoken to her since, but she'd been on his mind non-stop. So much so that he was finding it hard to do either of his jobs. The night before, he'd felt such a longing for her that he had gotten all the way to her building, but he stopped himself from knocking on her door. It wasn't until he left that he noticed the unmarked police car in the alley.

He hadn't told her about it.

There was no need to scare her.

Robert's attention shifted back to the ER. He glanced over at Sharon's desk and saw her gathering some papers and heading to room 11 for her next consult. He thumbed through the charts of people waiting to be seen and found one for a patient in the room next to hers. After waiting a few minutes, he grabbed the chart and headed toward the room, running into her on her way out.

"Hey," he said to her.

"Good morning, Dr. McKenzie."

"How are you?"

"I'm fine."

"'And you?'" Robert said.

"Pardon?"

"That's what you're supposed to say back. Someone asks you how you are, you say 'Fine. And you?'"

"Oh, but I'm sure you're doing fine."

"I'm not."

"This isn't the place, Robert. And this isn't easy for me. God, I've been miserable. But you made your mind up and left me, remember?"

"I made a mistake."

She shook her head and looked away. "People are starting to notice, Robert."

"I couldn't care less."

"Suddenly public opinion doesn't matter to you?"

"Listen, Sharon," he took her hand. "I miss you."

She pulled her hand away. "And you're sharing your feelings because…"

"Because I know what I want now."

"You don't know what you want."

"Sharon, I do. I want *you*."

"I wish I could believe you. But I think what you want is to be with me when it's convenient and then to fly around the city beating up bad guys the rest of the time. And if you can't do both, you'll pick the bad guys. You proved that the other night."

"I'm sorry about that. I'm sorry I stormed out. I'm not sure what got into me…"

One of the new travel nurses walked by. Robert stopped talking and flipped absently through the chart he was holding. Sharon nodded to the nurse, who smiled back.

When the nurse was out of earshot, Sharon pointed to something on the chart and whispered, "I've done a lot of thinking this week. As you told me on the bridge, I think it's not going to work out with us."

They stared at each other without saying a word. Sharon seemed to be holding back tears. Robert kept his face expressionless.

Then a resident hustled up to Sharon. "Is there any way you could talk to Mr. Berwald? He's asking for social services again."

"Sure," she said, "I'll go see him right now." She turned to Robert. "I'm sorry."

As she walked away, Robert tried to remind himself that his life had been fine before he'd met her. He didn't need her. He tried to convince himself that the hollowness he felt in his chest would eventually be replaced by something else.

He slapped the chart he was holding, took a deep breath, and headed to the patient's room. Back to work. He would survive this.

He had survived a lot worse.

And yet, he went through the next couple of hours feeling as if acid were filling his stomach. He thought about walking out of the ER and never coming back. He had plenty of savings. He could go back to Guatemala and live there for the rest of his life.

Then the ambulance doors crashed open and in clattered a pair of agitated paramedics doing CPR on a pregnant woman ready to burst. Rivera led them to resus and gave Robert a desperate look that said, Get to the bay—*now!*

Inside, the paramedics took turns doing chest compressions while one of the residents stood at the head of the bed bagging oxygen into the woman's mouth. She was at full term and coding.

A perimortem caesarian delivery.

This was a case Robert had never seen before: a pregnant woman in cardiac arrest requiring an emergency C-section. Without it, she and her baby had no chance to survive. His mind raced through dozens of medical journals and textbooks. He tried tapping into his hippocampus and prefrontal cortex, focusing on the pages he'd read years ago in Beckmann's *Obstetrics and Gynecology* and Shah's *Essential Emergency Procedures*. His head swam with thoughts that began to slow and distill. The light in the room grew brighter, his breathing steadied, and the familiar feeling of being in control returned.

"Okay, guys, move your hands an inch higher and continue compressions," Robert instructed. "Roll the patient onto her left side. Rivera, call the OB attending and tell her a coding woman in the ER needs a stat C-section. You," he said, pointing to Sanchez. "Intubate."

Resus went into frenzied action under Robert's intense watch. The paramedics continued chest compressions. Sanchez intubated the patient and connected her to a respirator. One nurse placed an IV line. Another inserted a Foley catheter inside the woman's bladder.

"Where the hell's OB?" Robert yelled.

"Dr. McKenzie," Rivera said, "the OB attending and senior resident are in the operating room, mid-case. The only person available is the intern."

There was no way he was going to let an intern do the procedure. Robert knew what he needed to do. "Stop compressions. Feel for a pulse."

He looked at the cardiac monitor and saw haphazard activity.

"No femoral pulse," one of the paramedics called.

"No carotid either," the resident called from the head of the bed.

Robert felt for a pulse himself and glared at the monitor.

"Keep compressions going. Keep bagging her. I need a delivery tray. We're going to get this baby out."

Robert poured a bottle of Betadine over the woman's abdomen, snatched up a pair of gloves, and told Rivera to get a scalpel and a sterile gown. As soon as he was prepped, he took the scalpel and made a perfect incision through the lower abdomen, right above the vagina.

Blood gushed through the opening, drenching the gurney. Robert pushed past the bladder and located the uterus. He pierced it with the scalpel, then used a pair of large blunt scissors to extend the opening.

A few seconds later, he gripped the baby's shoulders and pulled her out. He clamped the umbilical cord, cut it, and carried the infant girl to the neonatal station.

"Keep doing compressions," Robert yelled over his shoulder to the paramedics. He dried the baby, listened to her lungs, and began suctioning excess fluid from her mouth and nose. "Rivera, call the blood bank. Four units of uncrossed type O negative blood, stat. We'll start transfusing as soon as it gets here."

Sanchez had gowned up and was pressing the uterus with both hands, using a thick pack of sterile gauze to contain the blood. Robert finished suctioning the baby and went back to work on her mother.

"Good work," he said. "Rivera, give the patient a round of epinephrine and an amp of bicarb."

As soon as she did, Robert counted down a minute of compressions and checked the monitor. "Stop compressions. Feel for a pulse."

Robert stared at the monitor. There was a wide-complex, irregular rhythm.

"She's in ventricular fibrillation," he said. "We have to shock her." As Rivera ran across the room to get the defibrillator, Robert wound up his fist and plowed it straight into the middle of the woman's chest, hoping that the precordial thump would create enough energy to interrupt the life-threatening arrhythmia. Without pausing to check for a pulse, he resumed CPR and instructed the nurse to give another round of medications.

When he stopped compressions a minute later, there was a regular beeping sound coming from the monitor.

"I got a strong femoral pulse here," Sanchez called.

"And a solid carotid pulse," the paramedic added.

The obstetrics intern came down, got the information, called her attending, and wheeled the patient off to the operating room.

As Robert waited for the pediatrician to take the baby up to the neonatal intensive care unit, he continued to examine the tiny girl. He marveled at her perfect features and the arrival of a new life from the mother's dark ocean. With background congratulations fluttering around him, he couldn't help but smile.

He knew it was simply a matter of physics and practical action. When he removed the baby from the uterus, the vital blood vessels in the pelvis that supplied the mother's heart and brain with oxygen were no longer pinched, allowing blood to resume proper circulation.

Nonetheless, it felt like a miracle.

Robert continued to rub the baby's tiny arms and legs and noted her color pinking up, her breathing and Apgar score normalizing.

"You're a lucky little girl," he said softly, caressing her face with the back of his hand.

"Dr. McKenzie," the NICU nurse said as she approached him. "If it's okay with you, I'd like to transport the patient up to the neonatal unit."

He nodded, and the nurse took the girl. When he turned to see them out, he found Sharon standing by the door. Their eyes met, but she quickly looked away and walked down the hall.

Robert headed back to his desk. He knew the chart on the delivery would be reviewed with a very cold eye. Everything he'd just done needed to be documented precisely. He was certain he'd be criticized by the obstetrics and gynecology department for doing a procedure beyond his scope of practice, although he'd done what he had to do, and everything had turned out fine. He had already been reprimanded by the ER director for the thoracotomy. He didn't want to give Weiss any reason to criticize him again.

He sat down and began to write his account of what had just occurred. He looked at his watch and noticed that it was already six o'clock, an hour past the end of his shift. He felt surprisingly content; he had saved two lives and hadn't bitten off anyone's head.

"You're out of here a little early, aren't you?"

Robert looked up. Rivera was speaking to Sharon, who was dropping off her last charts at the triage desk.

"I have plans tonight," Sharon said.

Robert stopped writing and stared down at his hand. He was squeezing his pen so tight his fingers had turned white.

"That's my girl," Rivera said. "Who's the lucky guy?"

"That remains to be determined. I'm heading over to my favorite little hole-in-the-wall Mexican restaurant in my neighborhood. I'm going to sit by the bar and have a Dos Equis and maybe pick someone up."

"I have no doubt you'll be getting a little something tonight," Rivera said, laughing.

Robert loosened his grip on the pen and smiled.

Chapter 30

"Excuse me. Is this seat taken?" Robert asked.

Sharon's lips curled into a smile. "I was waiting for a handsome, intelligent, caring guy—but I guess you can sit there for now."

Robert laughed and sat down. He waved at the waiter, and a few seconds later he was brought over a beer.

"I saw you perform that C-section today. Nice work."

"I keep seeing that little girl's face and those tiny toenails..."

"Are you going to get in trouble?"

Robert shrugged and took a two-chug drink. "Ahh." He swiveled to look her full in the face. "I've missed this view."

Sharon's smile disappeared. "It's your fault."

"I know," he said. "I'm sorry."

"I still don't understand what happened. One moment you're sharing this intense, life-altering story with me, and the next you're running away."

"I don't know what got into me. I'm not used to talking about my feelings."

"You're going to have to start. I can't be with someone who keeps everything bottled up inside. It's destructive."

"I guess I'm used to suppressing my emotions," he said. "That's how I deal with things. It's worked for me so far."

"Has it?"

He didn't say anything.

"Look, Robert. You're an incredible guy. I don't like you going after people, and I hope that eventually you'll see my point of view, but you can't be shutting me out every time something bad happens. You need to be open with me. You need to let me in."

"Fine." He kissed her lips gently. "You look great tonight. How's that for starters."

"I'm serious, Robert."

"I know. So am I. I'll try."

"Thank you."

Robert sipped his beer and then pushed it aside. "Okay, let our first session begin. Ask me anything."

"Anything?"

"Sure."

After a moment of reflection, Sharon said, "Okay, here's something that's been puzzling me. How do you choose whom to help and whom to go after? You see hundreds of people a week, so how do you decide?"

"Basic triage technique. It's mostly based on urgency and immediate need or threat, but sometimes that's not enough. I often have to make my decision based on environmental cues."

"Like coincidence?"

"That's right. Like when you think of a friend you haven't seen in a long time, and the phone rings and it's that person. I have kind of a religious trust in these cues. Most people don't notice them or, worse, ignore them. I act on them."

"Okay. I get that, but you still have to look before you leap. There's something a little superstitious about always looking for signs."

"Not being stupid is also one of my prime directives."

She laughed. "Sometimes I worry it's not prime enough."

They stared at each other in silence.

"I've really missed you," he said.

"Me too," she said. "We're one big mess of irreconcilable differences, aren't we?"

"I was just about to say that."

He leaned over and kissed her.

"I get how you're good," she said, "but what I don't get is why you can't be more understanding with criminals. Almost all of them come from abusive households. They were beaten or raped or psychologically tortured as kids, so they grow up to do the same. You have to consider their upbringing and try to sympathize with them."

Robert grew quiet. His smile disappeared and his face took on that impassive expression Sharon didn't like. She was about to change the subject when he held up his hand.

"Bad things happen to good people," he began. "That's a fact of life. The good die young, the great die younger. Innocent people are murdered and raped every day. I figure that if random acts of badness happen to good people, why can't they also happen to bad people? There are criminals who grow up in wonderful, caring households, too. And there are good people who grow up in abusive households and overcome those obstacles to make something of themselves, without passing on the torture they endured as children."

"Some criminals can be rehabilitated."

"But some of them can't. Those are the ones I go after."

"How can you tell them apart? How can you be so sure?" She'd raised her voice and the people across the bar looked over. "Sorry, I'm a little worked up," she said to them, pointing to Robert. "I'm Yankees. He's Red Sox."

The group sent off a few playful boos and directed their stares elsewhere.

"Are you trying to get me killed?" he said, grinning.

She ignored him. "Seriously, Robert. How can you tell?"

"Guillermo taught me."

"Sorry, but that sounds like you're talking voodoo."

"Guillermo wasn't voodoo," he said. "If you met him, you'd know the man is nothing but practical. Recognizing the devils was part of basic training. Whenever we caught a group of enemy soldiers, we'd put them in makeshift cages. Guillermo would make me study them for hours. Then we'd talk about each one. There were always a few who were different. Something flat in their eyes. It wasn't how angry or docile they were, or whether they smiled or looked away. They had all sorts of personalities. But as we stood there, I came to know which ones had no conscience, and I have never been wrong about identifying these guys. Not in Guatemala and certainly not in New York. Believe me, I *know*. I know the feeling a psychopath gives me, like rotten wood inside of me crawling with termites."

"So you're a psychopath hunter?"

"The criminal psychopath. Not all psychopaths are criminals. The non-criminal ones break your heart. They're hurting and they're lost. It's going to take some genius to help them find their way. But the dangerous ones, they start a witches' brew in my gut. They don't want to break your heart—they want to tear it out, eat it, and lick their fingers. I know who they are. To these guys, I'm the messenger of Karma."

They were silent as they drank their beers. Sharon looked at the other families sitting and eating together. Fathers and mothers with their children.

"Why does it have to be you?"

"Look, Sharon, I want to make the world a better place as

206

much as you do. We just have different skill sets. You have your way, and it's strong. I've seen it. I love it. But I have my own way. I have to stop them. Ten percent of criminals commit ninety percent of crimes. Did you know that? That's staggering. If I can get rid of a few of these guys, then I've saved hundreds of people from murder, rape, assault, and psychological trauma."

"What about letting the police and courts do their job?"

"I wish you'd give up believing so much in the cops. Psychopaths have been going in and out of prisons for years, and they're becoming more dangerous. These are the guys that don't get rehabilitated. Even in your prisons, they wouldn't be cured. They need to be taken out of commission permanently."

"Don't you think the system can be changed?"

"The only way things can change," he said, "is if our society adopts the Machiavelli Plan."

"The what?"

"The Machiavelli Plan. It's how the Mafia deals with their enemies."

Sharon shook her head. "I have a feeling I'm not going to like what you're about to say."

"Hear me out for a second," Robert said. "Let's say next time a terrorist group attacks the United States, the government orders the Navy Seals to find and kill everyone affiliated with those terrorists—their family members, their friends, their acquaintances. Then the government orders the Air Force to bomb the crap out of every village or town each terrorist came from. Do you know how quickly terrorism would vanish? There would be no support system for terrorists. This is similar to how the Mafia operates, and everyone knows not to fuck with them."

"You can't be serious."

"I *am* serious. Those are the best options for fighting the war on terror—either we hire a vigilante or we subscribe to the

Machiavelli Plan."

"That's absurd," she said. "What you're proposing would hurt the innocent. Please tell me you don't honestly believe that's a valid option."

He shrugged and took a swig of his beer. "Criminals hurt the innocent all the time, and they keep getting away with it. I'm not necessarily an advocate of the Machiavelli Plan. I don't think hurting the innocent is ever justified. I'm not the Mafia, either. I was just trying to make a point."

"And what's that?"

"Sometimes," Robert said, "drastic measures need to be taken to ensure order in the world."

"I don't want to live in a world where the ends justify the means."

Robert put his beer down and held onto Sharon's hand. He lifted it to his lips and kissed it gently. "I don't either."

"You promise?"

"I do," he said, caressing her hand. "We're not there, and I hope we'll never be."

Sharon kissed him on the cheek. "No more talk of Machiavelli, okay?"

"Okay." He kissed her forehead. "For the record, you're the one with a copy of *The Prince*."

"Come over tonight. We can burn it together."

Chapter 31

When Sharon reached room 19 for her consult, she hovered by the door and listened to Robert instructing one of the residents. She and Robert had been back together for almost two weeks, and she'd seen the change she wanted: he'd taken another rest from his vigilante activities and he was being a lot nicer to people at work.

"Look at her shoes," Sharon heard him say. "You're a great resident, but you missed that. You need to start paying attention to details."

"I didn't want to stereotype, Dr. McKenzie."

"You can be respectful if you want, but don't let political correctness muddy your overall evaluation. Do you really think this patient needs a psychiatric admission?"

"I guess not," the resident said.

"Um, *hello!*" the girl in the gurney called out. "I can hear you guys. I'm right here."

Sharon had seen the fifteen-year-old being wheeled past triage a few hours earlier, texting madly. Rivera had briefed Sharon about the patient. "Suicidal attempt by intentional overdose" was the girl's chief complaint. Sharon was certain she'd be called to consult on the case at some point during the day, so she decided to get a head start.

"Relax, Alecia. Go back to your iPhone." Robert turned to the resident. "This girl did not seriously attempt suicide. Look at the lacerations. They're all superficial, half a foot from her wrist. She told you she ingested a bunch of pills from her purse, but all she has is an empty two-tablet packet of Advil next to a tampon wrapper. She's on her period, so she swallowed the pills and then decided she wanted her parents to pay more attention to her. That iPhone is the newest version. It just came out last week. And the shoes? Christian Louboutin snakeskin. They cost around a thousand bucks, which means her idiot parents buy her everything she wants, but she wants more. Of course she does. They're probably workaholic professionals who are trying to pay for her love instead of spending quality time with her. Right, Alecia?"

The girl looked up from texting. "My dad is a cardiologist and my mom is a corporate lawyer, and I *don't* want to spend more time with them because they're stupid and selfish and make my life a living hell. And you guys are incompetent idiots."

"What about the pills?"

"Whatever."

Robert shook his head and addressed the resident. "Are we in agreement? Cancel the two-thousand-dollar work-up you ordered for her, tell the psych resident not to bother coming down, and we'll get our social worker to have her parents sent away for life so this little girl can be put in an orphanage."

At this point, Sharon knocked and entered the room, putting on a fierce expression. "Good afternoon, Dr. McKenzie," she said. "I overheard you needed a social worker."

"What? An orphanage?" Alecia looked at Sharon and quickly pocketed her iPhone.

"Thanks for coming, Ms. Reede." Robert turned back to the resident. "Protocol medicine is bad medicine. You can't just order labs and consults based on a patient's chief complaint. That's how shitty doctors practice, and I expect much more from you. Study the entire person. Now go examine the guy in room 10 and be sure to pay close attention. He'll give you clues about what's really going on with him, but only if you let him."

"Okay, Dr. McKenzie." The resident hustled out.

Robert smiled and winked at Sharon.

"What's with you two?" the patient asked, a disgusted look on her face.

"And what's with you, young lady?" Sharon responded. "You think faking suicide is a game, like ditching school or making fun of kids who wear cheap clothes?"

Sharon's outburst caught the kid by surprise, and she burst into tears. "Oh shit, shit, shit!" She buried her face in her hands.

"I see a beautiful young woman here who doesn't know how to respect anyone, especially herself." Sharon placed a hand on the girl's shoulder as she sobbed. "We don't care about your shoes, your phone, or how much money your parents make. It's the truth we want, okay? You and I are going to have a little talk—and then we'll let your folks in on how you really feel."

When Alecia's crying started to quiet, Sharon continued. "We'll be fine now, Dr. McKenzie. I know you still have a lot of patients to see, so go right ahead. Alecia and I will clear things up here. Thank you."

"My pleasure, Ms. Reede. Bye, Alecia. Make sure you listen to the lady. She's here to help."

He left the room and headed down the hallway to catch up to the resident, who by now was probably in the midst of examining the next patient, an older gentleman with neurological deficits. Robert feared that under normal circumstances, the man's slurred speech and clumsiness would compel the resident to activate the stroke team, which would mean a massive mobilization of the ER's resources. Technicians, nurses, and residents would be called to examine the patient, get an IV, draw blood, and take him to the CT scanner for stat brain imaging. Depending on the results, a neurologist would rush to the ER and determine if the patient was a candidate for the very expensive, life-saving medication that treated ischemic strokes. The patient would be admitted for observation. He would spend a few days in the hospital for further testing, which would include an MRI of the brain and an ultrasound of his carotid arteries. In all, the patient would rack up a fifty-thousand-dollar bill, even though what he really needed was a liter of IV fluids, 100 milligrams of thiamine, and some time to sober up.

Robert was betting the resident had learned to pay attention to detail and hadn't called the stroke team. He hoped she'd caught the bulge in the man's right vest pocket and spied the flask of one-hundred-proof vodka. At the very least, she'd smell the alcohol on his breath, which the patient had tried to hide with a sub-therapeutic dose of mints.

As Robert passed room 13 on his way to meet her, he saw something that made his sense of contentment vanish. He doubled back, surprising Sanchez, who was about to suture the forehead of a thirty-something-year-old black man with blood all over his white shirt.

"What happened to you?" Robert demanded as he stormed inside.

In the weeks since his visit to Redbeard, there'd been no new incidents. Not at St. Jude's, not in the papers, not in the police logs. But still, Robert couldn't believe that his warning had really worked.

Sanchez reared back, almost scratching the patient in the eye with the suturing needle. "Jesus, Dr. McKenzie, you scared me."

"Sir," Robert said, ignoring Sanchez and addressing the patient again. "Who stabbed you in the face?"

212

The man looked surprised. Robert's insides were knotting. "Who stabbed you?" he repeated.

"No one stabbed me, bro."

"Listen, don't be afraid. You can tell me."

"I'm not scared of nothing, man. I'm just a clumsy dumbass, that's all." The man laughed a rich, bass riff. "I was watching this fine-looking honey bending over to pick up after her dog, and I tripped. I hit my face on a sharp piece of curb. No one stabbed me but that rock."

Robert scanned the man's wound and then looked at his hands. There were abrasions over the thumb pads, confirming the man's story.

"Hey, Doc," the patient said. "You all right?"

Robert was still calming down and didn't trust himself to speak. Sanchez stepped in. "Hey, man," he said awkwardly. "What about the chick? Did she come offer you any comfort?"

"Nah, she just went her way like they all do. Dog came over though, smelled my ear. Real dog breath, too, like bad meat."

"That's too bad," Sanchez said, looking sideways at Robert.

"Yeah, man. She was pretty hot." The man laughed again.

"Dr. McKenzie?" Sanchez asked.

Robert shook his head quickly and stood tall. "Okay, Dr. Sanchez. Keep up the good work."

The man continued to laugh as Robert walked out and headed to room 10, feeling lightheaded as his adrenaline wore off. His gut sensed something terrible, warning him. He'd been too long out of the justice game. He was a soldier burning to get back to the front line.

As he stood by and watched the resident examine the patient, Robert's mind kept racing back to the question that had surfaced a few days earlier.

What exactly was Redbeard up to?

Chapter 32

"Robert, are you okay?" Sharon called from bed. She got up, wrapped the sheet around her body, and stepped onto the open balcony.

Elbows on the rail, Robert didn't answer. He didn't move an inch.

It was three in the morning.

Another night of insomnia.

She quietly drew closer. He was wearing just boxers, the ones with the bottlenose dolphins she loved so much. She stood beside him, put her arm around him, and slipped her fingertips under the top elastic. Her hand was warm; his skin was cold.

He didn't react.

"Robert, it's freezing out here. You're going to get sick, and then I'll have to nurse you back to life again."

He turned and kissed her forehead. "That's not going to happen. My immune system is first class."

Sharon snuggled next to him. "Are you all right?"

"I'm fine."

"Do you want some tea or something?"

"Nah. I'm okay. Thanks, though."

She touched the wound on his shoulder. "Looking good here. Feel okay? Not sensitive?"

"Yeah, it's good. It doesn't throb anymore."

"No pus, no redness."

"Good to go."

"That's what I'm afraid of."

"I know you are." They exchanged knowing looks. Robert raised and lowered his eyebrows a beat, then turned to the silent winter nightscape. The New York City lights were like low-hanging stars.

"Were you having a nightmare?" she asked.

"How did you know?"

"You do that thing with your foot, as if you're pawing the ground."

He laughed dryly. "I never know if I'm running toward something or being prevented from running away."

"Probably both."

"Probably."

They gazed at shadowy Central Park and all of Midtown. Sharon could make out the black ribbon of the East River in the distance.

"Everything's so peaceful from up here," he said. "But it's an illusion. If we could see it all, we'd see all sorts of terrible crimes being committed out there."

"I guess," Sharon said, "but we would also see people enjoying each other's company, friends singing and dancing, and couples making love. That part is true, too. Maybe the key to happiness is having the discipline to focus on the positives in your life. Maybe it's about controlling your consciousness."

"I'm not sure if I buy into that stuff."

"There's been no activity from the neo-Nazis, right? Maybe they took your warning seriously."

"There's one problem."

"What's that?"

"I feel the same way I used to during night watch in Guatemala, right before an attack. I learned to wake everyone up when I felt this way."

"Really?"

"Yeah. Even though the jungle contained all sorts of sounds, of animals and bugs, I heard my instincts speaking clearly to me. Just like now. My gut is twisting over something fierce. It knows something I don't."

"What do you want to do? Dress in black and hit the streets?"

"Maybe I should."

"Please don't, Robert. Let's just go back to bed."

He sighed.

Sharon wrapped her sheet tightly around him and pressed her breasts into his back. His body relaxed as he turned to embrace her. They kissed slowly, passionately.

"Come on, let's go inside."

"Give me another minute," Robert said.

Sharon nuzzled his cheek and gathered the sheet around her again. She pretended to have trouble opening the sliding door back into the apartment and let the sheet drop. "Whoops," she said as she walked back inside, dragging the sheet after her like a wedding train.

Robert gave her a fleeting smile, then turned around and gazed at the horizon. His body tensed like a trapped animal's. He massaged his right shoulder and rotated his arm while staring in the direction of the neo-Nazi safe house.

He spoke in a whisper colder than the air. "Enjoy your last night of vacation, assholes." Then he turned and followed Sharon back to bed.

Chapter 33

The ER was a war zone. Dozens of paramedics, cops, and fire fighters lined the hallways leading from the ambulance bay to resus. The floors were dotted with blood, its stench everywhere.

Sharon dropped her bag under her desk and hurried to the triage nursing station. "What's going on, Michelle?"

"Rough night. Some neo-Nazi gangbangers went on a killing spree on the Upper West. Jumped a group of kids—a visiting choir from Atlanta heading back to their youth hostel after dinner. Two of them stabbed to death. Two up in ICU on respirators. One in the operating room all night. And this last one," Nurse Rivera pointed to resus. "The girl they're working on now..."

"What about her?"

"I don't know how she survived. She's alive, still conscious even. I'd love to say it's a miracle, but I can't. I don't believe in miracles. I don't believe in anything right now. How could any human being do this?"

Rivera's words should have prepared Sharon for what she found in resus.

But they didn't.

Inside, Dr. Sanchez, Dr. Donahoe, a respiratory therapist, and two nurses worked on the patient.

And then there was Robert, standing in the corner like a statue, his jaw clenched with fury.

Donahoe examined the patient while one nurse administered fluids and another gave morphine. A respiratory therapist placed a non-rebreather oxygen mask around the girl's mouth.

Sharon could hardly look at the victim, a black girl in her early twenties. Countless stab wounds covered her face, neck, and chest. Her hands and forearms looked like chopped meat. The cuts around her upper torso were superficial, but her abdomen...

Sharon gasped as Donahoe stuck his hand inside one of the girl's stomach wounds during his examination. She had never seen anything like it in her four months at St. Jude's. Suppressing her nausea was proving to be difficult. The girl on the gurney was moaning. Every so often her glassy eyes darted in Sharon's direction.

Detectives Landers and Macy stood in the back of the room, interviewing the paramedics who had been on the scene.

"Are you sure there were seven of them?" Landers asked.

"That's what I overheard," one of the paramedics said. "Skinheads. Jumped the kids as they turned the corner. Started beating them, cutting them with switchblades."

"What about this girl here?" Macy asked.

"Nobody's sure," a second paramedic said. "Bystander saw her run into a deserted alley, get tackled by a big muscular guy with a red beard. Based on how we found her, she was raped, beaten, and then stabbed repeatedly."

Robert's voice suddenly shot through the room like a rifle. "Enough! Rivera, get the propofol. We're going to induce a coma until the operating room is ready for her."

"But Dr. McKenzie," Donahoe called out, "the other girl won't be done with her surgery for another three hours. I have strict orders from Dr. Simone not to sedate the patient until then."

"Fuck Simone! The patient's in shock. Once the adrenaline wears off, she'll be feeling every one of those stab wounds. Morphine's not going to touch her. Dilaudid won't be enough, either. We're going to sedate her with propofol and intubate her. No discussion. I don't care if it's protocol or not. I want her in a coma. Now! Not in an hour, and certainly not in three hours when she goes to surgery."

Soon, Rivera was hanging the bottle of milky white medication on the patient's IV pole, despite the continued objection from Donahoe. Looking paler than the propofol, Sanchez stepped aside. Robert made his way to the head of the bed and intubated the girl on the gurney. A minute later the patient was asleep, connected to a drip and a respirator. Sharon felt her heart ease. The girl was unconscious and no longer feeling pain.

Robert stormed out of the room. She followed him.

"Dr. McKenzie?"

Robert didn't slow. He went right to his desk, grabbed the phone, and dialed. "Yeah, Valentine. You're on sick call, right? Great. I'm calling in sick. Be here in fifteen minutes." He hung up and put on his winter coat.

"Robert, you can't leave," Sharon pleaded. "We need you here."

He snatched up his bag and marched outside.

Sharon rushed after him through the ambulance bay double doors and into the frigid air. "Think, Robert. Don't do anything irrational."

He turned and glared at her in silence.

Sharon stood in the middle of the bay. "You can't leave the ER unattended. At least wait until Dr. Valentine gets here. Please, Robert!"

"This is your fault," Robert shouted, slamming his fist against the hood of one of the ambulances in the bay. "Goddamn you! I could've stopped that attack last night. I knew it was going down.

I should've trusted my instincts. If it weren't for you, those kids would still be alive. That girl wouldn't have been tortured like that. None of this would've happened."

"You're blaming *me*? I had nothing to do with what happened last night, and neither did you!"

"You're wrong. I could have stopped them."

"Robert, listen to what you're saying."

"I have to go."

"Be sensible. We need you here. Just wait until Dr. Valentine gets here."

"Fuck Valentine! I don't give a shit about him—or you. I wish I'd never met you. I wish you'd never come into my life," he yelled and stormed off.

Sharon began to cry. "I'm not the one you hate," she managed. "I didn't do this—and neither did you!"

She watched Robert until he faded from sight. Her body shivered furiously in the cold, and her mind flooded with images of Robert being tortured and killed at the hands of the neo-Nazis.

Sharon continued crying. She was so overwhelmed by Robert's departure that she didn't notice the man standing behind one of the ambulances.

"Trouble in the honeymoon suite?"

It was Detective Landers.

"Go to hell." Sharon wiped the tears with her sleeve and marched back inside.

Chapter 34

Sharon went to Robert's apartment as soon as her shift ended, praying she wasn't too late to warn him. She rushed to the elevator as an elderly couple was getting out and took it to the penthouse floor. She needed to talk some sense into him before he went on his rampage.

Sharon still felt nauseated from the morning's activities: fielding questions from Detectives Landers and Macy, dealing with the mayhem that followed Robert's abrupt departure from the ER, and trying to forget those last hurtful words he'd said to her before storming out.

She fought back tears as she approached his apartment and knocked on the door.

No answer.

She opened it with the key he'd given her, entered the apartment, and locked the door behind her.

"Robert? Are you here?"

She heard a noise coming from his bedroom and found him coming out of his closet. A large leather bag rested on his bed, filled to the brim with guns, knives, and spy gear. Robert started stuffing shells of ammunition inside the bag, rearranging the items to make more room. The arsenal of weapons on his bed seemed to be enough to equip a small army.

"You shouldn't have come," he said.

"I had no choice. Landers and Macy are onto you."

Robert stopped packing and looked up. "How do you know?"

"Because I spent the bulk of my morning answering their questions about you. They saw right through me. They knew I was holding back."

"It doesn't matter. They don't have any evidence against me."

"They *will* if you do something stupid."

"I have no choice."

"But you do," her voice grew louder. "Stop for a minute and think about the consequences of your actions. Either you'll end up dead, or in jail for the rest of your life. Is that what you want?"

"What I want is to make those scumbags pay for what they've done."

"Let the police handle it."

"There you go again. Jesus, Sharon. The police can't do shit. They have no idea whom they're dealing with. I know where these guys operate. I know what they do. I know how to deal with them. I'm taking them down."

"But the victims can ID them. The police will arrest them, and they'll pay for what they've done."

"How can you still say that after what you saw today?"

"The police saw it, too, Robert. They'll go after the neo-Nazis."

"Those bastards will have alibis. Even if they're identified, it'll take too long to put them away—and it won't be for long enough."

"What about the ER?" Sharon asked. "Are you willing to give up your career? You're already in deep trouble for what you've pulled off recently—and then you go AWOL this morning during a major crisis. The director himself had to come down to see patients and supervise residents until Dr. Valentine showed up."

"That's not my fault. Valentine should've gotten there earlier. I called in sick. In fact, I've decided to call in sick for the rest of the week."

"Personal time?"

"Very personal."

Sharon shook her head. "This isn't the best way, Robert. You're letting sadism inspire you, not justice."

"I want to avenge the innocent. I want to hurt those supremacist assholes as much as they hurt that girl."

"Are you listening to yourself? Can't you see that you are *not* the messenger of Karma? You say you're a psychopath hunter, but you sound just like them. You sound like a psychopath yourself."

Robert glared at Sharon for a minute. His eyes had that cold look she remembered from earlier that day.

She started to cry, but she forced out her words between sobs. "Please don't go out there. If you aren't going to stop this for your work, then stop it for me."

"I can't. Not now. Not after what they did."

"That's where you're wrong," she said. "You don't have to do this. Listen. I know you were hurt when you were young, and that's probably why you do what you do. But you're no longer that little boy who was burned by cigarettes. That's all over now."

"Spare me your psychological bullshit," Robert said, grabbing a box of bullets from inside the leather bag. He started to slot them in his SIG Sauer. "You know nothing."

"I know more than you think. I've figured out your past. Your father leaves you when you're young. The next man in your mom's life is a violent drunk. Cigarette burns are probably the least of it. What else happened to you?"

"That has nothing to do with it," he growled. "I do what needs to be done, and I don't trust anyone else to do it."

Sharon took a step closer and lowered her voice. "You need to have faith in people. You'll never even the score. You won't even come close without therapy. This all has a lot to do with your past."

"That's enough. Shut up!"

"You're supposed to be a doctor. You're supposed to be healing people, not hurting them. What you do in the ER is a gift, Robert, but what you do in the streets is total lunacy. You have to stop letting the things that were done to you when you were young turn you into a cold-blooded avenger."

"You don't know what you're talking about."

"I do," she said. "I know you were abused. I've seen the scars—"

"Stop talking about that. I'm warning you!"

"I can't imagine what you've been through," she pressed on, drawing closer to him. "But if you give me a chance I think I can help."

"I don't need your help!" he snapped, taking a step back. "What you softheaded liberals miss when you talk about how abuse messes up a child is how much it teaches him. Try getting beaten with an iron rod until you can't move off the ground. Watch your mother getting pounded senseless and your little brother getting raped. Try getting sodomized yourself by your stinking stepfather, knowing that the cops can't do anything to help because your stepfather would kill your entire family—and then himself—if the police ever showed up."

Robert stopped packing and went into the bathroom. His chest heaved, and tears splattered from his eyes onto the sink. He looked up into the mirror and watched himself when she came in behind him. "You don't know shit, Sharon. You have no idea about my childhood. You don't know half of what happened to me."

"Oh my God, you're right. I'm so sorry."

His arms clenched the bathroom counter tightly as tears continued to stream down his face. "Anger can nullify the pain. Anger can turn the poison inside into something useful." He lifted his head again to stare at the wreck of himself in the mirror, the image fueling his rage.

"I understand that," she murmured, "but there must be another way to make things right."

"There's no other way," he said, wiping his face. "Why can't you see that for each person I incapacitate, I save the lives of hundreds from rape, violence, and psychological torture?"

"That may be true, but you're stooping to your enemy's level. You talk about how horrible these psychopaths are, how they don't have any empathy for their victims. Don't you see you're killing off your own empathy? Revenge and hatred have turned your heart to stone. They've turned it into a place with no room for love."

"Go tell the girl on the respirator about how love will save her."

"Her friends are doing all they can for her," she said, "and that's more than you are."

"What her friends don't know is that the girl won't live past midnight."

"Robert, please don't."

"Don't what?"

"Don't go out there. Don't rule out love. What would your friend Guillermo do?"

"He would do exactly what I'm about to do."

"Please, Robert. I beg you. Don't go out there and seek revenge."

"Thanks for the advice," he said. "Now get the fuck out."

PART 3

Rape Statistics[1]

» *Every two minutes, someone in the United States is sexually assaulted.*

» *More than half of sexual crimes are never reported to police.*

» *Ninety-seven percent of rapists will never spend a day in jail.*

» *One in fifteen victims becomes pregnant as a result of being raped.*

[1]U.S. Department of Justice. National Crime Victimization Survey. 2006-2010.

Chapter 35

The subway slowed and the couple dry humping and slobbering all over each other finally disentangled and walked drunkenly to the exit door. It was 4:54 a.m., and the N train to Queens was nearly empty.

"Get a room next time," Robert called out.

"Mind your business, old man," the guy said, his eyes half-closed.

"You're just jealous," the woman added. Her face was smeared with brown eye shadow and her tattered sweater hung atop a big couch-potato fat roll. The doors opened and they exited, groping each other's asses.

Robert shook his head in disgust and turned his attention to the passenger across from him, a skinhead.

His iPod was blasting so loud Robert could clearly make out the violent lyrics. The target's eyes were closed and his head bobbed like a wobble toy's. Occasionally, he croaked a line out loud as if he were alone in the shower.

Only one other passenger remained in the subway car. He sat at the far end, reading an e-book. Robert couldn't see anyone in either of the adjacent cars.

A bell dinged, the doors slid open, and the passenger with his e-book skittered out, scaring off a rat by the garbage bin on the platform. An old, obese homeless man carrying two garbage bags full of empties started to waddle in. Robert blocked his entrance, wrinkling his nose at the man's sickening smell of excrement and long-brewed body odor.

"Outta my way," the man mumbled to the ground, not looking up at Robert.

"Sorry, buddy. This train's closed. Here's some money for the inconvenience." Robert waved a twenty-dollar bill, which got the homeless man's attention, and then crumpled it and tossed it back on the platform. The guy squatted to pick it up, his bags clinking and clanking behind him. The doors closed and Robert watched through the window as the man smoothed out the bill and looked at it curiously.

The skinhead sat with his eyes closed, noticing none of this.

Robert went back to the seat opposite his target. After a few seconds the guy must have felt the weight of the stare and looked up. Robert smiled and waved. The man across from him was the shortest of the band of skinheads Robert was after. He was in his early thirties and had a sunken chest, ferret-eyes, and a wheezy voice. Robert remembered him well from the safe house the night he was stabbed in the shoulder. He was the one who had suggested they cut him. The one who had squealed in laughter while his buddies kicked Robert in the chest and abdomen. The one who had fondled his pearl-handled knife as if he was stroking himself.

"What the fuck are you looking at?" his target snapped, taking off his earphones.

"I think you're a cutie-pie," Robert said, waving again.

The guy shut off his iPod and stood up. "Back off, faggot. You don't want to mess with me." He pulled out his pearl-handled knife and shook it at Robert.

"Oh my! What a big, beautiful, pointy knife you have."

The man looked startled for a moment. Then he shook his head violently. "And crazy, too? Queer and nuts? Shit man, stay the fuck away or I'll cut you."

The man walked to the end of the car and sat in the last seat. He looked back at Robert and shook his head. He put his earbuds back in, shut his eyes, and resumed bobbing and croaking.

The train screeched as it took a bend in the rails.

Robert got up and walked the length of the car, sat across from his target again, and stared.

The man burst up from his seat and held the knife tip three inches from Robert's face. "Stop staring at me, motherfucker!"

Robert laughed.

"You think I'm joking, asshole?"

"No, I know you're serious. I just can't believe you don't recognize me."

The target put his knife away and scrunched up his eyebrows. Then recognition struck. "You're that fuck who broke into our warehouse."

"Ding, ding, ding," Robert cried. "I thought you'd done too much meth to remember me."

"What do you want?"

Robert leaned back comfortably on his subway seat, cradling the back of his head with both hands. "I want you and your scumbag racist friends to pay for what you did to those kids."

Ferret-eyes looked around anxiously. "Fuck off. Didn't you have enough? Charlie cut you good."

Robert rubbed his shoulder and rotated it freely. "All better. See?"

Without warning, the man lunged, wielding his switchblade.

To Robert, teeming with adrenaline, it seemed as if his target were moving underwater. He easily grabbed the hand holding the knife and used the man's momentum to slam him into the beveled edge of the hard plastic subway seat. Never letting go of the man's wrist, he bent it backward, separating the lunate and scaphoid bones in the wrist from the ulna and radius. His opponent's scream was lost in the racket of the train's clatter.

Robert caught the knife as it dropped and used the butt end to pound viciously on the carpal bones of the man's wrists until they shattered into fragments. Next, he lifted his leg and snapped it down on the target's right knee, leaving the man's patella hanging by a ripped tendon.

"And this," Robert said as he stuffed the iPod inside the man's mouth, "is for playing your music too loud."

The train slowed as it neared the station. Ferret-eyes was beginning to keen, a noise louder than a boiling teakettle. Robert wrapped the earbud cord around the man's throat and tightened it until the vocal chords were silenced. The target's face turned blue, his veins popping visibly from his shaved head, his struggles subsiding as less oxygen fed his brain.

The announcement of the oncoming station blared overhead. Robert threw Ferret-eyes onto the floor. The man's body gave a loud thump. Robert wiped his prints off the knife and kicked it down the aisle to the other end of the car.

The doors thumped open and Robert exited. No one was on the platform. He got to a payphone and left an anonymous tip with the police that one of the men responsible for the attack on the choir from Atlanta could be found in the second-to-last subway car on the N train, along with a knife that would match some of the victims' wounds.

Chapter 36

Twenty-four hours later, the story had gone national.

On a bench in Riverside Park, Robert smiled as he read the article in the *New York Post*. He was never sure how the media got wind of a story so quickly.

The various papers had dubbed him all sorts of silly names: Righteous Avenger, Manhattan Vigilante, Prince of Payback. He knew he should be amused, but he was becoming anxious about being found out and linked to a long list of previous assaults.

He placed the newspaper down, took a sip of his coffee, and looked around. The park was always quiet at sunrise; the sudden cold snap had left it even quieter. His body shivered underneath his light sweatpants and hoodie, but he couldn't afford to be weighed down by anything heavier.

In the distance, he saw a runner approach. It was Kirk Gibson, the steroid-addled gym rat who'd held Robert's head while Redbeard slashed him. The man was muscle proud—strong as an ox, though likely not as smart as one. Robert was impressed that a low-life like Gibson had enough self-control to get up so early for a run along the Hudson, even after a hard night of assaulting, raping, and killing.

The man was probably driven by either discipline or her evil twin, obsessive-compulsive disorder.

The first rays of a cold sun cracked the brittle horizon. The sky started to take on a peaceful purplish hue, which reflected off the restless, brackish water of the Hudson River. Robert felt goose bumps rise under his gray sweatshirt.

A moment later, Gibson, in his shiny black running ensemble, huffed past.

Showtime.

Robert waited a few minutes for the man to get ahead of him, made sure no one was coming in either direction, and stood up. He was a bit unsteady on his new Rollerblades. He'd never been much of a skater and hadn't worn any kind of blades in years.

But he was always ready to fight.

He began a slow glide after the man. With each tack, he felt more confident. He began to gain speed, getting his thrill meter ticking as the pavement rumbled faster and faster beneath his feet.

Robert looked over his shoulder. All clear. Ahead, a woman jogged, but too far away to matter. He kicked into overdrive, hunching close to the ground, eating up the twenty yards left between him and his target. The speed felt dangerous and exciting. He crouched lower as he came alongside the man and then swerved violently, shoulder-slamming him over the crossbar and onto the jagged rocks that led to the river.

Gibson yelled and flailed wildly as he tried to brace himself. His bulging arms broke some of the fall, but his face hit a sharp crag.

Robert heard the thump from ten yards away where he came to a stop on the walkway. He looked around again, making sure he hadn't been spotted. The woman was still a long way off and hadn't slowed. He hopped over the rail and clomped his Rollerblades down the stony slope to where Gibson now sat cross-legged, punching a number on his cell with clumsy slowness. Robert did a hop step and kicked the phone out of the man's hands.

"What'd you do that for?" Gibson snapped. His headphones were askew on his shaved head, and he ripped them off. He had a massive body, but a small, pasty face with comically large ears.

He started to stand.

"Sit!" Robert barked and kicked the man's face.

Gibson patted his face with a beefy hand, feeling for broken bones and loose teeth. "Help! Someone!" he yelled, and Robert hit him in the same place.

"No calling for help," Robert said.

"What do you want, man? Please. Don't hurt me anymore."

"Lower your voice."

"Okay, I'm sorry," Gibson whimpered.

Robert nodded and sat on a large boulder nearby.

"What do you want? Money? I got a clip in my pocket. A few hundred. It's all yours. Take it."

"I don't want your money," Robert said. "I want to stop you and your neo-Nazi brotherhood from hurting anyone else." He stood and approached Gibson, who was cowering on the rocks and cradling his jaw. "I'm going to have to do it in a way that convinces me you'll never hurt anyone again."

Gibson gawked at him for a moment, trying to wrap his brain around what Robert said. Then he took in a sharp breath and his face lit up. "You're that fuck who broke into our warehouse."

"That's right," Robert said, tossing off his Rollerblades. "I'm the messenger of Karma, I'm the—"

Gibson's whole demeanor changed. He had lost any trace of fear. "Oh, you're gonna get it," he said between bouts of laughter. "We know all about you, Dr. McKenzie."

Robert stared at the man, startled and puzzled. Alarm shot up his spine.

"That's right," Gibson said, feeding off Robert's stunned look. "We know who you are. You can't stop us. We're part of a national movement. You think that my brothers and I are gonna let America continue to be run by some black president? We're gonna get rid of all the faggots, Jews, and niggers in this country."

Robert's mind raced to put the pieces together. "How do you know who I am?"

"Don't worry about how I know," Gibson said. "The brotherhood has its ways."

Robert exploded at the man, but slipped on the mossy rocks and fell on top of his target. Gibson's weight-lifting strength and hard-slab muscle kept Robert from getting any kind of hold on him, and soon Robert felt the guy's iron grip squeezing his stabbed shoulder. The pain flashed a red-blackout behind Robert's eyelids. He came to in time to see a rock fast approaching his face as Gibson smashed his head down to the ground. Instantly, Robert experienced more blinding pain, and then he felt himself being dragged up, gasping for air as Gibson bear-hugged him from behind and squeezed his life away.

Images of innocent people being tortured and killed by the neo-Nazis jolted Robert with the force that enables a hundred-pound mother to lift the front end of a car to save her pinned child. He threw back his hands and grabbed Gibson's ears and bent him forward with a roar, tossing him over his shoulders. Gibson's body hit the ground hard, his back pierced by a huge shard of shale, his legs flopping over the edge of the rocks into the frigid water. Robert fell back and kicked Gibson's lower lumbar, launching the oaf into the river. Without hesitation, Robert jumped after him, grabbed his handle-like ears and dunked his target under the water for half a minute, before pulling him up.

"Tell me what you know!"

"I know ... they're coming ... to get you," Gibson managed to splutter.

Robert yanked him under again. His fury easily resisted Gibson's frantic attempt to get above water. Once the struggling slowed, Robert pulled him up again.

"What aren't you telling me?" Robert said, shaking him violently. He grabbed Gibson's head and pulled it closer to him. Gibson didn't give any indication of wanting to talk, so Robert plunged him under again, his anger crackling into electric thinking.

They know my identity.

What else do they know?

When Gibson's body stopped struggling, Robert hauled him out of the icy water. His target was unconscious but still breathing. By the time someone found him, Gibson would be too dazed from hypothermia to provide any identifying information about his assailant. The scum would likely spend the next three nights intubated in the ICU and, Robert hoped, the next twenty years in jail, thanks to another anonymous tip.

Robert's legs trembled from the cold as he skated out of the park and caught a cab to the Upper West Side. He was certain Gibson was holding something back, and he needed to figure out his next plan of attack.

Chapter 37

The rooftop was packed with people in their late twenties and thirties—drinking, smoking, dancing. Despite the half-dozen heat lamps scattered around, people were bundled up in hats and winter coats.

Robert put his hood up and his sunglasses on, even though the setting sun was fast losing its brilliance in mild orange glory. He culled a can of beer from a washtub of ice and spotted Karl by the cylindrical chimney, talking on his cell with one finger in an ear.

Smiling broadly, Robert took a large gulp from his beer. Joining the rooftop party had been a snap. He didn't have to jimmy the lock or break down the door. He'd been buzzed in without question and then found himself in a crowd too large for anyone to notice he was a total stranger.

Robert would end it tonight. Karl was the second-in-command and Robert had a plan. If he could convince Karl to set up a meeting with Redbeard and the other neo-Nazis, he would surrender to the brotherhood and let them have their way with him.

But, of course, he wouldn't really surrender.

If things went his way, Robert would subject the neo-Nazis to the same surprise attack he delivered to his enemies in Guatemala.

He turned his attention to Karl, who started yelling loudly into the phone. He pulled it away from his mouth and glared at it, looking ready to squeeze it into pieces. Then he moved further behind the chimney, no doubt searching for a spot with better reception.

Robert took out his own cell and pretended to get a call. He walked past the crowd to the outskirts of the roof. When he was ten feet from Karl and closing the gap, he shouted into the phone. "Me? Oh, not much. Just looking for neo-Nazis and shit."

Karl shut off his phone and walked up to Robert.

"This is my roof, man. I don't know you."

Robert held up a finger at Karl and continued his fake phone call. "Yeah, I see him. What's his name?"

Karl's face darkened. He pulled a large switchblade from the pocket of his pants.

Robert tucked his cell away. "Is your name Karl? I was just on the phone with the prime minister of Israel. He wants you to go fuck yourself."

Karl started gently playing with the blade, facing off with Robert like a bullfighter. "You're the guy who took out Konrad and Gibson. You're that fucking psychopath doctor, aren't you?"

"Well, shit, Karl, who'd you think I was? I'm certainly no cop. A cop would just arrest your ass. After I get through with you for what you did to those kids, you won't remember your own name."

"Go to hell," Karl said and launched a one-two kick at Robert's gut.

Robert tightened his stomach and took the kicks, keeping his hands up. The knife made an arc around him, but Robert dodged it and then elbowed Karl in the throat. Gagging, Karl dropped the knife.

Robert picked him up and threw him across the three-foot gap between the buildings and onto the neighboring rooftop, away from any guests. Although his stomach was screaming where Karl had kicked him, Robert was careful not to show the tiniest wince. He glared at Karl, who was trying to get his breath back and stared back at Robert with a shade of awe.

Karl tried yelling for help, but his botched-up throat didn't allow anything but a rasp. He doubled over to catch his breath, then sprang up and took off.

Robert leapt onto the next building and ran after him. He could see that the roof they were on had no exit in the direction they were running except for a ten-foot jump to a window across the way.

Karl made the leap and crashed through the window.

Robert hadn't expected a rooftop chase, but he was more than willing to give it a go. He loved discovering what he could do once he threw himself into action.

Without hesitating, he flew up in the air and across the gap, scratching the sides of his biceps on the jagged shards still in the frame of the broken window and crash-landing on the carpeted floor of the apartment. From the corner of his eye, he caught an older couple sitting up in bed and holding each other in fear as he sped through the room, chasing the sound of pounding footsteps and a slammed front door.

He ran through the door and down the hall, past the recycling cans, out an open window and onto a foot-wide ledge, just in time to see Karl making his way down the fire escape. Then it was into the alley below and over a tall chain-link fence. Robert followed Karl's every move until he swung on the fence's top horizontal pole. Karl went up and over the razor wire above it, flipping once and landing on the other side without a scratch. Robert grabbed the pole with one hand and used the other hand to rip off his jacket. He wrapped it around his lower arm, slamming the padded arm on the razor wire and clambering over it.

Robert's arms were riddled with scratches, but all he felt was adrenaline. He chased Karl to the fire escape of the next

242

building and then up seven flights of steeply angled metal stairs to the rooftop.

Robert went up as fast as he could. It was getting dark now; the sun was just below the horizon. He reached the top of the tower and peered over from the scaffolding to the roof. There was no sign of Karl.

The dropkick came out of nowhere, hitting Robert square in the face. His left hand tore from the top rung, but the right one held on. Karl appeared a moment later from behind a cement tower and walked to the edge of the fire escape platform. He lifted his foot to stomp on Robert's hand, but Robert let go just in time and hooked his left elbow on the rung below it, buttressing his hold with his right hand.

Karl stood over the ladder's top rung like a squat column, confident he now held the upper hand in their battle. He launched his foot at Robert's forehead, but Robert had enough time to dodge it. He swept his right arm with all his might against Karl's pivot foot, tumbling him onto his back. Robert pulled himself onto the tower and got to his feet at the same time as Karl. They stood in the middle of the platform, watching each other hatefully and panting only slightly. Then they began to circle each other, each preparing for another attack. It was extreme fighting in its volcanic essence, lava about to blow.

Enough already!

Robert pulled out his SIG Sauer and aimed it at Karl. The skinhead stopped circling and reflexively raised both arms in defeat. "I had nothing to do with the attack," he said. "Charlie ordered it. He wanted to do something big, something that would attract a bit of media coverage. He's the guy you want."

"You were with him, Karl. You did those kids, too. And you guys were planning on going after me."

"It's Charlie, man. If I don't do what he says, I'm dead. He'll go after my family. I got twin boys at home, but Charlie doesn't care. He'll kill them. Honestly, man, you don't know who you're dealing with. It's not all of us—it's just one bad guy."

Something about what Karl said echoed Robert's philosophy and sent a weak wave of nausea through him.

Can I believe this guy?

Robert's heart pounded. His body ached. His mind raced. His normal decisiveness was gone. Maybe if he went after Redbeard and took him out, the whole brotherhood would come tumbling down. Redbeard, according to the witnesses, had cut and raped the girl who'd survived the attack. But what if—

Karl suddenly launched a kick that sent Robert's gun over the side of the building. He followed with a hammering fist against Robert's temple.

Stunned by the blow, Robert staggered back. Two more punches hit him quickly on the ribs from either side, then three quick blows to the face and another three to his stomach. As Robert doubled over, Karl slammed his clasped hands down on Robert's exposed neck. Before Robert knew what was happening, his face scraped the oily metal surface of the roof.

Robert saw double and he knew Karl wouldn't let up.

"You want a piece of me?" Karl hopped from one foot to another and then threw a few lightning-quick punches into the air. "I'm a former Ultimate Fighter, motherfucker. You want revenge for those kids? I'm gonna get *me* some revenge for the shit you did to my boys."

Karl's voice spun into Robert's clogged-up ears as if it were swirling down from a sky-high roller coaster. Robert forced himself to stand despite the crippling pain in his bones and began dodging his target's expert blows and kicks like some battered heavyweight in the final rounds. No thinking. Just doing whatever it took to stay alive.

Robert howled as he took three jabs to his side. He twisted his body to reduce the impact of the succeeding jab and allow himself to get in position for his own attack. As Karl wound up for another round of punches, Robert jumped up and kicked Karl's chest. He felt the cracking of ribs under the weight of his flying roundhouse. Robert sprang forward like a jaguar and double straight-armed two locked fists in the same broken place he had kicked, propelling Karl over the edge of the building.

Karl thudded onto the fire escape platform two feet below, then bounced to a standstill. Robert followed. Karl saw him coming and crawled away, not realizing how close he was to the landing's edge. He slipped off but managed to grab hold of an iron ring.

Karl dangled off the side of the building, seven stories of mortal darkness sprawled beneath him.

Robert stood above him, considering his options. Their eyes locked. Robert saw fear and pleading. He felt Sharon's presence commanding him to be a better man.

"Help me," Karl gasped. "Please. I don't want to die. I have twin boys."

Although certain he was making a mistake, Robert knelt and grabbed Karl's hand, then pulled him back onto the roof.

They both sat catching their breath for a moment.

"Thanks, man. You didn't have to—" Karl's voice trailed off as he sprang forward and, as quick as a rattler, got Robert in a chokehold.

Robert's vision slowly bled into the darkness of the falling night. Karl eased up a bit so Robert could understand his last words. "One of our guys was late the night you broke into our warehouse. He saw you get on your Ducati and followed you all the way to your girlfriend's place in Washington Heights. That's one piece of ass we'll all be enjoying pretty soon, Dr. McKenzie."

A nightmare montage of Sharon being beaten and gang-raped played instantly through his mind. Robert willed his hands to his throat and broke three of Karl's fingers. As soon as the chokehold loosened, he flipped Karl over his shoulder and into the bottomless night.

The sickening thud cut off Karl's ragged scream.

Without stopping to catch his breath, Robert bolted from the rooftop. He found his SIG Sauer by the sidewalk, ran down back alleys, and leapt onto his bike, speeding toward Hell's Kitchen, to the neo-Nazi safe house. Robert knew he was in no condition to fight, but he had no choice. The brotherhood would go after Sharon now that their second-in-command was out of commission.

Unless Robert took them out, she was as good as dead.

Chapter 38

After securing his Bluetooth audio enhancer and Eye-Spy high-definition heat sensor, Robert purposefully tripped the alarm set up for him at the roof of the warehouse.

"What the fuck was that, Bernard?" Redbeard demanded, two flights below.

"That's the alarm Damien and I set up," Bernard said, tugging at his ear nervously.

"What alarm?"

"We put a bunch of barrels under the roof access," Damien explained. "They topple over if someone cuts the wire and tries to come in."

"You two go get yourselves a vigilante," Redbeard said. "Brett and I will stay here and keep watch."

The two men grabbed their AK-47s. Each snapped a cartridge inside the slot, locked and loaded.

"He's probably gonna fry your ass," Brett said. "Wear him out so he'll be easier meat for us."

"You're kidding, right?" Bernard asked, eyeing him curiously. "Fuck you. We can take care of him ourselves."

Robert saw the two men climbing the stairs with their guns

turned sideways. They were now just one flight below him and he needed to change his equipment before they reached the third floor.

Still plenty of time.

As soon as the men reached the hallway of the second floor, Bernard went for the light switch.

But the lights didn't go on.

"Aw fuck!" Damien snarled.

"Anybody here?" Bernard called, his voice barely above a whisper.

"Oh, like he's really gonna say if he's here," Damien said. "You dumbass!"

"Right," Bernard said. "I don't think anybody's here."

"He could be standing still."

They both froze, straining their ears and eyes. Gradually, shadowy shapes could be made out. There were no hiding places. It was just a bare room.

They heard a creak from above.

"Third floor."

"Yeah. Careful now."

They headed up the stairs, their guns in front of them. Once they reached their destination, they flicked the switch on again.

No lights.

"Damn electricity."

Then a blinding brightness and a deafening noise.

Robert looked on as the two men threw their hands to their bleeding ears and fell to the floor, their eyes burning like little suns in their red-hot heads.

Covered in black except for his eyes and mouth, Robert whipped off his noise-reduction headphones and protective eye gear, which shielded him from any stun-flash grenade damage, and quickly wrapped the men's hands behind their backs with duct tape. As they started to recover and began to squirm, he trussed their hands to their ankles with long plastic ties. He dragged each of them to the top of the stairs, then he rolled them down, one after the other.

Below him, Robert heard Redbeard and Brett toting AK-47s up the stairs to the second floor. They found nothing but darkness and heard nothing but the floor creaking under their boots.

Then came a racket tumbling down the stairs that made them jump. They ran across the room. When the noise stopped, they opened the door and emptied their magazines into the stairway. As the smoke cleared, they saw they had turned their two brothers into steak tartare.

"Oh God," Brett said and threw up.

"McKenzie," Redbeard called up the stairs. "I want you to give yourself up. If I don't call my boy Karl in a half hour, your hot social worker friend is gonna suffer a fate worse than death! And you don't want that fine piece of ass to get hurt, do you?"

A single shot exploded from the doorway into the butt-stock of Redbeard's assault rifle, shattering it in three directions, making him yell and his hands shake from the shock. A second shot followed immediately, piercing Brett's trigger hand. He reeled back in agony, the rifle clanking uselessly to the floor. The blood from the gaping hole in his hand started to stain the area around him red.

Robert walked down the stairs, dropped his duffel on the floor, and tucked his gun away. "So you're the bad guys' bad guy?" he said, cracking his knuckles and glaring at Redbeard. "I get rid of you, the rest falls apart, right? Cut off the snake head and the body thrashes around like a spastic dick."

Brett had backed into a corner, holding his hand, trying to wrap it with an old jersey. His face paled and sweat covered his forehead. He used his teeth to tug the shirt into a tight knot before lurching to Redbeard's side.

Overwhelmed by the endorphins pumping within his body, Robert ran straight at them. As Redbeard dodged left, Robert veered, clapped both hands over Brett's ears, and stomped his heel over Brett's feet, causing multiple metatarsal fractures. Brett fell in a heap on the floor and started screaming in agony.

"I don't want any distractions," Robert said to Redbeard. He whirled rapidly and landed an elbow on Redbeard's temple.

It was a blow that should have knocked his opponent unconscious, but Redbeard merely angled his head and charged. He grabbed Robert by the hair and kneed him in the face. Robert saw stars. Before Redbeard could strike again, however, Robert's instincts made him throw his cross grip onto the hands in his hair, ripping at them and loosening Redbeard's hold just in time.

Bright bubbles were replacing the stars now, like planets in orbit. Two quick crotch kicks also failed to bother Redbeard, who slammed the heel of one hand and then the other up into Robert's jaw. Robert went along with the jolting pain and energy torque of the blows to do a back flip, landing on his feet with natural dexterity.

"Not bad," Redbeard said, pulling out the long steel of a switchblade.

Robert was hurting, but he knew from experience that he could push himself through the toughest fight.

I'm not going to beat this guy unconscious. I have to cripple him.

Earlier, a part of him had been standing back, gauging angles and studying his opponent's skills. Now he got himself moving and allowed the action to dictate his strategy. His gut told him what to do next. He was on adrenaline time, seeing everything in slow motion. His task was immobilization, and that meant knees or ankles.

Robert fell into a roll, and before Redbeard could deflect him, Robert clutched Redbeard's boot and twisted his foot a violent one hundred eighty degrees, then yanked the foot down on the floor. Redbeard put weight on it and keeled to the side.

The other ankle was next. It was a matter of following through and using surprise to his advantage. After the same quick crack, Robert pulled and twisted the unmoored foot. Redbeard dropped awkwardly to the floor, unable to stand.

But just as he dropped, he swung his knife into Robert's thigh and shook it viciously back and forth, probing for more and more nerves.

Robert kicked his thigh free with his other leg and wrenched himself away. He pulled the knife out in one swift move, experiencing a burning pain that was ten times worse than the original stab had been. Limping to his duffel, he pulled out a black scarf and made a tight tourniquet to stop the bleeding.

He pulled out a plastic bottle, prefilled with gasoline, and a box of kitchen matches.

He limped over to Redbeard, who scrambled to stand, and doused him with half the gasoline. He poured the rest over Brett's squirming body.

Then he took out a match.

"Don't do it. Please!" Redbeard pleaded. "I got a family. I beg you."

"You won, man!" Brett screamed. "Isn't that enough?"

"Come on, McKenzie," Redbeard scurried backward. "Have some compassion, man. You're a goddamn doctor!"

Robert stared at the match. His mind raced through scenes of Sharon being raped and beaten by Redbeard and the other neo-Nazis. He relived his own torture, re-experiencing the feeling of getting tied up by his drunken stepfather. He heard the screams from his little brother and his mother's pleading cries. His body convulsed as he recalled how desperately he had struggled to free himself, despite knowing that he was no match for his stepfather.

Robert stared into Redbeard's eyes. He saw the trademark flatness of the psychopath. He knew the boss of the neo-Nazis would never be rehabilitated.

With a flick of the hands, Robert lit the match. He stared at the brightness as the flame jumped around, ignoring his targets' appeals for mercy. The men were living, breathing incarnations of pure evil, motivated by an unshakeable desire to hurt the innocent. The remaining members of the brotherhood needed to suffer for what they did to those kids, to that girl.

It was Karma's way.

The flame had eaten up half the matchstick. Robert stared at his hand, his future held between his thumb and index finger.

Then he heard footsteps behind him and a voice he recognized. "You don't want to do that, McKenzie."

Robert turned around.

Detective Landers pointed a gun at him. "Trust me. If you burn these guys alive, there's nobody who will back you up. Right now, you have me and at least three-quarters of the NYPD behind you."

"These guys should pay for what they've done."

"And they will. I'll personally see to it." Landers took a step forward. He lowered his voice. "McKenzie, have faith in the system."

"The system's broken."

"That may be true," Landers said. "But this isn't the way you fix it. You can't go around subjecting people to your own idea of punishment. You need to let the police and the courts do that."

"I don't trust you guys."

"You can trust *me*." Landers took another step forward. "I promise to make sure these guys get put away for life. If they don't, I'll deal with them personally."

An unfaltering conviction in the detective's voice assured Robert that he would follow through.

He blew out the match.

Landers put his gun down. "Now get out of the building. My backup will be here any minute."

Robert's puzzled expression brought a smile to the detective's face.

"You don't really think I'm going down in history for putting away the Manhattan Vigilante?" Landers's laugh filled the room. "I say you have twenty-four hours at the most before my friends and I are forced to go after you. Get your things together, leave the country, and don't come back for a while."

Hearing sirens approaching, Robert grabbed his bag and fled the building. He jumped onto his Ducati and sped away, his mind trying to make sense of the night's events.

It wasn't the ending he had anticipated.

Regardless, the neo-Nazis were finished.

Chapter 39

"Robert, you look terrible," Dr. Weiss said as he took a seat in his big leather chair.

"It's nice to see you too, Mel." Robert stood in front of the director's desk. He realized now that it had been a bad idea to come to St. Jude's. He was wasting valuable hours and risking arrest, but he wanted to leave New York on his own terms.

"What's up with the limp?"

"I pulled a muscle doing Pilates."

Weiss laughed uncomfortably. "Can I offer you coffee or something?"

"I only drink espresso, so no, thanks."

Avoiding eye contact, Weiss fumbled through a dozen charts. "You really did it this time, Robert. I've always done my best to ward off your enemies. Everyone at St. Jude's has wanted me to ream you out in the past, but this time the complaint comes from someone I have to listen to."

"Who?"

"Me."

"I see," Robert said, giving Weiss a dismissive smile.

"I figure it's my job to talk to you, and I need to do my job. I like my job. It provides me with enough money to get by."

"I'd say you make a lot more than that," Robert said, sitting down on a plush chair. He looked around the room, taking in the massive mahogany desk and tasteful office furnishings. "You've come a long way, Mel. Last time I was here, we were sitting on wooden chairs from the cafeteria."

"Yeah, it's been a while since you came around to these parts."

"Remind me again. Why did you invite me to your office last time?" Robert brought his hand to his chin and stroked his slightly scruffy beard. "Oh, wait, I remember. I diagnosed your wife with subacute infective endocarditis and fast-tracked her treatment when a dozen brainless doctors couldn't figure out what was wrong with her."

"You know I'll never forget what you did for my wife, Robert. My whole family continues to be grateful."

"How's Francine doing, anyway?"

"Great. Lots of yoga, and her singing career is really taking off. She just got a gig in the chorus of the City Opera."

"Good for her," Robert said, crossing his arms.

The silence grew heavy. Weiss got up from his chair, poured himself a cup of coffee, and then sat back down with a fat man's sigh. He opened a thick file in front of him and started leafing through it.

"I trust my file provides you with action-packed reading?"

Weiss grunted and continued scanning the stack of papers, stopping now and then to shake his head. "You've been written up multiple times by practically every department. There must be a hundred letters here. Technicians, nurses, doctors—even patients! 'Rude.' 'Unprofessional.' 'Bedside manner of a threshing machine.'"

Robert laughed. "Was that the carpenter?"

Weiss read from a letter covered in wobbly cursive. "Nelson Grant."

"That's him. Has a drunk's nose. I sewed two of his fingers back on. Did he complain about that?"

"No, he complained about your lack of respect. You should read it. It's pretty convincing."

"He was roaring drunk. He tried to clean his chainsaw without turning it off!"

"What about all these complaints from the other departments? This month alone you did an open thoracotomy and a perimortem C-section without consulting surgery or OB/GYN. And what the hell were you thinking, letting a medical student perform a lateral canthotomy? Damn it, Robert! We have ophthalmologists in the hospital."

"Those patients are thriving. That's my defense." Robert's voice was getting heated.

"Following protocol would've saved them, too. And it would've covered your ass and the hospital's ass in case of any fuckup."

"The only fuckup was that none of those prepubescent residents or their attending physicians were anywhere near the ER to help those patients in time. That guy who was stabbed by some gang member was a hair away from death. That woman and her unborn child were inside the tunnel of light, and it was because *I* acted in time that they left this hospital a happy and healthy family. Protocol's fine when there's time for it but you, of all people, damn well know that saving a life is what's important. You should have enough balls buried in all that blubber of yours to tell those idiots to go fuck themselves."

Weiss stood abruptly. The secretary had just arrived and wanted to see what all the shouting was about. He shooed her away and shut the door. He walked back to his chair and plopped down again. "You do have one valid point," he said, patting his belly. "What can I say? I love pasta."

"If you want to play the friend card, Mel, don't invite me here for betrayal."

"Look, Robert, you know I agree with you. A life is worth more than a rulebook, and in an ideal world, you'd be thanked instead of sanctioned. Celebrated even. But we don't live in an ideal world, and I know you're not naïve enough to think we ever will."

Robert opened his mouth to answer, but a scalpel pierced his heart as he flashed back to Sharon leaving his apartment for the last time. He blinked hard twice to keep his eyes dry.

Weiss gave him a long look. "It's chaos in the trenches, Robert. I'm well aware of that. My job is to make sure the ER runs smoothly. We're not expected to be as orderly as the rest of the hospital, and I make reasonable allowances for that. But the chaos also means I have to keep a tougher watch to ensure that things don't spiral out of control. The rest of the hospital looks down on us as cowboys and grunts, but we need their help and cooperation to do what has to get done for our patients. The more they think they're walking into Dodge, the slower they'll come. We toe the line enough to keep the other departments from writing us off as hopeless. Well, guess what, Robert? They've written *you* off as hopeless."

"Who has? A bunch of suits who wouldn't know how to diagnose a sprained ankle? Or some old department director in red golf pants who hasn't set foot in the ER since the invention of aspirin?"

"It's not that simple, and you know it."

"So you tell *them* how it is, Mel, not vice versa! Have a spine. Do what you know is right. You tell them about the lives we save and the obstacles we face. The clock ticking, the blood gushing, the patients screaming—so many of them out of their mind with fear or pain. The overworked staff, the bumbling interns, our limited resources, and the inconsiderate physicians from the other departments, taking their fucking time and playing power games while people's lives are going down the tubes."

"That's not how it works."

"Don't tell *me* how it works. There are over one hundred fifty million ER visits each year in the United States. That number is climbing, but our resources continue to be the same. Why is it that overcrowding is an issue only in the emergency department? Why should we suffer and take the brunt of the abuse when the rest of the hospital and other services sit pretty with their quotas and so-called 'limited space'? What about that?"

"And what about the ER doctor who storms off his shift right in the middle of one of this year's worst crises?"

Robert grew quiet. Teeth grinding under tight lips, his mind flooded with images from the previous week's events.

"How can you possibly explain your behavior?"

"It wasn't good, Mel. I admit it, but I was sick that morning. I would've jeopardized patient care if I had continued to work."

"So you saw a doctor?"

"I didn't need one. I knew my diagnosis."

Weiss leafed to the last page of the file. "Yeah, that's what your old buddy Rivera says, too. 'Sick as a dog.' But the ER social worker, who also happened to be there that morning, gave a conflicting account. One of them has to be lying, right?" He took off his glasses, pinched his nose for a while, and then rubbed his eyes. "I've been doing this for thirty years. It doesn't take a genius to know that you and Rivera go way back. She'd do anything, including putting her job on the line, to cover your ass. So I'm going with the social worker's account." He paused to read the statement. "According to Ms. Reede, you were hale and hearty that morning, but your state of mind deteriorated after seeing all those kids in such horrible shape. She was pretty candid when the committee interrogated her."

Robert clawed the red leather armrest so tensely that his nails pierced the surface. He relaxed his hand and took a deep breath. "What else did Ms. Reede say?"

"She described the state of the young woman you treated right before you decided you were too sick to work anymore. Ms. Reede reports that your whole demeanor changed when you gauged the extent of the girl's injuries. That you didn't get pale or sick. Instead, you grew furious and couldn't stay at work because you couldn't think clearly. She made no bones about it." He glanced up at Robert. "She told the committee that your psychological well-being should be questioned and that you might benefit from counseling and anger management."

Robert stared at Weiss. He tried to smile, but his mouth was too shaky. He stood up and paced. He stopped at the window and looked out at a pearl sky, noting people starting to drift toward the hospital doors, bundled up. Everything was growing colder.

"Are you planning to sic a shrink on me, Mel?"

"Hey, who couldn't use a good therapist? You sure as hell could. You've always struck me as two salutes short of a fascist. Until recently, you've managed to come across as pro-human. But you crossed the line that morning, and I think you know it. You left a patient in dire need. A bunch of patients, actually. I tried to defend you during the committee meeting last night, told them you just needed a break, a forced sabbatical or something, but they were all in the mood for filet of McKenzie. Only one doctor, besides me, defended you. It seems like all the resentment the others have built up against you over the years just spewed out. To them, it isn't good enough that you are a smart guy who saves lives and can diagnose difficult cases. In their eyes, you don't like them, so they don't like you. Even the CEO and the PR people are against you. They claim our Press Ganey scores are way down mainly because so many patients polled were dissatisfied with your care."

"Press Ganey scores? Who the fuck cares about patient satisfaction? The only test that matters is who survives their ER visit and who doesn't. Do you know how many patients come into the ER with bullshit? You have to discharge them quickly. If you take too much time being nice, you could be too late getting to the sick ones. As long as I diagnose, stabilize, and treat the real emergencies, my patient satisfaction score shouldn't matter."

"You're absolutely, one hundred percent right."

"I'm glad you think so, Mel. I realize hospital politics are tricky. I know we don't live in an ideal world, but we have to fight bureaucracy, right? We have to stand up for our patients. We have to stand up for what we believe in."

"And that's why I have to fire you."

Momentary dizziness whirled through Robert, leaving him numb. Even though he half-expected this was coming, it was hard to hear. He stared into Mel's sympathetic eyes. Something he had known all along flowed back and forth between them, but Robert couldn't quite get it.

Then he did.

He shook his head and exhaled loudly. "Not because of the bureaucrats, but because I walked out. I abandoned those patients."

Weiss nodded and closed the file. "A lot of people don't see much value in the work they do besides their paycheck. In the ER, though, we know what we do matters. You've mattered to a lot of people, Robert. My wife is one of them, but I have no other option. I have to let you go. There's an army of people against you, and I can't defend your actions any longer. Maybe you'll never want to see me again. I would hate that. It hurts me to have to do it, but I have to fire you."

"It's okay, Mel. I'm ready to leave this place, anyway. You're right. I gave you no choice. I won't hold it against you."

Robert stood up, but he didn't move for a minute. He stared past the director's face at the window. White flakes were falling outside, sparse but steady. The first snow of winter. The city looked peaceful and beautiful.

After throwing his bag over his shoulder, Robert limped to the door and put his hand on the knob. "I hope you enjoy the little going-away present I left inside your briefcase. And tell Francine if she gets sick again and none of her Mickey Mouse doctors know what's going on, she can feel free to contact me."

Robert left the room and walked through the hospital administrative offices without making eye contact with anyone. At the exit, he smiled, picturing the director's face when he found Robert's resignation letter inside his combination-lock briefcase.

Then Robert went out into the quietness of New York City's first snow day.

For the last time.

Chapter 40

Sharon's first two consults were routine: a homeless guy needing a shelter and a drunk requesting detox. The third case, however, took a lot of care to write up.

The victim had gone out with her ex-boyfriend from college the night before. He called her out of the blue wanting to catch up. They went to a bar, drank, and talked for hours. Then they headed back to his place. Once inside, he proceeded to "teach her a lesson" for breaking up with him. He ripped her earrings through her ear lobes, broke four of her ribs, and raped her anally. Sharon grew furious with the tone the police officers took with her patient. She intervened three times because of how they framed their questions, almost as if they were blaming the victim for the crime.

She put it all in her report, read it over, edited it, read it one last time, changed a comma to a semicolon, closed the folder, re-opened it, and read it over again.

It was past noon and she still had eight other patients to see.

Dr. Valentine had taken over the ER, a tortoise compared to Robert. He was very kind to his patients and extremely attentive to his residents, doing his best to teach as much as he could manage during the busy shift.

But he was not as efficient as Robert with the difficult patients. Valentine also called for consults every chance he got, even in non-emergencies. Patients hung around the department longer, which meant the waiting room was twice as full and the flow through the ER had slowed to a crawl. Not to mention all the extra reports she had to do.

Sharon sighed and set about seeing her next consult. Despite her exhaustion, she didn't want to go home. At least all this work kept her from being alone with her feelings. Each time she looked at her cell and saw the list of messages from Robert, she was torn between longing and dread. She wasn't ready to hear from him. Deep down she knew that keeping her distance was the right thing. Robert needed more help than she could provide. She was over his vigilante stunts.

When Sharon dropped off the chart, Rivera was on the phone but cut her a hard look.

"What?" Sharon asked.

Rivera shook her head as if to say, *Nothing. Forget it.*

"Come on, Michelle. Just spit it out."

"Did you hear about McKenzie?" Rivera said, hanging up the phone.

"What about him?"

"He got fired this morning."

Sharon gasped.

"Yeah. Weiss let him go."

Then the floodgates opened, and Sharon started to cry.

Rivera put her arms around her and patted her back, telling Sharon it was all right. "A lot of us wondered if you two were, you know…" Rivera made gentle shushing sounds as she spoke. "I knew it all along. I just kept my mouth shut. I wanted to warn you about him, but it wasn't any of my business. Besides, the man looked happy for once."

"I think … he got fired … because of me."

"Because of you? Don't be silly, honey. All you did was tell the truth to those committee idiots."

Sharon nodded as she squeezed her eyes tight. The room was spinning a little. She felt lightheaded.

When they'd asked her why Robert had left the morning of the crisis, she thought the truth would do him the most good in the long run. She knew he needed to find a good therapist, and she thought the hospital could help him do that. Never once did she think her testimony would be used to get him fired.

"Listen to me," Rivera said. "Don't pull yourself apart over this. Weiss told me that McKenzie was planning on quitting anyway."

"Weiss is probably just saying that."

"No. McKenzie wrote his letter of resignation before he even saw Weiss."

This surprised Sharon. Relief rippled through her, followed by a new gush of worry. "What's he going to do?"

"I know if it was up to Guillermo, Robert would be on the next flight to Guatemala."

"Guillermo?" Sharon stared at Rivera, her heart fluttering. "You know Guillermo?"

"He's my ex-husband," Rivera said, putting an arm around Sharon. "Where do you think Robert gets all the fancy toys? And who do you think got him a job here?"

Sharon's mind raced with a hundred questions as she tried to piece together this new information.

"Go, honey," Rivera urged. "You don't have much time."

Sharon stopped crying. She looked at the remaining charts in her stack.

"I'll take care of those patients," Rivera said. "The floor social worker owes me a favor. I'll have her do the consults. You just go get your man before it's too late."

Chapter 41

Shaken and exhausted, Sharon entered her apartment. Her place was empty and cold. She dragged herself to the couch, turned on the lamp, and sat without moving for a few minutes.

Robert was gone.

Sharon had left work and rushed to his building like some love-crazed fool. She had rehearsed the speech. She had imagined the forgiving hug. But the place was totally vacant. There was no physical trace of anyone ever having lived there.

She took off her hat and scarf, stood up, went to the closet, and hung up her coat.

Collapsing back onto the couch, she stared into space.

She started sobbing like a child. Hugging one of the sofa cushions against her chest, she rocked back and forth, trying to justify her actions and hoping that the harrowing pain that plagued her was only temporary.

Should she have lied to the committee? Had she done the right thing? Would she ever see Robert again?

"You know, you really need to change that lock."

Sharon jolted her head up and found Robert leaning against the wall with his arms folded, a wide smile on his face. "It took me less than five seconds to break in here. I'm not going to be around to protect you anymore, so you have to take precautions."

She tried to speak, but couldn't. Robert came over and sat down. They wrapped their arms around each other.

"I'm so sorry, Robert. I got you in trouble. I should've lied—"

"Don't be sorry. Your honesty was one of the reasons I fell in love with you."

She pulled away and looked at him.

"Yes, Sharon. I love you. I'd be crazy not to."

"But you're still leaving New York?"

Robert nodded.

"Why?"

"Landers knows I brought down the neo-Nazis. He's willing to cover for me, but I need to get away for a while." He stood up and limped across the room toward the corner bookshelf and began browsing through the collection. If he noticed the two new books on post-traumatic stress disorder and anger management, he didn't mention it.

"You're limping," she said.

"I stabbed myself shaving."

She didn't laugh.

"Knife wound in the thigh. I'll be all right. Stitched it up myself this time. Didn't need your help."

Sharon made no response.

"I need to get therapy."

"You're really leaving, aren't you?"

"Yeah, I'm heading to Guatemala. I think seeing Guillermo again will be therapeutic."

"That's a start."

"New York's just too big for me—and too bad. In Guatemala, it's different. I can make a real impact."

She didn't know what to say. She knew it was the right thing, but she still didn't want him to go.

"You should come with me."

She studied his eyes. He meant it.

"You know I can't leave St. Jude's. I made a commitment."

"I know."

"But just for the record, I did beat the over-under."

Robert laughed.

"I'll tell you what," she said. "If you're still in Guatemala next year, I'll let you take me out for chiles rellenos."

"I know the perfect place." He held her hands. "Just get to Selaute and ask for Roberto. The villagers will know where to find me."

Sharon wrapped her arms around him and rested her head on his chest. She felt his heart beat and was instantly soothed.

"You know," Robert whispered, "you've changed my life. You've restored my faith in humanity. I realize now that no matter how many bad apples there are in this world, there's an army of saints willing to stand up and fight for a better way of life. As long as I know people like you are around, I'll be able to sleep easier at night."

He squeezed his eyes shut and began to cry. She hugged him. Then he was sobbing, his whole body heaving.

"Let it out," she whispered.

He hugged her tighter. She caressed the back of his head and kissed his cheek. He drew slightly away, then touched her lips and kissed her.

A minute later they both stood up and walked slowly to the door.

"Just promise me one thing," he said. "Get that lock fixed."

"I will. I promise."

They gave each other one last, long hug.

Sharon lingered in the doorway and watched him limp down the hallway.

"Hey," she called.

"Yeah?"

"Wherever you end up, I hope you find what you're looking for."

She smiled, waved her final good-bye, and went inside, locking the door behind her.

Robert stayed behind for a moment, staring at the door. "I think I already have."

Epilogue

Despite the police warnings, Sharon decided to walk home from St. Jude's.

It was cold, but the snow was light and pretty, and she wanted the sting and freshness of the winter night to scour the stale, bitter day from her system.

A large part of the day's grind had been dealing with child protective services over a six-year-old girl who'd been beaten by her mother and raped by her father. Thoughts of the girl's blank face and the unholy tangle of red tape Sharon had to wade through played like a long, blurry slideshow in her brain. She sloshed her way up a dozen blocks on Broadway, taking deep breaths of the crisp air.

Robert had been gone for almost two months. Landers and Macy were still coming around the ER from time to time to ask Sharon if she had heard from him. She wondered if they were the reason Robert hadn't contacted her—to protect her from having to lie to the police or become involved in any way.

Sharon suddenly heard running footsteps behind her. She twisted around, but didn't see anyone.

A serial rapist had been sending a number of women to the ER over the last two weeks, and the police had warned white women in their twenties to take extra precautions. The victims all reported hearing a hooting before being attacked, and the papers were calling the man the Owl. Sharon knew if Robert were still in New York City, the Owl would be an extinct bird by now. She told herself, though, that the police would catch the rapist soon enough.

She thought she heard something like a moan nearby and picked up her pace. Her heart pounded violently against her chest. She found herself looking over her shoulder every few seconds, making sure nobody was following her.

Sharon gasped as something brushed against her, then saw a stray cat shooting across the street toward a deserted alley. She heard a faint scream. She stared into the darkness but didn't hear it again.

A dog barked from a window, and she jumped an inch off the ground. She gathered her wits with a fierce rush of will and marched toward her apartment. She could hear footsteps getting closer, even though she couldn't see anyone behind her. She made it to her building and opened the gate.

Then she heard a hooting.

She sprinted through the lobby door, making sure it locked behind. She ran up the two flights of stairs to her apartment, pulling the keys from her purse as she did. She fumbled to find the right one and, as she went to unlock her door, remembered again that she had promised Robert to get new locks.

But she hadn't.

She entered her apartment, slammed the door behind her, and locked it. From outside she heard another faint hooting.

She ran to the window and looked out, then called the police to inform them about the hooting. They thanked her and said it was probably just some kids. They had been getting a lot of calls from different areas, and they told her "hooting" was becoming a very popular prank, but that she should be careful anyway.

She stared at the empty streets of Washington Heights. It was cold and dark outside—and filled with danger.

Sharon sighed, checked the lock on her window, walked across her apartment, and double-checked the locks on her door.

A calendar from St. Jude's Hospital that hung on her wall caught her attention. She had a week's vacation coming up. She had planned to head back to Indiana to visit family, but maybe she would go to Guatemala instead.

She walked back to the window and peered between the drapes.

Thoughts of Robert flooded her mind.

Maybe she was naïve, after all. With a lunatic like the Owl on the loose, torturing and raping women all over the city, maybe there was a need for a psychopath hunter, for a messenger of Karma. Maybe New York needed someone who didn't care about rules, someone willing to do whatever it took to eliminate the evil-doers wreaking havoc—

A reflection from the window caught Sharon off guard. Her heart fluttered as she whipped her head around and gasped.

"You were warned about getting new locks, weren't you?"

Acknowledgements

In my first month as an emergency physician in Las Vegas, a forty-year-old woman came to the ER after "tripping on a curb." Bruises and cuts covered her face, and she wanted an x-ray to see if any facial bones were broken.

I knew she was lying.

That part didn't bother me. Working in the emergency department, you quickly get used to lies—from patients seeking narcotic prescriptions, morphine shots, disability or work excuses, or just plain sympathy.

This lady was different.

But she was still lying.

Her tells: passive demeanor, hushed voice, inability to keep eye contact, erratic behavior—calm one second, irritable the next—and a physical exam inconsistent with her history.

Then the abuser showed up.

Her husband: a little older than she was, tall, well built, with a jewel-studded ring on his slugging hand.

Before long, she had decided not to wait for the x-rays and was leaving against my medical advice.

It was a busy shift. The ER was filled to capacity and so was the waiting room, but I pulled her aside anyway and found a private space to talk.

"I'm concerned you're being abused."

She didn't deny it.

"I'm calling Metro."

She started to sob. She didn't want the police involved. Her husband would find a way to kill her, she told me. She'd gone to the police before and that just resulted in things getting worse at home.

Then she ran back to him.

I watched as they left the ER. Right before they disappeared, the husband turned and smirked at me.

I will never forget that smirk.

The sad truth is that domestic violence, child abuse, and rape are rising in epidemic numbers. The statistics are staggering. They may seem inflated in this book, but I can tell you that, if anything, they underestimate how rampant these unfathomable acts of violence really are.

Apart from the statistics, this is a work of fiction. Any names, characters, places, and incidents are either the products of my imagination or used fictitiously. Any resemblance to actual events or persons, living or dead, is entirely coincidental.

I'd like to start off by mentioning here my debt to Daniel Goleman's *Emotional Intelligence* for its insights about the importance of emotion in our development, as well as its eye-opening information about psychopaths. It's a must read for anyone interested in this field of psychology.

In addition, there are many people I'd like to thank for playing a role in the development of this manuscript.

There is nothing I could have accomplished without the love of my parents, Ralph and Mercedes, and my siblings, Dave and Lisette.

Elliot Eigen, my ninth-grade English teacher, was my very first editor. He chose to show up to school early, leave late, and spend his lunch breaks editing my early works of fiction. For that, I will be forever grateful.

Robert Montgomery took a very rough draft of this novel and polished it into something I was proud to show. His advice, editing, and suggestions were instrumental in making Dr. Vigilante's story come alive.

Further thanks to David Berkeley, Kathleen Shea, Susan Wallach, Melissa Yourdon, Kristen Stieffel, Tamra Ann Rolf, Lindsey Alexander, Beth Wechsler, and Adele Brinkley for the copyediting and invaluable comments.

And to my mini-editors and close friends, those who read the earliest drafts and gave me honest feedback, I owe you enormous gratitude: Bridget Siegel, Eric Hess, Elad Bicer, Anthony Carrozza, Jung-Taek Yoon, Fahad Khan, Oscar Martinez, Sam Scheible, Marija Djokovic, Donald Reisch, Kass Cornia, Mette Adkisson, Robert Schofield, William Dubois, Chilembwe Mason, Craig Caviness, James Perrott, Darin Finkelstein, Evan Branfman, Sheri Grabert, Alana Mercer, Cameron Bird, Alissa Goldman, Tina Reynolds, Lindsay Roth, Michelle McDaniel, Tim VanDuzer, Alan Stanley, Elizabeth Tai, Sang Shin, and Sonali Ruder. Margo Murphy did a superb job designing the cover and Clint Sleeper turned the image I envisioned of a Dr. Vigilante-worthy caduceus into an awesome graphic.

Finally, a very special thanks to Becky Hanley, Ginger Herold, Alyssa Kapaona, and the rest of the fans of *The League of Freaks* series.

This book is dedicated to the courageous men, women, and children who have survived sexual, psychological, or physical assault and who are soldiering on.

Your calls for help have been heard.